HIDDEN EMPIRE

SAGA OF THE EAST

BOOK I

WRITTEN BY

MATTHEW CERRA

HIDDEN

EMPIRE

SAGA OF THE EAST

BOOK I

WRITTEN BY

MATTHEW CERRA

To learn more about how you also can be published

And to view more about this work, scan this QR Code and
learn about Half Light Publishing

Hidden Empire
Book 1 of the Saga of the East

Written by: Mathew Cerra

Copyright © 2018 by: Half Light Publishing

Book Cover Design by: Donald Semora / DonSemora.com

Interior Layout by: Donald Semora / DonSemora.com

10 9 8 7 6 5 4 3 2 1

Printed and Published in the United States of America

AKNOWLEDGEMENTS

Thank you for being so excited for the story Matt. Your faith in me gave me the confidence to finish this.

DEDICATION

To my wife

PRELUDE
THE TOWER BLACK

Winds swept across the plain, rushing toward the gnarled mountains in the north. Whipping around the few twisted trees of the grasslands, they tumbled ever forward, leaving the scents of the world in their wake. A wall appeared in the distance, a barrier to their smooth run over the valley slopes ahead. Moving relentlessly onward, they rushed headlong toward a solitary man walking along the stones. The force spilled over the wall, its strength broken, before gently rumbling past the figure and into the city beyond.

Kal walked along the ramparts scanning the fields that lay spread in front of the high sandstone walls. He pulled his black cloak tight to him and gripped the staff at his side. Its knots had long ago been baked white from the sun. The years hadn't been kind to his body either -- his hair was long gone, leaving only the smooth light skin of middle age behind. Kal looked to the west, his green eyes watching the setting sun dip behind the mountain that acted as a natural wall to this place. The shadows brought the valley into a foreboding early darkness.

Kal sighed deeply, and began to walk back towards the center of this fortress in the valley, its long wall bridging the gap between the hills protecting the small city within. As he stepped down, the guards on the wall nodded to him, one a veteran of the wars and the other a fresh young recruit. He could always discern the young recruits on the training field. Their over-zealous attempts at appearing at attention and formal address stood as a bright flag to their newness. He smiled at them both, waved, and continued tracing the steps down the high wall, careful not to slip on the stones worn smooth with age.

Kal walked through the city, heading toward the high black tower at its heart, where his council waited for him. He loathed his time with the council these days. His reporters from the corners of the land told of strange happenings, cruelty unbecoming of the lords and ladies of the towers. Even more troubling was the strange report of armies of orcs on the march. Not the usual disorganized bands fighting amongst themselves as well as against humans, but organized forces working together. Kal knew that something had to be done about them, and the inaction by his council worried him.

The city's stone streets were lined with torches that would burn through the night, and they came to life as he strode through the near dark evening. Kal had been living in this city for countless decades, coming as a young man to be schooled here. It was here that the council had chosen him to lead them, and where he had then stayed on as master of the black tower.

"My lord, out for another late night walk?" the guard at the keep asked of him.

"You know me Titus, restless even in my old years."

Titus seemed to smile through his own world-weary face, years of fighting and service to the tower having long ago marked him. "I also know you are not just restless. You look like you carry the world on your shoulders."

Kal smiled at his friend of many years. "Do I not carry the world?" With that Titus nodded and respectfully opened the door. Stepping into the well-lit entryway, Kal decided to take his secret stair and avoid any more of the council than he needed to before the meeting; his gut feeling was that it would go poorly.

~~~

"You are all fools." Kal stood facing the room containing his council. "To align ourselves with the forces of evil? What madness has come into your minds?"

Kal sat at the head of the council table in the tower. A stark round table dominated the center of the room, its heavy lacquer finish still shining after all the centuries of use Kal knew it had taken. The tabards of each of the thirteen towers hung behind the council members between pillars along the walls, stretching to the full height of the room six meters above their heads.

"Kal, think this through. As the head of this council you are supposed to see the wisdom of all things, and to not be limited by the simpletons who claim ownership of this world." Sinestra spoke. She was a tall strong woman who spoke with a calm and clear voice. She wore the clothes of her people from Adavad, a land of herders and traders. Her navy blue woolen leggings and colorful coat were a bright mark upon a room Kal felt was darkened by the discussion at hand.

"Ownership? You are asking me to sell the nations into darkness. " Kal paced near the door as he spoke. "Even if I did what you asked, which I won't, the dark tides will ask for slavery, and plunge this world into darkness for hundreds of years. There is nothing that can be seen as logical in this foolishness."

"Kal the orcs can be a great force of change. Just think; if we work with them we can bring a new order to Theron. Our order is what the world was meant for," said Natalie.

Kal looked over to her; her mastery of the Tower of Spirit had turned appearance the same as her stone's element. Natalie was translucently pale, to the point where one feared she would become clear. Her hair was dark and her eyes a light sky blue that complimented her white dress -- which seemed to move as if by a wind no one else could feel.

Kal looked at the faces of his brethren around him. He had been made their leader, but he began to think that perhaps they were realizing their error in judgment by choosing him. In the many years since he took the position he had grown into the role, learning and forcing himself to understand the ways of the council that sat ruling over the Towers of Theron. In the past few years the single most deadly enemy to humanity in Theron, the orcs, had come to terrorize almost every nation he could name.

Thinking for a moment, Kal put the pieces of the puzzle together in his mind. His messengers brought word of the orcs organizing, each of the nations was feeling their assault, and now his council was asking him to surrender the world to the orcs. In that moment of clarity the answer to who had been aiding the orcs was obvious; it had been the council all along. "You are the ones guiding the orcs, aren't you?"

Gilden, the opposing member of the council and leader of the movement to appease the orcs spoke. "It has been us Kal. I regret that you cannot see the *wisdom* in our decision. We command enough armies to take this tower from you by force." Gilden looked piercingly at him, his dark hair trimmed short, his yellow eyes almost shining with their own inner light. "Surrender the stone to us, or we will take it. Believe me when I say that we will scour and sear the lands with fire if you don't. Your choice will save millions."

Kal stood, locking eyes with each of the twelve members who composed his council. Each in turn gave back a visage of hatred and firmness that echoed what Gilden had stated. Kal had no allies left here. He had been picked for his unbreakable devotion to Theron above the other candidates; he had first and foremost sworn an oath to care for the lands. Turning towards the door he pulled opened the heavy maple and iron doors.

"Kal, do you not having something to say before you leave?" Gilden's voice oozed slimy and dark, like the pitch blood of the orcs he used to do his bidding.

Kal sighed, his hand still on the door. He turned to face the council. "Leave this tower, NOW!" Kal knew they could not take his controlling stone for the Tower without a fight, and they knew they needed more numbers than what they had to beat him.

"A childish mistake Kal, a simple child's mistake."

"Gilden, the only mistake that I made was in trusting all of you so completely for so long."

Being the last one out Gilden nodded his head as Kal let the door fall closed behind him. He retook his seat at the head of the chamber. Looking at the empty seats he knew that his decision might cost more lives than surrender. But he could not let orcs, the filth of Theron, rule the lands. Letting his head rest on his hand he spoke to no one in particular.

"I have brought the towers to war. The blood of Theron's children is now on my hands." Kal sat at the head of his table, resting his head in his hands. After a time there was a knock at the door. "Enter."

Titus, the captain of the Tower Guard and Kal's confidant of many years slipped his head inside. "I take it that did not go well? They all left in a hurry."

"They have chosen to walk a dark path Titus. I fear my choice will cost millions of lives."

Titus nodded. "Well my friend you have never been one to —" Titus stopped and listened as bells sprung to life in the city.

"What are they doing out there?" Titus said over the growing din.

Titus and Kal moved quickly, taking the stairwell that led to Kal's private chambers and the walkway that circled the tower. There they would be able to see the whole of the valley. Reaching the railing Kal looked out, Titus a few feet behind.

Titus cursed under his breath, but Kal was silent. In the surrounding valley of this black tower he called home, he observed the bobbing light of many torches. An army marched on his tower, and he knew who led it. Through the din of war horns and warning bells, Kal looked over at his friend and spoke firmly. "Bring me the stone."

CHAPTER 1

Theron is a world beginning to mature. It is not the ancient place of other stories, but one of a world just barely beginning to enter its second age. The elves and dwarves and other elder races are entering Theron and staking their claim on the lands left from the Zephyren; the first men of Theron. It matures in a time when magic is nascent and the darker races of evil are emerging from the shadows. The world is in a time of great change, and it is with these transformations where we begin our tale.

The Kingdom of Dalerad is a simple land. To its east lies the Silver Sea, whose shores are of fine black sands. The coastal villages are renowned not just for their sailing skills, but also for the beautiful violet glass they create from the plentiful sand found on their shores.

Crossing to the far side of the lands takes a rider across the hills of Gulthan, where the wheat and barley that feed the kingdom are found. For hours as the crow flies all one will see is amber wave upon amber wave, broken only by the stone lanes and walls that divide one farm from the next.

Coming at last upon the western edge of Dalerad, the mountains of Ironwood are formed of tall growth trees and waters cascading into hidden lagoons. It is here in this realm where the barbarian tribes trade their plentiful iron to the Friezen king in exchange for grain- and promises of peace.

To the south are the forests of dark pine. Deep and untroubled by the touch of man, it is said that the woods are haunted. Ancient witches of the first-born Gods cursed it to be a place where animals grow grander and stronger than in any other land. The greatest of elk are to be found here, and it is across this forest that the neighboring kingdom of Yulan, the Nation of Scholars, lies. Known as the keepers of books and paper, these men and women delve into their studies in their ancient libraries.

We turn west, between the plains of Gulthan and the western mountains, which hold the capital of Thylen. Its long line of kings is about to come to an end with the failing health of the last Friezen king. The whole of the kingdom cannot help but speak of this, as they worry about who their king will choose as his successor. Here in Thylen we come across a young man named Cael Firestorm, the young duke of the Firestorm family. He has been sent by his father to make an impression on the king, and to gather support for his family among the nobility, so that he can assume the mantle of rulership when the king dies.

Cael sits in the palace gardens, the early morning sun washing into the small courtyard. He is admiring the dewy drops of moisture on the roses and how they catch the morning light. Cael has made a point to learn all he could of the workings of the kingdom during his stay here in the capital. He even spent weeks dining and spending the gold his father sent with him to gather the support of the lords and ladies of the city. A dreary task, as more than a few of the older ladies propositioned him to some degree. He knew though that he had made his father proud so far.

Cael stood of average height, a little less than 6 of the king's feet. His dark brown hair hung in curls to the red cloak that wrapped around his silk shirt and black leggings. His family crest was stitched into his shirt, the tornado of fire eternally burning as it passed through time. As Cael approached the pathway towards the southern halls of the palace, he found an old servant waiting there, eagerly motioning for him to turn towards the king's meeting room.

Cael followed the old servant, whose wizened form moved with greater haste than should be possible for his age. He admired the hanging tabards on the walls, the frozen rose of the Friezen family embroidered on them. Following their short walk in the hall, Cael arrived at the door to the king's meeting room.

The servant pushed open the door, and Cael stepped through. The king was sitting behind a large desk of darkly lacquered wood. Across from him, a brightly dressed tradesman whom Cael did not recognize was speaking to the king. Their hushed voices did not carry, even across the small room. "My lord," said the servant, " I present the young Duke Cael Firestorm."

Bowing, Cael made eye contact with the king. "My king, it is a pleasure to finally meet you in person. "

"Please, don't be so formal, I don't have time for formalities anymore!" The old king stood, wrapped in a thick fur robe, though the room was quite warm. "Let me finish this business with this-" He paused, "-merchant, and I will discuss your reasons for our meeting."

The king pointed Cael to a cozy drawing room and shut the door between them. The room had a window overlooking the gardens that Cael had just enjoyed. He wondered if perhaps his musings had not been as private as he had hoped? He gazed at the simple furnishings, the chairs plush though still plain in appearance. Two large seats sat with a small table between them facing the fireplace, where logs were stacked and ready to be lit with oil and flint and steel. Seating himself, Cael prepared himself with patience, unsure of how long the king would keep him waiting.

Cael recalled his meetings with the nobility of the city; some of them had forced him to wait for hours before formally greeting him. Though he knew it was a game they played, he made sure to wait the entire time no matter how uncomfortable he had become. He was thankful that a reputation began to precede him and the last royal he visited wasted no time in inviting him in. They still were evasive and barely respectful but they learned he was not going to go away or be ignored.

He had barely the time to settle into his seat further when the door opened once more and the king entered the room. Cael could see the king was handsome with his age. He was still keeping clean-shaven, with his hair combed, obviously not letting age or illness cause him to neglect appearance.

Cael quickly stood, but was motioned to sit again.

"Now lad, no need to be putting on airs for me. By the time you finished using the proper titles I would have stiffened and not been able to sit at all! Please, be comfortable!" The king pushed Cael back into the seat, grabbing two goblets from a nearby tray on a side table. He offered Cael water with ice, a rare luxury this far from the mountains and winter a month past.

"My lord, you are too kind."

"Lad when offering a man water is too good, it will be when we are drowning in the sea." The king seated himself in the sofa opposite, while Cael stifled a laugh. "Now I know you have been spending all too much time in my capital—"

"My lord—"

"Now hear me out young man, don't interrupt."

Cael sat back and decided to listen, it would do him no good to anger the king with impatience, his father would have his head.

"No one in their right mind spends as much time with the lords and ladies as you have these past weeks. Why do you think I don't let any of them live in the palace with me?" The king asked with a wide grin on his face. Cael was unsure how to react to his friendly chat thus far. The fact he hadn't had to go into any memorized speeches made him relax.

"My lord," Cael started, thinking it was best to be honest at this point. "I am unsure how to respond. I can understand your choice to live alone, as dining with the other royal families has kept me quite bored."

The king kept his smile and leaned back in his chair. Seeing this as approval, Cael continued. "To be honest my lord I am missing a number of hunts in the hills north of the estates of my family. This is our one break in the year when the animals can run free while the orcs lie dormant in their caves further north."

"Ah yes, the problem of those filthy beasts. They haven't approached any village in years thanks to your father." The king sipped his water, "But please, call me Jonothon."

"Yes, Jonothon, but truly I have enjoyed seeing the capital. There are many more things here in this city than in our home and the surrounding villages. It is exciting to see the number of travelers here—"

The king cut him off with a wave of his hand. "This is but a town lad, at best a large glorified fortress. Have you never been to the great city of Calril? Ygdrosen? Pulrath? Those are cities of the likes of which every man wishing to rule should see." Leaning back, the king chuckled to himself taking a sip of his water.

"Truth be told Cael, our kingdom is a small dot in this world."

Cael blushed; he should have realized the king was wise enough to realize his father's intentions. "Sir I have never left this kingdom, other than the scouting parties my father sent me on into the northlands." Cael was sure the king noticed the red hue coming to his face.

The King observed Cael's discomfort and embarrassment, and smiled. "Lad, it's well known to me that the only family that can be trusted with the Friezen crown is the Firestorm clan."

Cael was left slack-jawed. He was wholly unprepared for this sort of interaction with his ruler. Though stunned, his only thought was of the letter he would write his father letting him know the good news.

"The only thing I have to ask of you, and your family, is for you to be sent away from the kingdom." The king stated it in such a relaxed manner that Cael nearly missed the statement.

"Leave my lo— forgive me, Jonothon. Why do I need to leave?" Cael was confused, why would the king ask him to depart?

Sighing, the king took a moment to compose his thoughts. "Cael, I have a mission for you that will secure the future of our lands. Rest assured this is no exile, but if Dalerad is to be kept safe for centuries to come there is work for you to do."

Cael sat back, setting his cup on the small table, and felt astonished. He had never left the kingdom, nor would he even know how. His father's maps had shown him every route into the northlands, and the main roads south into the great wood, but the rest of the world? It was unknown to him. He attempted to gather his thoughts again, forming a question that any good subject would. How would his father answer?

"Why away from Dalerad? Is there not something I could learn while I am here that would assist you?"

"Cael, rulership is dependent on tradition. When I was picked as my father's heir I had to do the same thing, and I came back with an alliance with the coastal cities that brings us trade along the rivers and connects us with nations further away than our roads lead to. This assignment is not to distance you, but to make you and the kingdom greater."

Cael bowed his head, thinking on the king's explanation of his being sent away. His father had taught him to follow tradition, and listening to the one who allowed you to be king would be one he would have to obey.

"What would you have me do?" Cael asked aloud, not sure where the confidence in his voice came from.

The king had been watching Cael very closely, and when he finally heard him speak, he grinned. Quickly rising, the king began to move towards a low bookshelf across the room. Cael saw a number of dusty tomes covering the cherry shelves. The king asked, "Tell me, have you ever heard about the Towers?"

Cael sat forward, paying closer attention. " I have heard the old stories, the legends of the seats of power for the first gods of Theron."

The king moved his fingers across the leather bindings of the books, their aged leather varying colors of gray and brown and each covered in some dust except the last one. Apparently it was the book the king wanted. "The towers' true story has faded into myth, as you were given the tale that makes them the seat of gods. That was hardly the case. The Towers were most definitely created by someone else: another race known as the Zephyren, an ancient ancestor of all mankind."

The king returned to his chair, wrapping the blanket draped on the seat around his legs and settling in with the book on his lap. Watching as the king placed his hands on the cover, Cael could see the leather cover was very old, but still looked as if it was fresh. All the books he had learned to read from were in far worse a state than the ones the king had in this room.

He watched the king open the cover, scanning the pages, turning them until he found the one he wanted. He then read what was contained there while Cael sat and listened in silence.

852 years After the Founding

The council is meeting this night to decide the fate of the Towers. Those eligible have been gathered into the city in secret, and the guards are holding them in the keep at the base of the tower. This is the first such time I have heard of the lords and ladies coming together to decide who will lead them. It has been a long while since they have created another tower to help protect and rule the lands.

When I was a lad they used the towers in the wars against the Dark Tide. The filthy orcs devastated much of our world while the council attempted to stop them. The heroes we picked to lead the towers fought back, bringing the orcs to their knees but they have never been able to truly drive them from the world…

The king closed the book, accustomed to ending the text at such an abrupt point. Cael sat in his chair, dumfounded, and could only think to ask one thing. "Where is the rest of the text?"

The king smiled back. "That is why I need your help Cael. I cannot travel to get the rest of the text. The text of this nature should have somehow found its way to the lands of Yulan, to our south. Whoever wrote this was preparing an early history of the towers, and all those who survived the fall would be known to the scholar nation."

Cael was unsure what to think. "My lord, what exactly happened during this fall?

The king sat back into his seat, and Cael could see the weight seem to lie heavily upon the aged ruler. "The fall is what happened to those who ruled from the Towers, the 'seats of gods' as we tell our children." The King stood and walked towards the window, Cael stood to follow him.

"Tell me please Jonothon, What happened?"

Jonothon looked tired, and Cael though he could hear his rasping breath as he stood at the window. "The fall is exactly what it sounds like. Those with such great power eventually will be destroyed by it. The stone keepers, or council as they were known, grew corrupt and then rebellions sprang up across the lands. Our kingdom was one of those that rebelled." Jonothon paused, and Cael could see he was weighing if he should say more.

"Yulan should hold more answers for us than I could ever hope to give you. If anyone was to have a record of what happened to the towers, they certainly would."

Cael spoke slowly in measured words. "So you want me to go to the nation of Yulan. But how will I know where to look my lord?"

The king drifted back to his bookcase and replaced the text on the shelf. "I have a signet I will give to you, a sign of the faith I have placed in you." The king came back to Cael's seat, handing him an object wrapped in soft leather. Opening it, Cael found a small black box with a clasp on the side. He looked up to the king who motioned for him to open it.

He unclasped the side and lifted the small lid. Inside was a gold ring, bearing the insignia of the Friezen rose. "To whom shall I take this, my lord?" Cael took the ring and began inspecting the small details of the insignia in the light. The gold seemed to glow in the rays from the morning sun.

"I told you, call me Jonothon. And take this to the capital of Yulan, the city of Pulrath. Ask a guard at the gate to take you to the Friezen post there. You should get all the help you need at that point."

Cael placed the ring back in the box, and started to wrap it back up when the king interrupted him. "You wear that ring. Don't keep it in some box to be lost."

"My lo— I mean Jonothon, the ring isn't my size."

The king smiled at Cael, motioning him to put the ring on his finger. Cael opened the box once again, and carefully took the ring from its case. Cael looked at the king who waited expectantly for Cael to comply. Cael held the ring on his right ring finger and pushed it on, expecting it to be too loose for him and to fall off again. To his surprise, the ring stayed, quite snugly on his finger.

"First lesson Cael, is that some items in this world are very special indeed. That ring is special in that it can change its size at will. So long as you do not wish it to come off, it will not."

Cael was still surprised, but his first thought was just how few uses a ring that could change its size would have.

"Also Cael, while you are in Yulan, you must take every chance you can to learn more about this world we live in. Even if you find the rest of the text, don't come back here until you have followed all the clues to the lost towers. Follow them and continue this search for our kingdom. If we are to survive the next 500 years we will need to find these towers and secure them for ourselves. Do you understand?"

Cael nodded his understanding, looking once more at the ring he now wore. This was definitely not the course of events he had imagined when he started this trip in his father's name. He had questions and felt he could push his luck to ask Jonothon for the answers.

"My lord, why am I being sent on this mission for you? Surely a sage of your own—"

"Cael, trust in me that I have my reasons. I have been keeping watch on you. Your father has done his best with your mother gone, and for a warrior you do well. Rulership, though, takes more than that. You must know the nations against which you work to better your people.

The King gave pause for a moment. "Lad this evening I am going to hold a small dinner party. I feel that since you have dined with the lords and ladies you should dine with me as well before you leave."

Cael's mind was whirling with everything he had left to do. He had to write letters to his father, prepare for a royal dinner, and he still wasn't quite sure what he was being sent to do, other than find some old books. Cael stood from his seat, his mind filled to bursting with plans and concerns.

"Cael, prepare for this evening, and I will send a carriage to get you later," the king said as he guided Cael to the door. "Also my dear boy, I hope you father saw it right to teach you to dance?" The last thing Cael saw was a grin on the king's face as the door shut, leaving Cael standing alone in the hall with the same servant that guided him here.

Turning away from the now closed door, Cael spoke, "This has been a fortunate, though strange day…"

Smiling while he motioned Cael to follow him, the old servant quietly began walking Cael towards the entrance to the castle.

~~~

With Cael gone the king returned to the first sitting room, where the merchant stood looking out the window toward the surrounding city. "My Lord, you are sure?"

The king took a deep breath, letting it out slowly as he took a seat in the cushioned chair nearest him. He replied, "Cael is exactly as the book foretold. I just wish I knew what he will face before he returns."

"The book has kept your line true for almost 5 centuries since the fall. I doubt it would be wrong now." The mysterious merchant turned from the window. "Do you wish me to warn him?"

"I believe it would be more prudent to send him with help. Perhaps lord Grim can be persuaded to send one of the barbarians he keeps along with Cael."

The merchant bowed deeply to the king and made for the door, but the king stopped him before he could reach it. "Make sure our hands remain unseen in this, Clarence."

"As always, my lord." Clarence bowed deeply once more and exited the room.

~~~

Cael stood in his room at the inn where he had been staying. Books lay spread out on his bed where he had been spending his nights studying. The bedposts held some of Cael's other attire, the riding shirts and coats he wore while entertaining members of the court in his stay here. The blankets still remained where he had left them that morning, a quick making of the bed before he had left.

Histories of Dalerad covered his bed, all part of his attempt to impress the members of the court with his knowledge of his nation's history. There had been, however, little he had not already learned from speaking to his father. Many of the higher nobles kept to themselves on their estates and it was their support that he had needed, and it was through the lesser nobles that he had been told to talk his way onto the throne.

Cael looked towards the curtains at the windows, the thick material keeping out the last vestiges of the fading light. They smelled faintly of the anise that the inn keeper grew in his small garden. He thought on all he had read and found that there was very little of the story of the "fall" that Jonothon had mentioned; it was as if those here had tried their best to forget it. Why would he be sent searching other kingdoms for the ancient relics when he would be ruling here?

Letting the curtains fall slack, Cael was reminded that the king made a good point, he knew nothing when it came to rulership. His father had only given him small bands of scouts, and while he knew how to fight with numbers of men, he was no tactician. Sighing, he looked to the mirror in the wall to straighten his formal attire. The carriage to take him to the dinner being held by the king would no doubt be arriving soon and he did not want to upset the driver by not being prepared.

Cael had a passing thought, wondering if his letters would reach his father in time for a message to return before he set out on the road. He had not been able to see his father for very long the night before he had left their home. Shaking off the nervous feelings in his stomach, Cael turned his attention back to how he was presenting himself

Retying the black sash he wore at his waist, Cael double-checked to make sure he was properly attired for the evening. His white cotton shirt was freshly pressed, the tornado of flame for his family brightly stitched over his heart, and the crimson of his slacks matching it perfectly. As he straightened himself his eyes fell on the very obvious icy blue of the Friezen Rose adorning his finger. He was given no more chance to think on it as he heard a carriage in the road below and moved quickly to the stairs. Cael was unsure about the small dinner the king was having, but he knew it would be his first appearance as heir.

CHAPTER 2

As Cael stepped out the door of the inn he saw the carriage from the king waiting for him. A deep burgundy in the dim torchlight of the street, he could make out that the carriage was highly decorated. The knob on the door was gilded in gold and underneath was a carved Friezen rose painted in the light blue and white of the colors of the house. A coachman dressed in fine clothes that seemed too plush for a servant stood at attention near the sleek white horses that would be pulling the carriage.

Seeing that Cael had come out of the inn, the coachman stepped over and silently opened the door. He motioned Cael towards the now open door that revealed the cushioned interior, as he bowed slightly and spoke.

"Your carriage awaits my lord."

"Thank you. How long will it take us to reach the palace?" Cael asked stepping towards the carriage.

"It will not take longer than half the hour, my lord."

The man motioned for Cael to get inside with another wave of his arm. Cael stepped up and ducked his head to make sure he did not hit it getting inside. After he was seated, the coachman closed the door and quickly jumped up to join the other man that had been holding the reigns of the horses.

Cael felt the carriage jerk to a start and had to catch himself. He felt somewhat awkward at having been called 'lord' by the coachman, but he knew that if the king was honest in his words from earlier, it was a term he would have to grow used to.

The soft cushions made the trip a smoother ride then Cael had thought possible on a stone street. The horse's hooves clacked steadily on the stone streets, lulling Cael somewhat as he rode along. He watched the torches pass through the screens in place at the window of the carriage.

Sooner than he realized, they arrived in front of the well-lit palace just as the last of the others were entering. The palace struck an imposing figure as it was lit with the light of torches and lanterns to the top of its towers. Cael tried to count the different towers rising into the sky above him, but in the darkness he was unable to see their numbers against the night sky. He wondered how many rooms this palace would have. The more interesting topic would be learning who resided in those rooms. His own home had a great room for meetings with the local leaders but it was a small corner of what he could see the palace taking up for space.

The carriage rolled to a stop, and Cael opened the door and stepped out, unassisted. He could see from the look on the coachman's face that this was a breach of protocol. Cael smiled nervously and stepped away, hurrying up the steps and pausing at the entryway to look at the grand hall beyond. Cael guessed that nearly a hundred people were in the room. When the king had said a small dinner party, he was unaware he meant a number that felt as though the entire court were present. Nervously he smoothed his shirt, silently hoping he had worn the proper attire for such an event.

Cael stood near the doors, taking time to let the lords and ladies and assorted guests be announced ahead of him. He was not anxious to enter the hall. He noticed that many of the nobles handed cards to the herald as they advanced. He didn't know what they were, but he was left with little time to think about it as soon it was his turn to be announced.

"I don't have one of those cards." Cael whispered to the servant.

The man tucked his brass horn under his arm, fixing his gaze on Cael. He was attired similarly to the coachmen, but with shoes instead of the riding boots, and the house's colors setting the tone for his attire.

"My lord what have you done with your invitation?" The herald looked at him. Stepping in from behind the banner hanging behind the herald, the wizened servant from earlier whispered into the herald's ear. "He is what? Oh well that makes sense."

"Wait, what makes sense? What are you talk—" Cael was left with his confusion as the herald began his presentation seconds later.

The herald lifted his horn and blew a short series of notes and then spoke to the crowd gathered at the base of the steps. "The Duke Cael Firestorm! The Guardian of the Northern Steppes!" He bowed and moved further off to the side to allow the crowd a better view of the formally attired Cael.

He took a moment to stand there, the eyes of the room measuring him to see if he was worth speaking to. He was snapped from his reverie as the servant appeared to nudge him forward. Taking a few steps down into the room, he allowed the surprise at being announced to a room full of nobles pass. Though he was technically the son of a duke, he knew that his station was well below the company he kept tonight.

In that moment he was reminded of how preposterous it seemed that his father had sent him to try and gain their favor. To them his father was but a provider of men for their personal armies – not a viable option to take the throne.

His thoughts were interrupted as Jonothon approached, and the crowd returned to its murmuring with knowledge that a duke from the harsh north had appeared in their party. Cael was sure rumors had already started about him and the reasons for his presence.

"My lad, welcome to dinner." The king's voice was comforting in the noise of the room. "I have to apologize, but I felt it best to announce you this way. You should not shy away from letting these bloodsuckers know who you are."

Cael laughed nervously at the statement. "I have to agree with you my lord- I think..." he added much less sure of himself. Jonothon turned away as he spoke, motioning Cael to follow him.

The king found his movement unrestricted as he passed through the crowd. As Cael followed, he heard occasional comments and greetings made towards him. He carefully waved off all the entreaties to speak and followed the king to a small sitting room curtained away from the rest of the guests. He saw a few of the nobles were here as well. Aside from what looked to be a large barbarian in the room, everyone looked like they belonged there. The large hulk of muscle stood a full head and shoulders above the nobles, with a surly face that would seem comical if it hadn't been for the sizable axe the barbarian standing next to him carried.

"Alright lad, it's time for the formal introductions." He motioned to the tall surly lord standing with the barbarian. "This is Lord Grim, his lands lie near that of the barbarians in the mountains."

Cael bowed. "A pleasure, lord."

"An honor, Duke Firestorm. I have heard many tales of your father's endeavors to protect the northlands." He stressed the words with great displeasure.

Cael saw that he wore his hair closely cut to his head. He was somewhat gray in his beard and at his temples, and his clothes were simple but elegant. Cael was curious if black was the only color his house had picked or if it was his personal preference, considering how disapproving he seemed to look. Grim was lithe and carried himself with a firm stony grace that Cael knew was from years of being a commander of armies. Cael turned from his piercing blue-gray eyes to greet the next noble.

"Ah come on Grim! Be a little more festive; people of Dalerad rest easier knowing warriors protect them from the beasts of the north," said the strange man. He appeared to be the exact opposite of Lord Grim in both appearance and temperament. He wore a huge smile and appeared quite rotund around his middle, no doubt the result of years of enjoying himself. His clothes were bright greens and whites, but more refined than those of a jester. While Grim had piercing eyes, his companions were brown and seemed to be filled with a child-like cheer.

"This is Lord Kingsley, Cael. I would say where his lands are but I doubt he could find them once he starts to drink." The king smiled at Kingsley though the smile had a strange sense to it, a hesitation. Kingsley took Cael's hand and shook it heartily. Cael inspected it to make sure it had survived the grip unscathed.

"Aye a strong lad! He will do well!" Kingsley turned away to continue a discussion with a young lady servant who carried a jug of wine.

The next few lords Cael paid little attention to, as he was distracted by a dark haired woman at the far side of the room. She was wearing a red dress and seemed to be following Cael as he walked around the room completing his introductions.

The king finished his last presentation, letting the noble walk away when Cael finally had a chance to ask about the young woman.

"My Lord—"

"Its Jonothon lad, and the young lady you have been eyeing is my niece."

Cael stiffened; his attempts to sputter out a response were silenced with the king's hand. "Cael, believe it or not, I was young once."

Kingsley cut in abruptly, appearing out of nowhere, "Jonothon can you even remember that far back?" He laughed along with all the other nobles at the joke- all, that is, but Grim, who maintained his stoic appearance with his barbarian.

"Ignore Kingsley, either way she is just your age as well, Cael, so I see no problem with her speaking to you. I do warn you though, she is a very independent creature."

"Independent?" Cael asked.

Jonothon looked over at his niece. "I let her have more freedom than it is custom for women to have. I would warn you to be careful with her, but it is you who I am concerned for."

Hearing the king had a niece had made Cael start to think on why the king did not have an heir picked from his own family.

"My lord, why is it that you don't let your niece or her father take the throne? Would they not be next in line as part of your family?"

The king looked across the room at his niece in silence. After a moment he seemed to put his answer together. "Her father passed on many years ago and she cannot take the throne because that is just not the way things are here, Cael. When the time comes you will understand. Come, let me introduce you."

As the king led him across the small room, Cael straightened his shirt and prayed he wasn't blushing. As they approached the king's niece, he regained his composure. Cael felt less anxiety facing the orcs in the mountains of the north than he did walking up to the beautiful young lady who was the king's niece.

As they came closer, Cael tried to not to stare at the woman as she stood speaking to a pair of the many nobles Cael had been introduced to. He could hear her laughter and saw her smile at a joke they all shared. Her dark hair was pulled up off her neck, and seemed to be pinned up in ruby encrusted plaits. Her dress was red with gold corseting and Cael saw her eyes shone brightly with the deep green of emeralds.

"My dear Thera, allow me to introduce Cael Firestorm."

Cael bowed as he gently took her hand. "A pleasure, my lady."

The young woman bowed as she spoke, "An honor, sir. It is not every day my uncle actually introduces me to one of the other royalty." A playful grin played across her as she turned to face Jonothon.

"I mean no harm dear, it's just— "

"Just that you are overly protective. I forgive you uncle. Now, leave Cael to speak with me alone." Thera watched her uncle walk away smiling. Cael felt rather entertained by the interaction thus far and thought that informality must be a family trait. He watched Jonothon walk away and caught a wry smile on the king's face as he did so.

"Now that we are introduced, let's take a walk while we talk, shall we?"

Cael grinned, "You know the palace better than I my lady. Perhaps you should lead us to ensure we get the best sights."

Thera took Cael's hand and started off to a large set of side curtains that decorated the wall. They avoided the conversational attempts of several lesser nobles by finding their way quickly across the room. Stepping behind the heavy velour panels, Cael was about to ask where they were going when she pulled a key from the lace at her wrist and slid it into a lock that seemed built right into the stone face. He realized now that they were completely concealed from view by of the rest of the large room.

Cael didn't get time to ponder it, as Thera took his hand in hers again, leading him through the opening in the wall. The door shut quickly and quietly behind them, something Cael was impressed by given the size of the stone door they had passed through.

Thera gently pulled him along. Cael noticed a faint torchlight lit their path through the small hallway. He tried not to pay attention to how soft her hand was in his, nor of how nervous being alone with her made him. Cael's experience with women was short and consisted of some rather rough innkeepers' wives that struck fear into the rowdiest of men.

"Where are we?" Cael asked of his guide.

"We are inside the palace walls. The first king of Dalerad was a very paranoid man. Though I admit he had reason to be," Thera said.

"Why is that?"

"Dalerad was one of the first new kingdoms after the towers fell. Once the old rulers were gone their subjects found themselves with armies to command and land they had liberated, they realized someone had to rule so many of the generals picked themselves." Thera smiled at Cael in the dim torchlight. "You don't know much about our history do you?" She stopped them at what appeared to be an intersection.

"I know some of our history. I started to read our histories when I came to the Thylen. Your uncle mentioned the fall of the towers but I can't find anything on it in the histories I have."

Thera made a noise to herself, and continued straight into the next section of hall. He couldn't tell if she was angry or just in a hurry. She didn't say anything else as they moved along, and Cael had to admit he was impressed she could move so well in the mass of lace that comprised the dress she was wearing.

Finally they came to the end of the hall where the torches stopped, but a light similar as that from the moon illuminated the stairs. Looking up the stairwell, Cael saw no windows, but the steps were lit as if a full moon was right above them. What struck him as even more strange was the fact that the moon had almost faded to nothing the night before; there should not be this much light.

"Is that moonlight? The full moon is weeks off yet."

Thera smiled and motioned Cael to follow her up the winding stairs. It got brighter as they moved upwards further than Cael could see, and quite suddenly Thera stopped at a landing where he guessed another door awaited them. A tall thin glass window with the light that Cael had been seeing was next to the door.

The window glowed with a light that mimicked the moon. The window itself was ornate, with designs of the stars and the sun and moon worked in iron.

Thera pushed on the door lightly, letting it swing open to reveal a room with a domed ceiling covered in stars. High on the dome a moon-shaped item hung near what should have been the ceiling. As Cael stepped in, Thera moved to a pedestal in the center of the room. Cael looked above him, realizing that from this angle he couldn't see the ceiling; it truly looked like he was under the night sky.

"What is this place?" he asked.

"This is an observatory. The old kings found it to their benefit to know the paths of the stars. I think at times they felt the stars were just as much their playthings as a map of the heavens." She looked at him with a smile that Cael could feel melt his misgivings about being alone with her.

"So this machine watches the stars, and shows where they are?" Cael was very curious how this place could see a moon that wasn't full or stars from inside a palace.

"You might say that. What you see now is the night sky a thousand years from now." Cael felt a momentary wave of shock and denial. How could anyone see a thousand years into the future? Thera kept that same melting smile and Cael felt it better to believe her.

"An observatory can predict star movement my young duke. Once you know part of a star's path, you can see the rest of it through time."

Cael looked up at the simulated night sky above him. He stepped closer to the pedestal in the middle, finding that the floor was replaced with a wide circle of grass around it. A few cushions and pillows were in a pile to the side.

"So how does this place work?" He asked, his surprise giving way to curiosity.

Thera shook her head. "Other than the controls here on the pedestal, I have no knowledge of how it works. My uncle says it is one of the relics from the first kingdoms, a small portion of the powerful creations made before men went mad with their power."

Thera twisted one of the small spheres that were on the pedestal, and as she did so, the moon faded to near-black and the room got very dark. Cael could just barely make out her shape in the darkness now that the moonlight was gone.

Thera walked over to the pile of cushions while she said this, grabbing a large pillow for herself and one for Cael. Cael didn't know what she intended until she threw the pillows down, grabbed a blanket, and tossed it at Cael who caught it roughly.

"Roll out the blanket for us over the grass. We are going to watch the stars for a time," Thera said, going back to the pedestal.

Cael unrolled the wide blanket and Thera tossed her pillow to the end of the blanket nearest the center of the grassy circle. Laying her-self down, she gazed up at the sky. Cael stood for a moment, unsure of how proper it was to be lying next to her in such a place. Thera sensed his discomfort and broke the silence.

"It will be alright Cael, no one will be here save for us. Come, relax and speak with me."

Cael joined her, and as they lay still in the silence, he felt a bit strange and out of place. He noticed the night sky was different from his own, at least a little. He had learned to navigate with the stars but this sky would not lead him true. Thera was the one who spoke first.

"Cael, can I ask you something?"

"Anything you wish my lady."

She paused as she weighed her words. "How fierce are the orcs you fight in the northlands?"

Cael sat up and leaned on his arm looking at Thera; wondering what reasons she would have for wanting to know about the orcs.

"That is a strange question to ask."

"It is the curiosity of a little princess trapped in the castle." She said playfully, which made Cael think it was only a half-truth. He took a moment and thought on what his answer should be.

"The strength of the orcs is without question; they are fierce and savage in their attacks. They are cruel and show no mercy to humankind." Cael started to push the memories of old battles out of his mind. "They customarily use poison arrows, preferring to let us humans die slowly and painfully. They never take prisoners for long."

Thera was quiet in the darkness, and Cael began to worry if he had said too much to the young woman. The cruelty of the orcs was something he knew keenly and was aware of in a sense that few others could understand. He had seen men die even in his young years, and he had faced the beasts and had come out from it as well.

"I am sorry. I forget that others are not as aware of them as my family is. I will stop — "

"No, no! I was just," she paused for a moment thinking of what to say. "I was just taken by surprise. The fear of orcs here in the city is like that of a child's tale. Most have never even seen one." She rolled up onto her elbows to face Cael. "That is much different from you. You are so young but you know them and fear them for what they really are."

Thera's eyes seemed to be looking *into* Cael and he felt somewhat less than worthy in that moment. She was right for saying he knew them; he was the one feeling out of place here in the city. He was barely able to follow the proper etiquette the court required. It was sad to know that many of the people here would be lost if they lived near the harsh northlands where the orcs roamed. The icy winds that preceded every attack were the only warnings they gave of their coming. Why the winds accompanied them, no one had ever explained.

Cael laid back down to look up at the false night sky, his mind losing itself in the expanse that the stars filled above him.

"Thera why are you not picked to rule?"

"It makes no sense to you now Cael, but I promise in time the reason will be clear. The high lords would never stand behind my family. Even though I am the niece of the king, my father and mother were not high born."

"And what of your father and mother? What happened to them?" Cael asked, feeling brave.

Thera was silent in the darkness. Cael leaned back up on his arm to look at her again and she rolled back on to her elbows.

"My family was killed in an orc attack. I have only the dreams of my mother to remember them by now." Cael watched as she smiled sadly.

"Tell me Cael, since we are asking all these questions, why did you accept my uncle's quest to leave?"

"My father has always told me to serve the king in totality. I was sent here in his place and I know he would have accepted. How can I do any different?"

"This does not seem strange to you at all? You get told that your family is going to inherit the throne but you have to leave to get it and you just accept that?"

"You seem to know a lot about what will be happening for me very soon. Why did you really bring me up here?" Cael asked playfully. Her questions were honest and did not feel as harsh as they sounded in his mind.

Thera leaned in closer to Cael, looking directly into his eyes. Cael could see her eyes catching the thousand sparkles of the stars above the two of them.

"I wanted to make sure you had a reason for coming back."

Lord Grim was doing his best to remain wary. Jonothon had informed him before this party that he was going to announce his heir to the throne and wanted to ensure that the lords maintained the peace. Grim had been acting on behalf of the king for years, becoming more and more his right hand in the ruling of the kingdom. While some of the other lords felt he should be picked as heir, Grim had been well aware for some time that he was not the choice to be made.

"Grim, do you think I will get a chance to fight with Lord Kingsley's henchmen?"

Grim looked up at Herth, still a full head taller than Grim's height of over six of the king's feet. His lightly curled blonde hair and clear blue eyes gave him the look of a child-- a stark contrast to his position as one of the best warriors the western mountains had to offer the world.

"No, I doubt they would be stupid enough to try anything with this many of the other lords around. Besides, the king has yet to announce his heir." Grim grimaced as he thought of the long shot that Kingsley would be picked. Herth took notice of the grimace that passed over Grim's features as he looked over at Kingsley being so jovial amongst the lords and ladies.

"You don't actually think Jonothon would pick him do you?" Herth swilled the ale in his large mug about while he spoke, watching the room.

"I certainly hope that is not to be the king's choice. I would hope that Clarence would be voice enough in his ear to stop that from happening." Grim thought about how much he truly hoped Clarence would stop such a thing. Though he had only met the strange man a few times, he did trust him in a way.

Herth listened to this and looked out into the room at all those present. Though he was considered nothing more than a barbarian by most of the lords in the room, Grim knew he was well aware of the political scene into which he had escorted Grim.

Kinglsey was suspect in more shady activities than anyone would think a man capable of. No matter how many times he was under suspicion though he was able to keep a clean slate and came out without any charges of guilt. Herth had accompanied Grim to a few of the other cities following the paths of men known to be faithful to Kingsley over the king. Never did they ever reveal the dark path they were suspected of walking.

Grim looked again through the room and noticed the absence of the king's niece and Duke Firestorm, a very young man in terms of the experience his title suggested.

"Grim, what do you know of this Firestorm Duke? I don't think I have ever heard of his clan."

"No, I don't suppose you would; the Firestorm clan are not lords so you would rarely hear them mentioned. They are also the only clan or family allowed to answer directly to the king. The Firestorm name carries great weight because they have always borne the burden that is the northern steppes."

"They are the ones keeping the orcs at bay?" Herth looked questioningly at Grim.

"Yes. In every confrontation they are the first to strike and unerringly take the hardest hits in return. It's been a surprise throughout our history how they remain so trivial politically, and yet they are the greatest keepers of our peace." Grim seemed to weigh his own words in his head while Herth watched him.

"Do you know the reasons for this?" Herth asked.

Grim shook his head. "I know nothing for sure, but it has been this way since the founding of Dalerad, so far as I know."

Grim scanned the room and saw from the back that both the king's niece and duke Firestorm had now returned. They carried themselves with a different look. She scanned the room and Grim could see her compose herself and put on the front that all the lords and ladies expected her to have. The duke, however, seemed awkward and lost, and was undoubtedly at a loss for what to do with the finery of the party. Grim noted that Herth saw it as well; undoubtedly he was pleased to see that the Duke was so out of place. Grim thought that perhaps he considered the young man a kindred spirit for the evening.

"I think I want to spar with the young duke. Grim, could I have your permission?" Herth looked over at his master and Grim saw the barbarian's playful eyes already cheering at the thought of someone he could fight with.

"I think we should hold off for now on challenging a young man less than half your size to a contest of arms."

"Fine. I will wait, but I still want to challenge him."

Grim shook his head at the sentiment of his friend and servant. "Let us start by having you stay here and watch the room, and I will speak to him at greater length."

Lord Grim gave Herth a look that conveyed he meant what he said. Though Herth was a large and playful man, he knew there were serious moments to be had. Grim knew that Herth was well aware he was using the impression of others who said he was only a barbarian to his advantage. It allowed him freedom to act and never quite have to follow the rules of propriety that Grim was bound to.

As Grim approached, he noticed the Kingsley had made a similar move, and was coming with a few of his less than honorable minor lords. Grim was the closest to his target, and waited for Cael to finish getting a glass of wine from a passing servant before approaching him.

"Duke Firestorm, I hope you are finding the party tonight to be enjoyable?"

Cael looked surprised that Grim was even speaking to him. Grim knew his face almost always held a dour and intimidating glare, but he was doing his best to appear friendly.

"My Lord Grim, the pleasure is mine. And the party..." Cael seemed to think on this a few moments. "I can't say I even know what to think; it is a little beyond me for all the finery."

"It is alright, it takes us all some time to get used to the regalia." Grim managed his best smile as he sized up Cael in his mind. He was about to ask what had brought Cael to the city when two things occurred. The first was that Grim caught sight of the signet ring carrying the Friezen rose, an important symbol of the king's favor, and the second was the untimely arrival of Kingsley.

"My dear boy, a fine welcome to the palace party isn't it? I do say I have enjoyed the evening thus far." Kingsley jumped in as if Cael and he had known each other for years and not for mere hours as was the case. "Tell me lad, what have you liked most this evening?"

Kingsley purposely ignored that Grim was standing there speaking to Cael, and though Grim held his temper, he was bristling with the knowledge that there was nothing he could do to warn Cael or to interfere with Kingsley speaking with him.

"My lord, I don't think I have decided yet what I enjoy more."

"Right I know, there is too much to choose from." Kingsley gave Grim a wry smile and continued speaking. "You will hopefully not let Grim get you down will you? He is aptly named, given his demeanor."

"If only the same could be said for your own name Kingsley." Grim returned the same smile back towards him, and he noticed Cael was starting to look as though he was felt somewhat awkward while the two lords exchanged looks at each other. "Duke Firestorm, I will bid you good evening, and will see you at the feast very shortly I am sure. Lord Kingsley, until another time."

Grim paced off, leaving Cael to fend for himself with Kingsley. Not knowing much of Cael, he was worried about what pressure Kingsley would be able to bring to bear on the young man. No man should have to face the choices Cael would have in his life if he stayed at court.

He was so young that Grim almost thought he shouldn't have to bear the weight of his family legacy like he had been directed. Grim wondered if he himself had been ready to bear the same weight at that age; what boy could truly be ready to bear a sword and know how to rule at the same time? His thoughts on the differences of birthright were interrupted by the appearance of Herth in front of him.

The interruption was welcome though, since Herth gave Grim an opportunity to pull himself away from the ball for a few moments and go to a side hall where they could speak privately.

Though everyone considered Herth a servant or guard for Grim, he was much more than that.

Following the path that the crowd made for them at Herth's advance, they quickly emerged off to the side where the clamor of the room died down a bit. They stepped into the cover of the hall Grim where felt it was safe to speak, as well as it could be with the palace full of revelers.

"Did you note anything strange while I was speaking to Cael?" Grim asked.

"Other than the fact you let Kingsley push you out of the way, nothing unusual. I should assume you learned something though?"

Grim nodded. "The young man wears a signet ring bearing the Friezen rose."

Herth's eyes narrowed at this news, he was well aware that if Cael possessed a symbol of such importance from the king then he was indeed a player to be wary of in the events of the night.

"Do you think he is the king's choice for an heir?"

"I am unsure. If it is so, then the king is asking for a bit of trouble. It would explain why Clarence came to me and asked for you to be present this evening."

Herth crossed his arms in a mix of contemplation and disgust. He did not trust Clarence, the merchant advisor to the king, and had good reason. He was never around long and when he was, he felt it his right to supersede all boundaries and normal rights and go directly to the king. While Herth had little interest in doing so himself, he would take offense at any time that Grim was not shown what Herth considered his proper respects. Grim appreciated the sentiment from Herth as it was a sign of his loyalty from the tribes to Grim's family.

"Then Clarence knew who the king's choice would be. Or he helped make it."

"Herth, not even I am aware of how the king is going to make his decision. Everyone in the council of lords assumes he is to choose among them, or at least among the highest lords in the king's favor. We can't even look to some precedent since the line of kings has been unbroken since before any of us were born."

Herth looked back out into the room, watching the exchanges between the lords. Grim followed his eyes to observe the movements of the crowd. Servants were coming out from the other side of the room to guide guests into the dining hall where dinner would be served for the lords. Grim watched with Herth as lords and ladies began to file into the other room towards their dinner with the king, and wondered how many of them expected the surprise he and Herth were starting to be able to predict.

"So it is during dinner that the news will be given to us all." Grim looked over at Herth, "I want you to sit next to Cael, make sure that nothing happens to him after the news is given, I am sure there will be some who are going to be displeased with the decision if that is how it goes."

Herth nodded his understanding. Whenever a task presented itself he grew quiet, focusing on nothing else. Seeing a servant coming to guide them to their seats for the banquet Grim, nodded back to Herth and walked off towards the dining hall.

Cael found himself being led into a large hall filled with tables covered in food. As he grew closer he saw roasts and potatoes and carrots steaming in ornate dishware. He saw the rare sea-oranges with strawberries and grapes. There were also mints and some small decorated squares that he assumed would be the chocolate he had heard about as a child.

A servant stopped in front of him, and motioned Cael to sit down in a high-backed chair with carved arms and a red silk cushion. Complying, Cael looked around himself at the different people at the table and noted that he was just a few seats down from the king. Jonothon raised his glass to him and smiled and Cael smiled back almost automatically.

Cael looked expectantly around the room, trying for another glance at Thera. He was still caught up in the time they had spent in the observatory. He did not find her immediately, and his search was cut short by more lords coming to the table at which he was sitting.

He was interrupted by Kingsley being seated between himself and the king. On his other side, Cael was surprised to find Grim's barbarian settling into a chair. Cael had to wonder if he could even fit in the seat.

"Ah lad, don't stare at Herth, he tends to not like it." Kingsley smiled as he spoke in Cael's ear. If Herth heard his comment, he didn't make any reaction suggesting as such. He continued merely to try and make himself comfortable while looking for the best place to leave his large axe during dinner.

"Does he always carry that thing with him?" Cael leaned over to inquire of Kingsley.

"I think he may even sleep with it. You can never tell with the tribesmen. They are, after all... " Kingsley seemed at a loss for the word he was trying to use.

"Savage. Quite savage is the word you are looking for Lord Kingsley." Herth's voice was smooth and strong, and without any sense of irritation. Cael thought that Herth must not be anywhere near so savage as Kingsley had suggested, as reflected by his ability to keep his composure. The large man had been obviously insulted, yet made no change in motion or voice to suggest he cared.

"Anyways young man, if you look around here you will see a number of lords waiting for the announcement the king is to make tonight. Many of them support one lord or another, each believing he knows who would best rule. Just remember that the choice of an heir is an important thing in this land. The council of lords requires a strong king to guide them. In the past they have struggled for control with the king himself, and Jonothon has done much to stabilize that power struggle."

Kingsley grew silent though as all eyes in the room turned to the king. No one in the room was eating yet- they would not eat before the king took his first bite, as it was was the tradition of this ceremony of announcement. Cael took a quick moment to ponder the sea of faces at the tables of the lesser nobles scattered about the room. Though he was not a high noble, he was sitting on the raised platform at one end of the hall with them.

The stone room had high walls, each with a pair of banners bearing the Friezen rose insignia of the king. The roof of the hall rose above them, high enough that Cael was sure his family's estate home could easily fit inside before even touching the lower rafters.

"Lords and Ladies of the kingdom, I welcome you to this rare occasion of feasting in the palace. My father always taught me that all news sounded better with a full stomach and a full glass of wine at hand." Jonothon paused as he let the small murmurs of laughter die down. "We are all here this evening because I must make a choice that will secure the kingdom for our children, and our children's children. And I have made that choice. In making this decision, a king must choose carefully, with great diligence and care of thought. I did not make a choice on whim or by flight of fancy. Nor did I make this choice based upon the favor that one lord may have earned over another."

Cael saw a large grin grow on Kingsley's face at this last statement. He began to straighten his shirt and cuffs as the king pause to let the room take in the words he was giving them. Cael was unsure at this point if the king really was going to choose him over someone in this room and if the talk they had earlier in the day was merely a front to give him the strange idea that he could rule.

"Today I finally honor the greatest loyalty this kingdom has known since the fall of the council and the founding of Dalerad, almost five hundred years of duty and diligence and sacrifice of life."

"Just tell us so we can get to the wine!" A voice yelled from across the room. The king smiled at his subject but did not let him interfere with his speech.

"I will announce it. Tonight henceforth I want the whole of the kingdom to know that with my passing the Friezen Clan ends, and in its place as rulers of Dalerad will be the Firestorm Clan of the Northern Steppes." The king faced the lords and the sounds of a confused crowd slipped across the room. Cael was stunned in his chair; he noticed that Kingsley was half-standing looking surprised at the king. His head slowly turned to face Cael.

"Duke Cael Firestorm, please rise." The king motioned for Cael to stand, and he was surprised he was able to keep his feet underneath him. Cael felt the tension in the room. He could feel the surprise of the room as well as his own. Cael was certain that he was as surprised as the nobles had been by the announcement.

"My Lord." Cael gave a small bow, unsteady in front of the many eyes staring at him just a few seats down from the king.

"Your family has protected Dalerad for centuries. I welcome you no longer as a duke of the realm, but as the first Prince Firestorm." The king began to clap, ignoring the near silence of the rest of the room. The next person to stand and begin clapping was Lord Grim, seated on the opposite side of the king. Though his face was still a grimace, Cael noted it had a strange mix of relief to it. The other lords and ladies began to stand, their singular claps soon fading together in a room full of applauding men and women for Cael. He took note that Kingsley had remained seated, not clapping and seemingly unsure of what to think.

Cael felt a pat on his back as the applause began to fade; the large barbarian seemed to give his approval with just a nod of his head as he sat down. Cael looked back to the king who looked like he was about to make another announcement. While the lords retook their seats Cael noticed that wine was being passed around, though no one took a drink quite yet.

"Tradition dictates that each king must bring something new to the kingdom. I brought greater trade with the shipping lanes for the eastern coast. Yes, Cael is a younger man than most of us here. He is awkward at times with formality and has seen no more of this world then most of us." The king let this statement sink in for emphasis. "But this young man has been in the northern steppes for all his nineteen years, where he has faced orcs in battle. His family as a whole has asked for nothing from this kingdom for all the centuries their blood has protected us. But I must ask one final task of you Cael, that you must accept in the audience of your lords." The king put added emphasis on the 'your lords' to ensure that the room understood his point.

"I will do as you ask my liege, as any loyal servant would." Cael stumbled through the response.

"You are to be given a quest, to ensure the longevity of this kingdom. Do you accept?"

Cael felt as though the eyes of the crowd were boring into him when the king announced him as his heir. It was nowhere near the feeling of being examined that he experienced now as the room awaited his response.

"I will go my lord. I will return with the means and knowledge to protect Dalerad so long as my family is to rule."

The king smiled and raised his glass. "To the journey that is life, I raise my glass. To the flowing river that we follow to our life's end, I drink." With that the king raised the wine glass to his lips and drank. The rest of the crowd murmured the same chant, and the feast was on. Cael had no sooner sat down then the merriment was on at the tables surrounding him. Herth was already tearing apart the legs of a large bird he assumed was a roasted turkey. Watching him, Cael wasn't sure if he should be hungry, or disgusted, or impressed at the rate that the large man was making food disappear around him.

Looking the other way Cael saw that Kingsley had disappeared, his absence apparently unnoticed by the revelers around him. Cael was unsure what to think of the lord. He had been very friendly, almost to the point Cael felt he was trying to get something from him. His reaction to the king's announcement had caught him by surprise though; he had risen to his feet as if he thought it would be him.

"Cael, is this seat taken?"

Cael turned to see Lord Grim standing next to him, respectfully with his hands behind his back.

"I suppose not, please sit." Cael rotated himself and adjusted his chair to be able to speak with Grim who pulled the seat in next to Cael.

"I want to be the first to let you know that I am on your side in anything that happens." Grim began to inspect the wine glass in front of him as he spoke, the smoky glass evidence it came from the east of Dalerad.

"I am confused, why would you need to say that to me?" Cael inquired, watching Grim pour himself some wine and filling Cael's glass.

Grim placed the bottle down and picked up his glass, rolling the wine around the bottom and looking deep in thought. Cael was about to ask if he was well when Grim spoke.

"The life of a King here is not going to be easy. You could have probably noticed earlier that Kingsley and I are not on very good terms."

"That much was obvious. You looked like you were about to stab him." Cael let himself enjoy a short chuckle thinking back on the situation.

Grim took a long drink of the wine and set the glass down on the table, meeting Cael's eyes. "The kingdom is held together by the delicate thread that is loyalty to the king." Cael looked out at the crowd, feeling suddenly unprepared for the eyes gauging him. The unnerving thought of wondering who could want to get something from him came to his mind.

"I can keep them loyal to you here, but in your journey you will need help, and I wish to offer it. I want you to take Herth with you."

Cael looked to his other side to the barbarian drinking a mug of ale, his plate covered with a stack of bones larger than any Cael had seen. Herth looked at him and smiled, taking another drink of the ale.

"I don't know Grim, is he not your guard?"

Grim followed Cael's gaze to look at Herth. Leaning back in his chair now, he didn't look like he could be intimidating, nor did he look like he could have stood up after all the food he had eaten.

"Whether you want him to come along is not an issue, as you will require help on the road ahead. Herth will be able to part from my side for a time if it ensures the kingdom will survive."

"Didn't you say the barbarian tribes were loyal to you? Shouldn't you be their first concern?"

Grim smiled, well as much as he was able to. "They are loyal to me but they know I would give my life for the king and Dalerad over anything else, so their loyalty is also to that end. So long as you keep their respect, the tribes will be behind you."

Cael looked around the room noticing the other lords and ladies enjoying themselves. Their first care and concern was their own stomachs it seemed. Cael wondered if this was the game of politics where everyone would pretend to not be concerned while secretly they planned what to do next to protect themselves. Cael looked back to Grim and nodded.

"I will accept, but I have a question and a request."

"And that is what, my lord?" Grim asked rather curiously.

"First, is the kingdom in danger?"

"Nothing more than usual Cael." Grim answered a little too quickly, which troubled Cael.

"That is a fair answer. I also need maps of the south, do you know of any I could use? I am afraid that my own go no further south than Dalerad."

Grim thought for a moment, leaning back with his wine glass still in hand. "I think I might just know the maps you would need. I will have them sent to your inn by the morning."

Grim took one long drink from his glass, finishing the wine. Standing, he looked around the room preparing himself to leave.

"You are leaving already?" Cael asked, feeling somewhat abandoned to the crowd who had thus far stayed distant while Kingsley and Grim were near.

"Yes Cael, I have duties I must attend to. Herth will stay with you tonight and until you return. I don't want you to fear for the kingdom in your absence, I will ensure your father gets word of this day and your lands will be kept safe."

Grim began to walk away and Cael stood and called after him again. Something about this all bothered him. "Lord Grim."

Grim stopped and turned back to Cael. "Yes, Cael?"

"Who did you want the king to choose?"

"I didn't have anyone I wanted him to choose Cael. Anyone was better than the one I feared." Grim bowed and continued into the hall towards the exit. Cael watched him fade into the crowd and looked back at Herth, who appeared to be snoring as he reclined in his chair.

Cael thought on the events of the evening and noticed that some of the lesser lords felt safe enough to come close and greet him in a much friendlier manner than they had before. As he went through the formal greetings and the preening he had grown used to from them, his mind was distracted by thoughts of Thera, and his hopes for the long road ahead.

CHAPTER 3

Jonothon was doing his best to distract himself as he walked along the stone walls of his castle. As he paced, he tried to memorize the patterns in the polished stone floors to drive out the rambling thoughts of his worries. It wasn't working. It had been a few days since his soldiers confirmed that Cael and Herth had left the city, beginning what he knew would be a very long journey. He had been asking himself if what he had done was just, sending Cael out from the kingdom nearly blind and without any more guidance than a few cryptic words from an old book he held on his shelf.

He still had not come to some terms that made him comfortable with what he had done. It would be troubling indeed if he could never find a way to live with it. Catching himself, he noted that he had found his way to the same gardens where Cael had waited for him just a few days ago. He could still smell the scent of the roses in bloom, even at this late point of the afternoon. He took pride in the large rose bushes his city was known for. The flowers covered so many different colors and combinations it would take an outsider years to memorize them all. He stepped down onto the stone pathway that would take him to the bench in the middle of the gardens, careful not to lose his footing. Though he kept active, his doctors had already had to set a few broken bones- part of the secret of his failing health that the lords were not allowed to know.

Jonothon came to rest on the bench, the smooth stone firm but not entirely uncomfortable. The sounds of the songbirds picked up again as he finished moving and interrupting their days. Jonothon closed his eyes and relaxed for a minute, taking a deep breath of the scents that lingered around him. He caught the rose, pygmy moss, hyacinths and the woody smell of the mulch coming to his nose. He tuned his ears to concentrate on the chirping and chatter of the birds and the squirrels he knew had made their homes in the garden. The wind swayed through the branches of the oak tree towering above the garden. Jonothon was unsure when it had been planted, but he knew it was well before his time as king. It was already large during his childhood, as he had spent many days climbing in the branches and hiding from his own father.

The distant sound of footsteps in the hall caught his ear. He recognized the shuffling but smooth gait of one of his closer confidants. He came closer. Looking towards the entrance he saw that his old manservant Felsath was there smiling, two steaming mugs in his hands.

"My lord, would you care to join me in having some tea?" He lifted the two mugs higher, accenting the flowing steam rising up from them.

"Felsath, why do you ask questions you already know the answer to?" Jonothon smiled at him, motioning for him to take a seat next to him. Watching his friend amble over, Jonothon was reminded of the years they had spent sitting here talking about the problems of their lives, their trials and joys. Felsath was very old, as he was already a man when the king was still young. His hair was gray and had thinned slightly as time passed. Though somewhat hunched, he was still strong enough to get around. His eyes were sea green and revealed very little to those who did not know him.

Now seated, Felsath handed the king a mug, and the scent of sharp spices caught Jonothon's nose. Taking a sip Jonothon felt his stomach warm, and his joints loosen a little. Felsath had earned a reputation in the palace for the potency of his teas, and their flavors. Jonothon was sure that Felsath could have won a contest had one ever been held in the art of tea brewing.

"The Firestorm duke is quite a young man isn't he?" Felsath noted, seemingly to no one in particular. The king knew better than to miss the opening his servant had given him, but he played along for the moment, their old game still practiced almost daily.

"I guess. He *is* quite young…"

"Yet your niece was taken by him I saw. I hear she showed him the observatory in the palace." Felsath kept his face straight, still not betraying what his true thoughts were as yet. Felsath had always been able to maintain a sense of holding his observations to himself. When he showed his thoughts and emotions it was always with great care as if they were very dear to him.

"So I had heard. I spoke to her about it and I guess he spoke to her about the orcs. It gave her quite a fright realizing that some of the kingdom lives in constant fear of those nasty beasts."

Felsath had a wry smile on his face. "And you think that is all they discussed?"

Jonothon thought on what his niece had told him of the conversation; she certainly had her chance to hide something from him.

"I can only hope that is what they discussed."

Jonothon was also worried about how his niece would take her wish for revenge. Ever since she was a child she had wanted to make the beasts pay for what they had done to her family, though whether she ever could was an entirely different story. He wondered if the girl would use Cael to that end in some way. The young girl had been more sheltered from the rigors of the world than Cael had been, and Jonothon had to think he may have done her an injustice in that regard. But it had been his duty to defend his niece from any more events that could have befallen her. How could he have done otherwise after the loss of her parents?

"Do you think Cael will make it?" Felsath asked.

Jonothon was not looking forward to this question. Doubts and worry had nagged at him, driving him to seek solitude in the garden. "I don't know, Felsath. I have never held so many doubts about a choice I have had to make." Jonothon set his mug down on the stone bench and stood up, beginning to pace again. "I have sent men to war, and into situations when I knew they were going to die. I know the cost and the difficulty in decisions that a king must make. I know these things, but sending Cael on this quest still brings me such concern that I am uneasy."

Felsath looked upon his king, Jonothon could see him contemplating what had been said. He had sat there and been at Jonothon's side for almost every decision he had made; being uneasy and uncertain were things that a king was never allowed to be. Felsath had in his own mind given his trust over to things larger than himself years before. And while he loved his king, he knew that Jonothon struggled with letting things be taken under the care of others, especially when he knew it had to be done right and was difficult.

"Why are you so uneasy this time Jonothon? What makes this any different from when you have given men quests or goals that risked their lives for the kingdom?"

The answer was an easy one, but it still bothered Jonothon. This was the first time he had to rely solely on the most deeply guarded secret artifact of Dalerad, the Book of Kings. "You know why I can't feel comfortable with this. The line of kings has been kept intact for over 500 years. I am the first childless king and my father knew before I was even born that I would be the last Friezen king. Cael shouldn't have to bear this sort of weight and yet he is the one being asked to do it."

Felsath kept quiet, he could see the frustration in the eyes of his king, and he let him continue to vent. Felsath had been there when Jonothon had learned his queen was pregnant, contrary to the prediction of the book of kings which said he would never be a father. The months of excitement had been cut short as she had died unexpectedly in her sleep.

Felsath had been there to comfort his friend and make sure he was not consumed by the anger he saw inside him. Jonothon seemed to become tired suddenly; the thoughts of his loss weighed heavily on him. The frustration was beginning to fade from his body as he held himself silently in the gardens. The swaying plants behind him were setting a gentle, natural rhythm to relax to.

"He is taking the path he is meant to take though, isn't he?"

Felsath nodded. "All men bear the weights placed upon them. It is not whether one carries something lighter than the others, but whether he can keep moving even with the weight there. You know better than to panic and fret over something like this Jonothon. Your people cannot see you question yourself if they are to keep their confidence in the transition to another king."

Jonothon turned to his friend, weighing his words. He knew everything he said to be true, and Felsath knew it. Jonothon recalled a few of the times where their roles had been switched, and Felsath had been speaking to him about his daughters and sons and the tribulations of family life. Even in those moments of trouble, Jonothon had been able to steer his friend towards the right action, to soothe Felsath's misgivings and to help him be a good father. And what of the stability of the kingdom, the ultimate level of parenthood? Jonothon would do anything to assure his people had peace for many years longer. Other than guarding the northern slopes from marauding orcs, they had had little to fear when it came to war and their fields had been plentiful.

"Perhaps it is the fate of old men like ourselves to one day question our purpose."

"And to question our choices." Felsath added.

Jonothon returned to the bench to sit next to his friend. Holding his mug, he again stared into its depths, looking for answers to the thoughts racing around in his head. Still a singular question swirled and came to the fore of Jonothon's mind. "Do you think he will make it?"

Felsath seemed to consider the question. Jonothon knew he had only spoken a few words to Cael, but he had always been able to know people, to see into them. His eyes could pierce into a man and see who he was deep inside and it was an ability that Jonothon had relied upon in the past.

"I think we have done everything we can. To worry at this point does nothing for our health, and we have to care for the kingdom until he returns."

Jonothon nodded. He lifted his mug to his lips taking in the sharp aroma of the tea as he took a small sip. "Yes. We do have to care for the kingdom while he is gone." Jonothon took solace in knowing that he could still be sure of his decisions in the defense of his lands. "Tell me Felsath, has Clarence gathered all the lords for the council?"

Felsath seemed pleased that his king was distracted by this new topic. Jonothon knew Felsath would be satisfied with the change, even if it was only for a while. "Yes, he has made the preparations. They will be meeting shortly after nightfall. I have had a table and chairs prepared for the meeting."

"My dear Felsath, how would I have ever lived without your assistance?"

"Hungry, cold, and very alone I would imagine." Felsath grinned. "Come my lord, let us go inside. These gardens don't need two more statues of old men in them scaring the birds."

"Speak for yourself, old man!" Jonothon playfully spoke to his friend. "You are skinny as a scarecrow." The two walked together side by side. Felsath helped Jonothon find the step up in the fading light of the garden as they left their place of solitude from the world at large.

"If I am a scarecrow then you are the witch who scares children in the fall festival."

The two continued like this for some time, laughing, with each trying to outdo the other. It was a game they had used for years to entertain themselves and release the stress they both felt inside. Old friends, though servant and king.

Lord Kingsley was sitting next to a pile of books in the library of the king, staring intently at the pages of an old text written before he was even born. Placing the book down, he grabbed another, once again looking at the pages looking for the telltale sign of his goal. Still, he was forced to grab another book and begin searching again. He was looking for something very specific and he was growing more irritated with himself as his search went on.

Looking around at the piles of books on the table, he absent-mindedly brushed dust from his shirt as he thought of what he had been searching for. "This Alfred, is why we should never have waited so long. We are simply too old to spend all this time reading the histories." Alfred Kingsley was a stout man, and though he was still just reaching his later years, decades of life were catching up to him. The voice in the back of his mind was piping up once more from the madness he had kept a secret from the world.

"Alfred my dear friend, I tell you it's not going to be here."

"That may be true, but a reference, a key, a bit of information for the secret of it all...."

"You tease yourself. Something like this the king would keep in his own chambers. How many times must I mention this?"

Alfred looked up at the cloaked figure that he feared was his own mind. Sitting crouched on the table, its black cloak hid its face from sight as it spoke to him. Alfred was unsure when the voice had first come to him, but he had been sure that he could trust it. Something in the way it knew him so well, the way his very nature was laid bare. And the truth-- it always had spoken to him about the truth of the Kingsley line in history.

"There has to be another way. You know this. I cannot gain entry to the king's rooms!"

"How pitiful you are, that a simple door and key keep you from securing your rightful place in history. You know as well as I that you are the true king of this land."

"So you have always told me. So you have shown me."

The apparition interrupted Alfred's words. Raising his head, he looked past Alfred and seemed to be listening intently for something beyond the door of the library.

"There is someone coming." With the fading of a light mist from the room, the voice from Alfred Kingsley's mind was gone. He quickly pushed the conversation from his thoughts, busying himself with his work once more. Only through dedication and planning had he been able to keep his madness hidden for so long, and whatever this voice was, it knew things that Alfred never had.

Standing up, he ran a hand through his beard, he could smell of dust from the old tomes. Ignoring it, he picked out another shelf with histories written about Dalerad.

"Now Kingsley, let's not be too hasty... Bah!" Kingsley spoke to himself. All he could remember were the stories he listened to as a child, about how the Kingsleys had once ruled these lands, until the Friezens had beaten them. They had been attacked out of the east during the Council Wars. The voice had told him so much of that time it seemed like Alfred had lived it himself. The knowledge he held within his head had let him build up his family's position greatly, though the means were less than honorable. Of course, the original wars were the first act of treason.

The aftermath of those wars had upset the very balance of the first kingdoms. When the rebellions began, they spread like wildfire on dry pines, and few nations were left untouched. He knew the legends of the Towers, and he had been able to learn that the young duke Firestorm had been sent on a mission to search for the items of legend. Even if Cael found something, he would be too far from the kingdom to stop what he had planned. If he returned, he would come home to a kingdom no longer his own.

Kingsley climbed up the ladder a few steps to grab at another book. He was paging through another when the firm footsteps and the metallic clink of a sword he knew very well. Turning, he was not surprised to see Lord Grim had entered the room, locking him with his typically piercing glare.

"Alfred, I don't suppose I could help you look for whatever it is you are searching for?" Grim did not try to hide his displeasure, but maintained a civil tone.

Kingsley turned back to the shelf, replacing the book in his hands with another. "I am unsure if I would dare trouble you for such a small favor James. I know the king's business keeps you well occupied." He began flipping through another book, its ancient pages crinkling in the open air as he thumbed them roughly. "Tell me, how do you find time to keep that lovely wife of yours company when working this much?"

"Perhaps if you did something to help the king once in a while, my load would not be so heavy to bear, and my wife not so lonely." Grim still had not moved from his place in the room.

Kingsley smiled to himself. Grim had been the much-favored lord for years and some believed he would be chosen to take the throne. It was a rumor Kinglsey had a small part in spreading. "You know, Grim, that I would go anywhere the king asked me to." He began to climb down the ladder, stepping and turning to face Grim's accusatory face full on. "Have I ever left you any doubts as to where my loyalties lie?"

Grim walked closer, coming down the second set of steps to face Kinglsey, just out of arm's reach. "Do not try to be coy Alfred. I know that you are more than just lazy in lifting a damn finger to help the king."

"I ask you again, do I give you any reason to doubt my loyalty?" Kinglsey met every bit of Grim's glare with his own. He knew there was nothing that Grim could do to him and his slate was clear. While he was planning something, he would appear as innocent as a newborn to any who tried to find reason for betrayals. "Always you try to find fault with me James, as if I had done something to give you reason to doubt my loyalty."

Grim stiffened, and if his glare could have deepened any further, it would have done so. Hefting the book in his hands, he let it drop onto the table, kicking up more dust and making Kingsley jump. Grim took a certain satisfaction knowing he had spooked Kingsley, if only a little. "Take note Kingsley, I am watching. If I detect for a minute that you have betrayed my king, I will—"

"You will what?" He looked Grim straight in the eyes. Grim smiled at the fierceness of Kinglsey's face, a stark contrast to his plump spoiled form.

"Take care." Grim turned and went back up the steps. He stopped at the doorway leaving the library. "Enjoy your reading, but do not be late for the meeting of the lords."

Kinglsey watched Grim leave, the footsteps and the clanking of Grim's sword fading down the stone hall of the castle. When he was satisfied that he had passed far enough down the hall, he returned to the books on the shelf. The shadowy voice from his head reappeared on the table, its black cloak hanging in gloom over his face.

"Good, the dark one leaves us."

"And you are one to talk of darkness, shadow…"

Jonothon stepped into the hall where the lords were meeting to discuss the kingdom. He felt the room Clarence had chosen was fitting. The hall bore the weapons of past kings, their personal tabards handing along each of the long walls. At each end were the high stained glass windows made as a gift from the eastern coastal cities when he brought them into the kingdom. Long tables ran the length of the room, though only one was set, with the high-backed seats of the lords surrounding it. The lights from the candles in the chandeliers were doing their best to light the spires of the ceiling. The hall was built as an expansion to the attached chapel to Portus, the god protecting Dalerad.

He noted a fair number of the lords had already entered and were friendly in the greeting of their brethren. The Council of Lords was an old tradition that had started in Dalerad's first years. Jonothon knew that while power was supposed to be balanced between lords and king, each had their time when they were the true ruler of Dalerad. Jonothon was happy that his rule had been one of balance, and he had come to rely on the lords as they did on him.

Jonothon did not have to be able to read the minds of his lords today to know that they were not pleased. His decision to follow the Book of Kings had forced him to choose a minor Dukal family for the heir to the throne, instead of one of the council lords. While they were civil, he could tell they were troubled by his choice, and by the meeting they were to have this day. Jonothon knew most were loyal, but some had begun to look after themselves before the kingdom and that concerned him.

"Harris, Jenoa, my good friends, it has been so long since we spoke last."

The king looked over at the two friends walking up to join him near the table. Jenoa smiling widely as he always had, no trace of the wariness his other lords had met him with as he entered the hall. At about the king's height and with jet black hair, Jenoa's cheerful disposition was a stark contrast to his dark features. Jonothon had been Jenoa's mentor when he was a child and they had always kept the close friendship he had earned in those years of mentorship.

"My lord, I am sorry to have been given lands so far from your city, but you understand my responsibility to my family."

"Yes I do, but isn't your son old enough to take your position yet?" Jonothon playfully inquired. He knew fully well that his son was still a baby.

"Well lord, he might want my position, but it is hard to get a toddler to be interested in affairs of the court. He just reached his second year a month past."

Jenoa laughed with the king for a moment as they had always been able to do. Harris cleared his throat, trying to enter in to their conversation.

"I don't mean to interrupt, but it would be nice to also greet the king."

"Of course Harris, I would never have thought to keep you from him." Jenoa playfully responded.

"Harris, ever the serious one are you not?" Jonothon asked being coy.

Harris bowed, his light brown curls catching a dull shine in the light from the torches on the walls. "If I am not serious, than there is no one to keep my cousin Jenoa under control my lord."

"If you ask my wife, I believe she says she is the one in control." Jenoa said while chuckling.

"Jenoa, that is as it should be. My wife…."

Jonothon looked with surprise at Harris "You are married? When did this occur and how was I not invited?"

Harris blushed, but their conversation was interrupted by the arrival of Lord Grim, his face matching his name more than ever. All conversation halted as he entered the room. Murmuring conversations began to break out as he moved into the room, all eyes drawn to the large scroll of leather-bound paper under his arm.

"Jonothon, what is this meeting about anyways?" Harris asked. "Jenoa and I are barely in the city a few days, hear that you have a successor, and now we see James Grim in the darkest mood of his entire life."

"I wonder if he has ever smiled?" Jenoa inquired to no one in particular.

"My young lords, all will be revealed soon enough. I must speak with James if you can excuse me."

"Of course, my lord." Harris bowed.

As Jonothon moved to Grim's side at the table, he could hear Jenoa already poking fun at the overly serious Harris about his constant bowing. Jonothon put that out of his mind as he reached Grim's side, motioning to the scroll under his arm as he stood next to his seat, which was next to the king's at the table.

"I hope this is good news?"

Grim looked at the king, offering what Jonothon knew to be a slightly softer, but sadder face. "Sorry my lord, but I have little good news to deliver today."

"Is it as the scouting parties said?" The king had been getting updates weekly for the past few months. More and more, the news from the north bothered him.

Grim took his time responding, and the king knew than that his news was not going to be good. "It is as we feared, though if we act soon it is not beyond our ability to respond."

Jonothon nodded. "Good, than let us begin." On the table next to his chair was a mallet. Used to bring the meetings to order as the lords grew heated, it was also used to bring everyone to the table. Lifting it, he handed the wooden handle to Grim, motioning him to take it.

"This is your news, and you are my most trusted. Take it."

Grim slowly reached out, taking the mallet from the king while looking in his eyes. Jonothon noted he seemed reassured by this, so he smiled and took his seat in the king's place. Grim rapped the wooden mallet on the table three times and the conversations of the lords faded as they took their seats at the table. Jonothon noted that Kingsley took an extra few moments to sit, staring a bit at both Grim and Jonothon.

"My fellow lords, we have called this meeting to discuss the defense of the kingdom. I have reports from northern hills of large bands of orcs moving south into Dalerad." Murmurs began to work their way down the line of lords as they heard the news, some of them had lands far from danger of orc raids and had heard no news of this threat.

"Lord Grim, are you to tell us that they are invading? Or did a paranoid scout see a few of them from a hilltop and report it as an invasion?"

"Lord Heath, I assure you it was not a single scout that brought this news to me. We need to work quickly to address this movement of their forces into our lands."

Kingsley spoke up, drawing all the eyes at the table to himself. "I think, James, if you showed us the map you hold under your arm and then explained the situation to us, perhaps we could better assess what you will be asking of us."

Jonothon watched this exchange carefully. He knew the animosity that sat between the two men at the table, and he felt the tension on Grim as Kingsley had spoken, especially speaking in his defense to the other lords so he could plead his case. Nonetheless, Grim began to speak, rolling out the map as he did so all the lords could see the points he had marked.

"The orcs are assembling forces in hills near the older cities in Dalerad, threatening Gloston, Holk, and Iven Crossing." He pointed to sections that had been outlined in black ink. Before speaking, he pointed to a set of lines crossing the map, coming out of the mountains north of the plains. "These lines here are the paths they are taking. Each of these is a new route that until a few weeks ago we were unaware they were following."

"One of those routes lies a day's ride from my lands, how is it that we are being caught so unaware of this movement?" Jenoa asked suddenly. His lands were not very close to the northlands, but his family had helped keep the eastern sea and the plains free of danger for some time. Jonothon knew that for him it was a matter of pride that orcs could not easily pass through his lands unopposed.

"The orcs are traveling at night, and are being very careful. Also, they are staying away from their normal invasion routes. The lands here," Grim pointed at the central point of the northern edge of Dalerad near the mountain, "in the lands of the Firestorm Clan. They have been in most every battle we have fought with them and it has been their main route of passage. Of all the leaders we have that clan has the most experience, and has paid the highest price for every encounter."

"Grim, why was the Duke not invited here?" Grim looked over at the lord asking.

"He was invited. However, this time of year he leads the hunts to the north for dormant groups of orcs. In other years the orcs take the start of the summer months to regroup and prepare for their winter assaults."

"Has there been any reason found for their sudden change in habits or pathways of attack?" Jenoa looked more concerned than he had before, and he was leaning intently towards the map looking at the spot Grim had been motioning towards.

Jonothon kept quiet; he was curious what his lords would try to do without his immediate involvement. He was also watching to see which lords would use this time to advance himself over the kingdom. He thought of it as a test to see which lords had only been trying to impress him before he chose an heir, and which were really loyal to him and the kingdom.

"There have been no reports from any of my scouts as to why this has occurred. In the past they would move only once, and that was to attack." Grim responded.

"Grim we all know the 'typical' orc behavior; few of us here have not faced one in battle. I also want it to be known that orcs have behaved this way in the past, and it was always under guidance and assistance of a greater strength than their own." Kingsley spoke matter-of-factly and it stunned some of the other lords. Just as fast as they had been shocked into silence, their conversation rose to a low roar at the very suggestion that anyone would ever think to help the orcs.

"Lord Kingsley, the last time such a thing occurred was during the Council Wars and it was the council themselves who were the villains guiding them."

"The council leaders were demigods, how could anyone else have the power to control the filthy creatures?"

"The council are more myth than real."

Jonothon had not come to listen to his lord debate mythology, and was growing tired of the infighting between the lords once the Council Wars were mentioned. Taking the wood mallet he had given Lord Grim, he slammed it onto the table three times. He had no time for the kingdom to be wasting away on an argument of who the council really was.

"All of you keep silent. What does it matter who or what could be driving this invasion of my kingdom?" Jonothon noticed the somewhat impatient glances he got from a few of the lords around the table. "Yes, it is MY kingdom. Your lands are yours because I see fit to keep status at the same level of your fathers before you. I had this meeting called to decide how best to defend the land, and you are all more concerned with fighting about the Zephyren from our past. Decide how to write history later; today decide how you will protect the women and children of the nation in the present day."

Jonothon sat himself down again, his mug of tea appearing at his side as Felsath predicted his king's need. The lords sat in the chairs, though Grim remained standing and looked out at the faces surrounding him. Some of them had the look of rebuked children. They knew they were wasting time and many of the lords had lands near the spots Grim had marked for buildup of orc numbers.

"I need lords to volunteer men at arms. I plan to have two forces patrol the northlands with the help of the Firestorm clan to slow or stop the flow of more orcs into Dalerad. The others will work to attack the forces already building in the plains and near the great wood in the south." Grim looked at each lord in turn as he spread his plan out in front of them. Pointing to another set of red lines on the map he continued to speak.

"When we do we attack the orcs already in Dalerad?" Harris asked this time, his face matching the concern of Jenoa. Both were among those Jonothon knew maintained loyalty to him even with the strange choice of heir.

Grim sighed, looking at the map in front of him weighing the answer to the question before he spoke. "The orcs cannot simply be driven out of where they are. The last thing we want is one group of orcs becoming a few dozen roving bands to terrorize the lands surrounding their bases. When we attack they must be surrounded and they must be destroyed outright. It is in this task that more of us must put our strength."

Jonothon watched the lords breaking into small conversations. Their talk was needed, as it would relieve some of the tension from the news that Grim had reported. He knew that some would quickly volunteer, and the others would wait to see where the favor was to be had before they decided to help or not.

Harris and Jenoa caught their king's gaze, each smiling at Jonothon. Standing together, Harris spoke. "Lords Harris and Jenoa volunteer to defend the northlands."

"How many men at arms will you take?" Jonothon asked of them.

"Between us we have 750 men, give or take what the latest enlistment adds." Harris answered.

"Lords, I am sure the king appreciates your service to this cause. You may decide amongst yourselves which of you will guard the east and which will guard the west," Grim stated with thanks, and the entire table heard the gratitude in his voice. He did take a moment to look at Kingsley and a few of the lords he knew favored him while he spoke to Harris and Jenoa.

"Gentlemen, though Grim does not mention it, I want news of the duke Firestorm sent to me. His help will be invaluable as his people know the northern steppes better than any."

"I am sure he would also want news of his son." It was a lord to the left of Kingsley, greasy in his appearance and his voice. His name was Galiad Jurshon, and even Jonothon knew him to favor Kingsley more than his ruler. Jonothon looked over and saw Grim glowering with rage at the implications everyone at the table heard in his voice.

"Do you think that no one sent word of his son being chosen as heir to the throne, Galiad?" Grim kept his tone civil.

"I think we all are curious how just a couple days after he was picked to succeed our..." he paused for sarcastic emphasis, "gracious king that he would be sent out of the kingdom with none but one of your primitives to accompany him." The other lords were showing mixed expressions to Galiad's very obvious rebellion.

"I don't think it is your place to question the decisions of our king, Galiad." Grim stated with a sharp edge to his voice.

"I speak only what everyone is thinking, and wondering. Why is it that an heir was chosen from outside the lords, and what could possibly be going on that he would not even stay to learn more of the kingdom he is to lead?"

Jonothon stood, and though he was near the end of his years he still moved quickly and spoke with authority. "Galiad you have said enough. If you wish to question my rule than you can learn to do so without your title, since if I remember correctly, it was I who gave your family such rights to be here." Galiad sat back, rebuked and fuming that it had been done so publicly and with such finality. "If you wish to take your own path, than I will gladly grant your lands and title to the Firestorms. Then my *heir* would not be outside the ranks of lords would he?"

Jonothon looked around the table at the lords present gauging each in turn. "If there are any others who wish to question me, then do so now." The lords stayed silent, each turning to his own council on the situation at hand. "In that case I will take my leave of you. I want an army to be marching for those strongholds within a week, and I want the plan for their activities by the end of this evening."

Felsath was already behind his king's chair, pulling it out and helping him with his cloak as he prepared to leave the room. He knew that a few of the lords watched him leave and a few more were too ashamed of their own thoughts to dare catch his gaze as he left. Felsath pulled the door shut behind them as they reached the stairs, and the king heard the debate begin on how best to fight the orc menace.

The king awoke sitting next to his fireplace, his large chair covered in pillows and warm furs lying across his legs. A stool kept his feet off the floor, facing towards the corner of the roaring fire behind the metal grate. He felt the stiffness of the cold in his feet and legs, and grimaced as he tried to pull himself into a comfortable position.

He looked around, sensing someone nearby. Standing near the door, Clarence awaited, his blonde hair and red suit with gold lace a bright marker in the room. The room was lit only by the light of the fire, revealing the king's bed and some of his treasured possessions. His sword and armor hung on their stand in the corner, and the windows were dark, as the moon was not up this night. Seeing that only Clarence was with him he waited for the mysterious merchant to speak.

"It's getting worse isn't it?" Clarence spoke to the king with more of a statement than a question.

"Why is it you always seem to ask me questions you know the answer to? Couldn't you ask me something new or unknown?" Jonothon looked at the man who had come to him as a Merchant Chief years before. He knew better than to believe the story, but Clarence had still maintained his trust, and his knowledge was invaluable in caring for the kingdom.

Clarence sat down across from the king, letting his coat open up to his sides as he settled. He reached out to pull the blankets from Jonothon's feet gently, but with a firm surety that few would ever have in coming to touch the king. The sight revealed to him was just as disturbing as it had been the first time he had seen it. The king's feet were appearing more and more like they were frost bitten. No matter how warm they were, the disease eventually killed all the Friezen line. Bit by bit their bodies would mysteriously be stricken and eventually they would die.

"You haven't been keeping me updated on the progress Jonothon. You know better."

"Clarence, you know how long I have left. I picked the heir I was supposed to. What else do I have left to do before I am to die?"

"You can at least try to last long enough to greet Cael upon his return."

Jonothon laughed, not a laugh of joy but one filled with sadness and a certain resignation that one carries when they know their days are short. "Clarence, we both know he will be gone for a long time. His role is not going to be played out so readily or in such short time."

Clarence sighed deeply. "Are you sure the Council of Lords can be trusted to care for the kingdom once you are gone? Kingsley alone is not to be trusted."

"Yes, so I have heard. Felsath said he was in the library searching for the book again."

"You have secured it for the time being?"

Jonothon grinned. "Kingsley will not be able to retrieve the book if that is what you are asking."

Both men looked over as a small side door opened to reveal Felsath, carrying a pot of warm water to bathe the king's feet. Clarence knew it to be a nightly ritual. Though some of the persistent cold could be chased from Jonothon's bones it always came back worse than before.

"Felsath, perhaps you have had some luck in convincing this stubborn old man to at least try to survive longer?"

Felsath walked silently over to the stool, placing the bin on the floor, and pouring the water into it. "You should know by now Clarence that I am loyal to my king. Neither of us is long for this world."

Clarence stood and began to pace again about the room. He watched as Felsath gently placed his king's feet into the warm water and saw some of the mysterious frost fade, but it left the marks behind of the damage it had already done.

"So Clarence, what bothers you so much you have come to visit me late this evening? I am not far enough gone to not realize that something is bothering you."

"The lords have made their decision, but I am unsure of how their plans will succeed. This situation comes at a very poor time for your lands."

"The orcs have invaded before, Clarence."

Clarence interrupted forcibly, probably more so than he intended. He spoke not with anger, but with the voice of someone very concerned. "The Council is back. One of them is driving the orcs towards us."

Jonothon felt his blood freeze quicker than it ever had since the advent of the disease he now fought. "How can you know? Are you sure?"

"I am sure of it as I can be. They were lost to the pages of history after the wars were over. Most were imprisoned, some were banished, but a few just disappeared." Clarence sat back down across from the king. "We may have made our move too late, and I don't know if it will be enough to save what you have here."

"Tell me Clarence, are any of the lords involved?"

Clarence shook his head. "Though I would suspect Kingsley to be involved, his hands are still clean. I can help make sure to save what I can with the lords' help."

"Whomever it is can't be stopped now. We have nothing to face the masters of the towers with."

Clarence looked into the flames of the fire. "There may as yet be a way, and hopefully Cael learns of it."

"What are you speaking about Clarence?"

Clarence continued to gaze at the flames, lost in his mind in a way Jonothon had not seen before.

"In the time of the council the orcs were obviously defeated. To do so requires a weapon equal to their power, and if they are able to return I believe something must have happened to the weapons as well. If Cael's journey takes him to a tower he will hopefully find the weapons to defeat the other council in the process."

"It is a hope that we both now share, Clarence. Cael will do fine, the book of kings has never failed to be correct, even when I had hoped it would not be."

Jonothon felt the concern in Clarence's heart, and felt it as he would from a close friend. In truth though, he knew not the origin of the strange gold and red dressed merchant, though he did know that he was always honest and had been a loyal aid to Dalerad. It felt odd comforting him for once.

"My dear friend, that is the state of being for anyone who sets down roots and tries to build a life. We always wonder how long we will live and die. We never know if it will work out or go poorly, but we still keep trying."

Clarence nodded, understanding that in some way the king was not going to allow his final days to be fraught with fear and uncertainty, a trait he was sure he could be impressed with under any circumstance. "So, refusing to give in, are we?"

"Hope is all I have these days. You wouldn't condemn a couple of old fools like Felsath and I to end our days with little hope for sunny skies? I would have never thought you so cruel a man."

Clarence waved off the attempts at cheerful sarcasm that Jonothon attempted. He stood, his face betraying the thoughts he felt inside. Jonothon saw, and adjusted himself before he spoke.

"Clarence you knew for some time that my days were numbered. I have played my part in this dance we call life and I am happy for what I have done." Felsath looked up at his king, and Jonothon was reminded of their conversation earlier in the day. "I am sometimes unsure of my choices, but I have done my best to never regret them."

Clarence stood in the light of the fire, looking down at Jonothon as Felsath cleaned and warmed his feet with the basin of water. After meeting his eyes for a few moments, he spoke. "My dear friend, our time together has been too short. I regret that I must leave again and I don't know if I will return before your time has come to an end."

"That explains the rush you have been in these past few weeks," Felsath interrupted as he began to rewrap the king's feet with cotton warmers.

"Yes, it is part of my sense of urgency these past days; too much to do and too little time to complete it. Jonothon, I will be heading south. If I get a chance I will return but it could be some time before I am able.." Clarence stepped forward from his place near the fire, and kneeled next to the king.

Jonothon took his hands as they had been offered. "Clarence, I know you have hidden much from me, but still I trust in your guidance and assistance. Even if you return after I am gone, please make sure that Cael is cared for, would you?"

"It will be my top priority. Cael's rule will a great one if I am able to help him."

Jonothon smiled at this and closed his eyes as he leaned back in the chair. Felsath had just finished placing his feet back on the stool and covering them in the thick furs and blankets the king had to always wear to help ward off the disease.

"I will hold you to that Clarence. And if I can't, than Felsath will."

Clarence smiled at the sentiment, and began to head towards the doorway. He looked back at Felsath caring for his king in the light of the fire, two old men doing their best to keep up with a world soon to pass them by. Clarence opened the door and stepped into the dimly lit hall, most of the torches were now out for the night.

Clarence began to walk from shadow to shadow, passing by a servant on their way to another room. The servant turned to catch another glimpse of the red and gold dressed master merchant, but by the time they had turned he was gone.

CHAPTER 4

Cael was standing beside his horse, looking across the last stretch of road before he entered the forest that marked the southern border of Dalerad. His companion from the barbarian tribes, Herth, was sitting on a boulder next to the road waxing the string of his bow. Cael felt a breeze brush by him and the eerie sensation was followed closely by a dark chill down his spine. Herth continued to work as if nothing had occurred.

Cael turned back to the woods, searching the green depths and wondering how far they stretched. He had been given maps by lord Grim to guide him, but they had few of the details he truly wanted to know. No source of water was marked, nor were there any markings of villages along the way. All he could discern was a long thin line marking what turned out to be a dirt road; it wound generally southward to the lands of Yulan. Cael wrapped up the map, placed it in the sleeve on the back of his horse and tightened the saddle straps.

"Come, let's see how far we can make it today." Herth silently complied with Cael's request, packing up his wax and bow while Cael climbed on top of his gray courser. Sitting atop the steed, he felt more secure, and the dark green wood's stood like a wall stretching out of sight and fading into the mists.

Cael tapped his heels to bring his horse into a quick trot, and tried to think on the legends and myths he had heard about these woods. As he approached the forest he recalled the fantastic stories of elk with silver antlers and bears that could stand taller than a man while they were on all fours. Cael didn't know if he was less at ease with Herth's silence or the imposing forested landscape slowly coming towards him.

Cael looked back at the large war stallion that Herth straddled. The behemoth seemed to carry him with little difficulty, and Herth rose tall on its back with his armor and weaponry making him appear even more imposing.

As they moved along, Cael also took a moment to look back at the last of the rolling hills of southern Dalerad, wondering when would be the next time he could lay his eyes on his homeland.

"I guess this is how you must have felt leaving the mountains." Herth watched Cael for a moment, but went back to scanning the road ahead. "Some companion you are supposed to be," Cael mumbled. Turning his attention back to the hills, he noticed some birds being spooked into the air. He squinted as he looked at the far hill, but saw no more motion, so he returned his eyes to the road to follow Herth into the woods.

They approached the border, and it seemed that the whole world disappeared behind them as they pushed onward. Cael could see decaying leaves of the mammoth oaks littering the forest floor. He could smell the scent of the maple trees hidden further in, and see the white bark of the birch trees growing between the oak. The tall trees blocked almost all of the morning sun, but the light green rays of leaf-filtered light reached the ground below, illuminating their path like an emerald sun.

The road was still easy to follow, and was as wide as two carts for ease of travel. Along the sides Cael saw the ferns of a typical forest floor, which put him at ease. Perhaps these woods were no more dangerous or magical than any other he thought, and the soothing trot of the horses kept him calm as they walked.

After riding in silence most of the day, Cael decided to make camp in the fading light. The dusk came and their fire burned brightly with a few small logs that Herth had found in the surrounding woods. Cael prepared his rolled mat for his bed and had no sooner closed his eyes to relax than he heard the sound of a sword being unsheathed. Sitting up quickly, he looked towards his horse to see Herth springing toward him, his large axe in one hand, and Cael's sword in the other.

Cael spoke quickly as he stood "Herth, what are you doing?" Cael was silenced when Herth tossed his sword to his feet. He didn't have to ask what was next because Herth had already hefted his axe into a fighting stance, and silently motioned Cael to come towards him. Picking up his sword, Cael carefully shook the dirt off the blade. "I don't know what your prob—" Cael ducked as Herth's axe passed through the space where he had stood a moment before.

"Herth!" Cael dodged again, his sword still in hand. Stepping to the side, he brought his sword up and made a quick lunge forward to try and catch Herth on his unarmored side. Herth continued with his forward momentum, letting the axe arc around and brush Cael's weapon to the side. The pair took two steps backward, and adjusted themselves. Cael stayed at the ready, his training kicking in before any assumptions over Herth's intent at this point.

Herth stood silent, a short grin coming across his face as he stood with his axe held high above his head. Without a warning he moved forward, his axe swinging up and under the defensive stance Cael had taken. Cael barely caught the massive blow on his sword and then pushed out with the hilt of the sword striking Herth on the shoulder. Cael took a step to the side, swinging wide to the offside of Herth's axe, coming a few inches from striking the quiet barbarian's side. Cael watched as the unavoidable elbow of the heavily ironed and muscled barbarian smash into his head.

He staggered back, trying to shake off the stars in his head, and then Cael heard laughter fill the small clearing in the wood.

"Very good Firestorm, let us continue!" Herth rushed at Cael once again, this time swinging across his body with the axe. As Cael ducked under the blade, he set his foot on the rocks of the clearing and pushed off hard, up and into Herth's chest with his shoulder.

Cael felt the wind knocked from Herth's lungs as his strike sent Herth stumbling in retreat.

"What in bloody blazes is wrong with you?" Cael panted. "What offense have I given you to cause this?"

Herth spoke with a smile. "This was good. I am pleased that you only looked soft." Still laughing a little under his breath, the barbarian leaned heavily on the black haft of his axe. Cael noticed the axe was covered with runes that he assumed to be from the barbarian tribes. Dramatic red runes were etched into the steel blade. Pushing himself up, Herth held his stomach with one hand.

"You can truly fight, that is a good thing." Herth began moving back towards his horse while Cael collapsed on the ground, exhausted from the few minutes of tussling. His head was still throbbing from where Herth's elbow that connected.

"That was just a test?"

Placing his axe on the ground and laying down next to it, Herth stayed quiet. He was massaging his shoulder where the hilt of Cael's sword had dug into the flesh. He had returned once again to his silence as the fire burned on.

"Barbarian, you are being spoken to!" Cael needed answers. "You keep silent for days while we traveled just to attack me without provocation and don't allow me any questions?"

"Well did you want me to wait until you had been killed?" Herth asked, opening one eye towards Cael.

"Excuse me?"

Herth continued, leaning up on one arm. "Perhaps it would be better if we fell under attack and I learned too late that your sword skills were not up to the task of defense? How am I to know that you can wield the sword instead of just carrying it as a trinket?" Herth gave a glare in exchange for Cael's anger.

Cael felt himself calm as he found reason in what Herth was saying, realizing that he had a point. They now both knew they were capable of defending themselves. With that comfort, it would be easier to trust each other if they met with any problems. Life on the northern steppes had taught him the value of being able to trust the man next to you.

Herth saw this realization come to Cael, and stopped glaring, letting his smile return. "Besides my young Firestorm lord, at least you know you can take a hit from a barbarian twice your size. Now, get some rest, we have weeks of travel yet."

Cael sat in the silence, and after a few moments he looked away from the pleased smirk on Herth's face. He stood to grab a few more pieces of wood to feed the fire. Keeping his sword close, he pulled his traveling blanket over himself and looked up at the forest above him, searching through the canopy for glimpses of the night sky.

He thought back on his father, and wondered if he had received his letters yet. He knew his father would be proud of him for acting on his behalf. Refusing a quest from the king would have been as good as stabbing his father in the heart. Content with knowing how his father would react to the news he had succeeded, Cael fell off to sleep to the crackling of the fire, hoping for dreams of Thera. He wished that somewhere she was doing the same for him.

Cael found himself standing on a path of stone, suspended in space. At its center was a stone portal, with what looked like the slow rippling of air between its two arches. Barely taller than he was, its surface was scarred with scorch marks, and black soot covered the dark runes in the gray stone. When he reached out to touch it the ripples turned to flames and he saw that their core was black. Cael was unable to pull away; instead he felt as though he was being pulled closer to the portal of fire. He struggled against the slow drag with no success. A few moments later, he tumbled into the vortex— and found himself awake on the forest floor.

Cael sat up, rubbing his eyes. Herth looked at him, not saying a word, nor giving any hint to what he thought at Cael's sudden awakening. Herth had seemingly been awake for some time as he was already packed and sitting on a rock, sharpening the axe he had used to test Cael the day before.

Cael pulled himself from his blankets and into the cool morning air. He stretched and gazed skyward, where he saw the form of a white owl perched in the canopy. Its eyes took in the scene of Cael and Herth in the clearing as if suggesting they had intruded in its space.

"Come young lord, we need to get moving." Herth stood up from his seat and began putting his sharpening tools away in his pack. Cael had only to wrap up his blankets and place his sword back in its sheath and they could be off. Scratching at the short stubble on his face, Cael began to pack his things while Herth mounted his horse and sat in silence.

"Herth, is there a chance of you actually speaking today?"

Herth's response was to merely smile from the back of his horse. It appeared it would be another day of silence for the two once more. Cael placed his sword in the scabbard strapped to his mount and kicked some dirt over the last of the embers from the fire made the night before. He looked up again where the white owl was perched, and found its piercing eyes locked on Cael. This time the bird dropped from its perch and flew further into the forest, quickly fading into the shadows of the woods ahead.

As Cael pulled himself up onto his horse he wondered what thoughts ran through the mind of his companion while they traveled. As for him, he let himself settle into thoughts of home and the night with Thera while the horses trotted along the dirt road south through the wood.

They continued like this for some time, traveling during the day, and sleeping at night. Cael was thankful that Herth found no more need to test him. Herth's words were short, though Cael was slowly prying some small bits of information from him. He heard the tales of the barbarian tribes of the mountains, their dreams and their sufferings in the pine-covered hills they called home. Though Cael had never traveled into the mountains west of the kingdom, he could begin to picture the place that Herth called home.

In between bites of an apple he was eating as they rode along, Herth finally started to ask a question about Cael's past.

"What about you young Firestorm lord, what sort of place do you call home?" Herth asked of him as they rode along, still under the canopy of the forest.

"I am from the hills that border the northern range of the mountains you come from. We have rolling green hills stretching out as far as you can see in a day's walk. Beyond that are the crags and plateaus of the steppes, a barren and frozen landscape the orcs call home. Though it's not an easy or kind place, many winter there. The orcs of Ledun harass the towns that border the northern waste every winter and my family defends them."

"I see. Then you have fought battles with the man-eaters then?" Herth inquired his mood suddenly dark on his face.

"Many times, though only small bands and never without aid. Why do you ask?"

Herth motioned Cael to be silent, and urged his horse forward into a quick trot to get around a bend in the road. Cael followed and kept quiet, beginning to hear sounds he had hoped would never reach this part of the world.

Rounding the bend he heard and then saw the guttural savagery of the Orcs. He was not sure what they were squabbling over beneath their hands; he counted five of the gross creatures, with ragged rusted armor painted black as the blood held inside their green flesh. Cael drew his sword, and dismounted from his horse so it wouldn't be frightened further by the commotion. Herth dismounted and pulled his bow free, an arrow already knocked.

They walked together along the edge of the trees, both careful not to disturb the brush or make any extra noises. Cael was happy for his choice of leather studded armor beneath his travelling cloak, he had learned early in life to keep it close, if not already on.

Herth stopped and began to pull back the string of his bow, carefully aiming his shot for the closest of the monsters. Cael hefted his sword in his hand, relaxing his arm and readying it for a fight. He heard the hiss of the arrow from Herth's bow fly towards its target across the small clearing.

A squeal of pain-laden rage filled the clearing. The creature's brethren stood, stunned by the anguished cries. Staring at him in surprise, they quickly noted the arrow and began to look frantically for their attackers. Herth stepped clear of the bushes they had been hiding in, releasing another arrow which struck its target square in the chest. A gurgling squeal rose as he fell to his knees driving the other three into frenzied action.

Cael looked at their twisted forms, just a tad smaller then himself; he knew them to be just as strong, and more vile then anything. He knew from their armor that they were orcs from the steppes, though how they had gotten so far south was beyond him.

Herth dropped his bow to pull his axe free, and Cael lunged from the brush with his sword drawn. Whipped into a rage by the death of their comrades, the orcs rushed the two warriors. Herth raised his axe and Cael stepped outward giving them both room to use their weapons. Cael dropped his sword to prepare a low defense.

The largest of the three orcs ran towards Herth, leaping at the last minute. Herth swung wide with his axe, bringing it up to catch the orc in his side, which threw him and his twisted blade into a tree next to the road.

Cael was left with the two smaller orcs, which rushed him just as quickly as their larger companion had done to Herth. Deflecting the rusty pike of the first, he rushed in close, slashing open its chest. At the same time Cael shoved him out of the way, he quickly turned to block the weapon of the other, and countered by catching its leg. The swift movement allowed Cael to then drive the orc to the ground with his sword in its chest.

Herth had already begun to calmly clean the gore from his axe.. "Seems too far south for these orcs," he commented before dropping the blood-sopped cloth onto the chest of the first orc Cael had killed.

Cael began walking over to the corpse the beasts had been tearing to shreds. Not much remained that their blades had not already defiled, and he was forced to cover his mouth at the smell. Death filled the air around the creature and it looked like the acid burns covered his arms and hands. They let their poison ravage the poor soul before they had killed it.

"Herth, do you know this creature?" Cael asked of his companion. Herth walked over and knelt by the body, seeming to not notice the stench. Herth drew his gaze upward toward the being's hair and ears, neither of which Cael recognized. "I know of nothing with ears like that, or hair the color of gold."

Herth brought his hands up to touch both the ears and the hair, or what was left of it. Cael could see that hiss heart was heavy with the loss of what must have been a beautiful figure. The golden hair and the pale skin with a hint of the color of the trees surrounding them would have indeed been a memorable sight in life. "Whatever it is, there is nothing further we can do for it. Let us let it rest in death, and bury it properly."

Cael nodded in agreement and they set about to digging a grave to the side of the road. Without proper tools they were hard pressed to dig around the roots of the trees they were stuck in. Herth drew out one of his smaller axes and chopped his way through the soil and roots to ensure they made the proper depth to keep small animals out of the grave.

Cael stood, stretching out his back after being hunched over to dig the grave. The smell of earth filled his nose as he wiped his brow with his arm. This place carried a scent that was vibrant with life, rich and pungent like the ground after a spring rain.

Cael stepped over to the creature now that they had prepared its final resting place. It seemed sad to him that his life had been taken, especially in such a quiet place as the woods he now stood in. It seemed wrong to him somehow, though he could not place a name to what he was feeling. Herth came and stood at the other end of the creature, scooping his hands under his shoulders while Cael took his legs. Stepping as carefully as they could around the hole they had dug, they gently lowered the corpse into the grave. Cael and Herth began to cover the body with soil, pushing the rich earth over the void. Within minutes the body was covered and the hole filled.

After seeing their work complete, Herth seemed to lose himself in his thoughts. Cael turned his mind back to the road and what might lie ahead. As he stared at the soil on the top of the grave, his thoughts were interrupted by panic from the horses tied up nearby. Cael felt the same cold chill he had on the plains.

A low rush of wind moved towards them, and Cael saw the leaves and dirt of the forest floor being whipped into small flurries. He glanced to Herth who was tending to the horses, and saw he was holding himself with caution as though he felt the chill this time too. The horses' hooves began to frantically beat the ground, nervousness giving way to outright panic in the next few moments.

Herth grabbed his axe and moved to his horse's side, trying to calm it but it continued to grow agitated. Cael followed and grabbed the reigns of his own, trying to put his hand on its head to soothe it. Rearing up on its hind legs, Herth's stallion pulled its reigns from the Barbarian's hands and took off into the deep forest, ignoring the path they were on. Herth then tried to help Cael calm his mount, but it had already reacted to the panic of the other and pulled free of Cael's hands.

Snapping back on the reigns the horse pulled away, the leather teared at Cael's hands as it freed itself. Cael grabbed at the pack containing the maps and few supplies he had inside as the horse turned to run. He barely held on to it as the horse broke into a gallop and was gone.

The two men stood for a half-second looking at the direction their mounts had run into the woods. Herth turned to face down the path behind them, trying to hear or sense something that Cael could not. Finally, he placed his axe back into its hardened case on his back and turned towards the path that led deeper into the forest.

Herth and Cael waited in the gusting wind on the road. As Cael watched, the ground on the path they had passed through began to broil, and dirt and leaves and needles from the pines and firs began to twist into a cloudy mass and slowly move towards them.

"We must go. Whatever is coming down the road is nothing I want to face." Herth said as he began a quick jog down the road.

Cael didn't question him, as he also felt a growing dread come upon him even though he could not hear with the same clarity that Herth could. The image of the maelstrom churning its way through the wood was enough to make him want to keep moving briskly forward.

As they ran, the gusts continued to pick up behind them, and the cold sensation struck deep into their bones though the wind felt warmed by the sun. It was picking up in strength and Cael felt the panic in his chest grow at this strange occurrence. Herth did not look panicked yet, but Cael saw that he quickened his pace. Pushing forward to keep up, Cael began to feel that out running this foul wind would not be an option.

The path turned and twisted, and with each passing moment Cael felt the maelstrom growing and inching closer. He could hear the groaning of the trees behind them, the snapping of smaller branches as they were pulled in. Cael saw a tight group of trees ahead, seemingly growing right on top of each other in the same patch of soil.

"There!" Herth yelled over the wind.

Grabbing Cael, Herth pulled him off the road and into the patch of trees that stood close enough together to provide some shelter against the wind battering down upon them. They huddled together and listened to the wind howling around them, and as quickly as it had come, the gale passed on ahead and further into the woods. A short distance down the road, Cael could hear the wind fade into nothingness, leaving them with the relative silence of the woods.

Cael and Herth uncovered their heads and listened cautiously, wondering if the maelstrom would continue or if some other evil would be following. Cael stood and stepped out into the path, the battered branches and leaves of the trees littered the forest floor. He caught sight of nothing unusual as he scanned the path in both directions.

Cael caught the mild scent of pine, realizing that the forest had changed somewhat from where they had begun their frenzied run. He was bewildered by the strange occurrence. Panting, Herth stepped out and joined Cael, his face betraying very little of the concern Cael felt he must have at the loss of their horses and packs in the middle of the forest.

"We must continue on foot." Cael noted with dismay.

"How much farther do we have to travel Cael?" Herth asked.

Cael took the map roll out of his pack, unrolling the flexible leather on the ground in front of them. The old leather was barely marked, though Grim had told Cael that the map was much older than even he could know.

Herth and Cael followed the lines of the map, finding the road they now stood upon. Cael looked at the road finding its way into the forest that was dividing Dalerad from Yulan, but the map did not reveal anything for how far they had traveled or how far they had left to go.

"From my best guess, we are just under halfway through the forest." Cael said, "Anything more then that I cannot guess at since I do not know how large the forest really is. This map was old even to Grim's memory of when it came to the castle."

"Do we have enough food to walk the journey to the Yulan borders?" Herth seemed to already know the answer when he asked.

Cael reached over, looking inside his pack. He saw that they had a week's worth of dried meat, but only a few apples and two water skins remained to keep their thirst at bay as they walked.

"No. Not without scavenging and hunting while we travel."

Herth nodded. He had some arrows left with which to hunt, and Cael knew he would have to be sure of his shots with no way of replacing the arrows in the woods. The arrows were a valuable commodity outside a city with a fletcher to make more of them.

Cael continued to search the map for clues as to how far along they were and what they could find along the path to help themselves. He traced the lines etched along his ring as he stared at the map, but in his peripheral vision, he saw Herth check his weapons while keeping his axe at the ready. Herth looked over at Cael and his eye caught a detail he hadn't asked about before.

"The ring, why did the king give it to you?"

Cael looked down at the ring, following Herth's inquisitive gaze. "He gave it as a sign of his faith in me. All the lords recognized it at the ball."

"Yes, but has it ever been told to have any powers other than being just a ring?" Herth came over to look at it closer. He continued to speak. "My people know of ancient relics, from the Zephyren, the original people who lived on Theron."

"You speak of those who sat in the towers?"

Herth nodded. "My people were the first to rebel against them, but we remember the things they made and many of them were created with great powers. Did the king think this was one of them?"

Cael tugged at the ring and noticed that unlike the first time it slipped on, it refused to adjust size and come off. "It was supposed to adjust size as needed, to stay on my hand. Jonothon said nothing more of its use."

Herth looked down at the map again, tracing his hands over the lines. His rough hands were still dexterous for their size. Grabbing Cael's hand he gently but firmly pushed the ring over the map and the two men watched carefully as the vague lines and borders began to gain color and detail. Cael tried pulling his hand back, but Herth kept his grip firm.

"Herth, what did you make the map do?"

"Hush, let us watch what it is doing."

Herth motioned for Cael to continue, and Cael ran his hand along the path they had followed into the forest. As they watched, they saw the details of the path reveal themselves on the old leather.

Like pictures appearing from the mist of a memory, the map revealed their path, the images fading as they progressed further. They saw images emerge of the orc bodies along the path, the spot where they buried the strange creature, the spot they lost their horses and then finally the clump of trees where they hid while the maelstrom passed them by.

Cael let his hand rest in the spot where he now saw the image of themselves, looking down at the map as they were now. He started to notice the details spreading out and a larger image being revealed around them. Herth stood quickly, axe at the ready. Cael felt him tense at something but continued to watch the map, as it revealed cloaked figures surrounding them in the trees.

"Herth, we are not alone." But Cael saw that Herth was already focused on something, his face just as impassive as the first time they had met. Looking away from the map, Cael saw the same cloaked figures surrounding him as he had on the map. Some had bows that stood as tall as they did at a full 6 of the king's foot, the surface of their bows a white bark wrapped in a bright green. Others held swords at the ready, with blades the color of leaves and hilts gilded in black steel and a red substance like opal on the blade guards. Cael knew that no matter their skill, he and Herth could not keep themselves from capture.

One of the figures stepped forward silently; Cael did not even hear the leaves and needles break beneath his feet. His hair was a metallic bronze color and his skin was white with the hint of a vibrant green tone.

"Cael, I think we found who those orcs had been fighting with." Herth said

Herth was grunting with exertion. Cael had seen him hooded and his hands bound behind him just before his own head was covered with a similar hood. They had been marching some time and Cael knew that he was no longer aware of his location in this forest and was now at the mercy of his captors.

He could feel Herth being kept close to him; occasionally they stumbled into each other as they followed the rough path their captors laid out for them.

Cael felt a staff brought against his chest to stop his pace. He braced himself for Herth to bounce into him, but instead heard him curse through his hood as he tripped. Cael wondered if they would help Herth stand, but he received a swift kick to the back of his knees that knocked him down roughly to the forest floor. Cael said a short prayer of thanks that the leaves beneath kept his knees from the hard soil and stones.

"Remove their masks." A smooth but ancient voice filled Cael's ears. A quick tug of the hood left Cael facing the light of the forest without the mask over his head. Though the light was not bright, the sudden change from darkness stung his eyes and forced him to blink and look away. His face felt cool in the air of the forest, and his nose was chilled by the mix of pine and cold air in contrast to the stuffy hood he had worn.

When his eyes refocused he was facing what appeared to be a man taller than Herth. Dressed in silver plate armor, with the whitest hair he had ever seen streaming down his back, Cael knew him to be the same race as the creature in the woods. If not for his strange white hair, his gray eyes and pointed ears gave away his lineage.

The large man walked forward, inspecting Cael and then Herth for imperfections. Cael's mind wandered for a moment thinking that a horse at market must feel similarly. He felt that even their souls were being checked for flaws as the creature circled them slowly.

As he came back around, he stared Cael in the eyes, holding them with the light gray of his own. Cael felt it was not proper to speak yet, as the man seemed to be coming to some decision in his own mind. Cael looked at him and believed him to be cut from a solid piece of stone. His gleaming armor and features flowed as one, emanating a smooth and natural strength. Cael realized in this moment that the woods were silent and sensed that the stillness was the forest's way of giving reverence for the being standing in front of him.

"I want to ask why you two are in the lands of the elves." The ancient voice indicated he had been the one speaking while they were hooded.

"We are passing through to the lands of Yulan, we did not know the Forest was yours." Cael got it out clearly enough.

The "elve" appeared to believe what Cael had to say, though he was far from satisfied yet. "I am Qonos, king of the elves, and leader of the kingdom of Pentath. What are your names?

"I am Herth, of the Westrom tribes. I am a servant of Lord Grim of Dalerad given the charge of protecting this young man."

Qonos looked at Cael. "And your name is?"

"Cael Firestorm."

Qonos seemed pleased, but not fooled by the simplicity of Cael's introduction. "Such a simple introduction. Do you not have some purpose to your journey? You seem a little out of place travelling all this way with the help of such a—" he paused, "'large' body guard."

"He is the chosen heir for the Friezen throne, and on a quest for the tools to save and rule his kingdom."

Cael shot Herth a dirty look. He was confused as to why the barbarian was being so open and vocal about their purpose and names. He had spent the trip in silence and now chose to speak readily.

"The king of Dalerad chose an heir? My scout would have returned with news of that already."

Cael knew in that moment that they had found the origin of the man, or elve, that they had found slaughtered along the road. He must have been the scout the king was waiting on.

"My lord, sadly we found the corpse of one of your people upon the road during our travels. It had been set upon by the man-eaters and though we killed the orcs, he was already dead." Herth stated blandly.

"What did he look like?" Qonos was still almost expressionless. Though you could tell he was feeling many emotions, he bore them with a kingly state that Cael was strangely jealous of. Qonos's hands were resting on the black hilt of a sword at his side, loose in the scabbard and ready to be drawn. Cael saw the scabbard was carved with vines and leaves of the forest.

"His face we could not make out, but he had the only true gold hair I had ever seen." Herth continued to be the speaker for this conversation.

"And the body, what did you do with it?"

"We buried it as best we could, a mile or so up the path your people found us on. It is near the bodies of the man-eaters that had killed him."

Qonos nodded to some of the elves behind Cael and Herth. Cael felt more than heard the others leave; only the two holding their bonds remained with Qonos. Qonos stepped towards them, kneeling and looking them each in the face, first Herth and then Cael. Pierced by his gaze, Cael felt his very soul being probed for its worth to this gleaming lord of the elves. As quickly as it had begun, the gaze broke and Qonos stood.

"Untie them, and return to them their things," Qonos said as he turned away. "You two will come with me, so that we might speak at greater length."

"My lord, where are we going?"

Qonos did not even turn around as he answered. "To Pentath."

CHAPTER 5

Not every part of Theron exists in a space of wide fields and sunny skies. Lying in the vast ocean that divides Theron in two is a storm that drives the deep currents of the ocean and the winds of the sea, and strikes terror into even the most seasoned sailors. The tempest gives this ocean its name, the Storm Sea. The great storm tosses ships and tears through them like silk ribbons, and has been blowing since the end of the Council Wars. It has tested the courage of sailors and the strength of ships, and in over five centuries the storm wall has never been broken.

Until now, that is. A ship of the nation of Iliana, the nation of a thousand isles, has bested the wall and is now sailing into a sea unseen by any outsider. At the heart of the sea lies what will soon be known as the lands of the Eternal Emperor, Tyrnor.

The wind was howling and tearing at Timothy's cloak. Standing next to his horse on the cliff overlooking the ocean, he was exposed to every whim of the surf and winds. The smell of salt and the chill rain that would be falling soon filled his nose. Holding the reigns in his hands, he sought the ocean for signs of an unknown sail.

Timothy stood of average height for a man of Tyrnor; at just over two of the Empirical meters in height he could look over his horse with ease to scan the horizon. His blonde hair carried a platinum sheen, and he wore it short-cropped and his beard shaven. Unlike the stout soldiers of the emperor though, Timothy's family carried themselves light, lithe and agile. He was the son of the mistress who led the Thieves Guild. His family had spent generations perfecting their craft and Timothy was known as one of the best students of their teachings.

"Well Jintol, I see nothing on the promontory, should we continue on to the south from the watchtower?" Timothy spoke to his horse. Its response was to look at him and bray while nodding it head.

"Something tells me you agree because you know it means you get time in the stables, while I stay out in the cold." Timothy chuckled as he pulled himself up into the saddle. The horse whinnied and began a quick but careful trot from the promontory to the path leading to the watchtower.

As he moved down the path, Timothy took time to gaze at the lands surrounding him. Rolling green hills, many of which held the ruins of fortifications from times long past, spread out from the coast inward to the Sapphire Mountains. Small pockets of forests filled the lowlands and the edges of the mountains, all strongly controlled by the Emperor's administrators. The patches of rain coming in from the sea stretched in shadowy lines across the landscape in the late afternoon light.

Reaching the lowest point of the path, Timothy turned his horse across the field towards the paved roadway. He let his horse Jintol play a little, and as they reached the road, he directed the steed southward. In less than an hour, he would be at the watchtower and enjoy a short respite from his search.

Telnor was staring into the fire burning brightly in the fireplace where the dancing blaze cast shadows of his minotaur form on the stone walls. The hair covering his body was mostly hidden by his leather armor, but the flame-red of his mane was in sharp contrast to the black hair of his limbs and face. He grabbed a sharpening stone from the mantel, and began to polish the points of his horns. Like all Minotaur's, he took great pride in the care for his horns and his carried a sharp gloss from their white bases to the sharp blackened tips.

Turning from the flames, Telnor tossed the stone back on the mantle and eyed the stairwell across the room. Feeling it was time to return to his search, he moved to the base of the stairs and eyed their lower curves before he started up for the lookout above. He stepped lightly, two treads at a time, and yet the sound of his hooves still echoed in the stone tower.

"Well Telnor, it is time to check the horizons is it not?" the bulky minotaur grumbled to himself. "I am unsure why Timothy has sent me on this mission. I could cover as much ground as he and that horse any day. Poor simple beast...." Telnor shook his head as he climbed the steps, thinking on the sad state of what it meant to be a horse.

Telnor passed the first of three landings, this one holding the kitchen and pantry for the tower. Stocked with dried meats and sealed jars of pickled radishes and beets, the tower would never produce a meal fit for the nobility, but it would keep a garrison well fed for many months before provisions would have to be brought.

At the next landing he held his nose to the acrid stench of the soldiers' belongings. He was always curious how the soldiers could stand the smell but Timothy had reminded him each time that humans could generally not smell themselves. Telnor had thought it strange since his people always knew the scents of those around them, including their own.

Coming to the top of the stairs, and the last of the three landings, he grabbed hold of the latch bar and swung it sideways out of the slot holding the hatch shut. Pushing upwards he lowered his horns and carefully brought them past the stone floor which the hatch opened up into. Stepping up Telnor left the hatch open, feeling the warmth of the room below flowing upward as he stood near it.

Telnor thought on the warmth of the air rushing around him, and how he preferred it to the heat coming from the pipe works inside the stone floor beneath him. The pipes kept the room warm, but in his mind they could never replace the feeling of sitting close to an open fireplace in a large room.

Moving towards the center of the platform on which he now stood, Telnor looked out at the ocean surrounding the watchtower. The dark frames for the window glass were shaped wood from the tree farms of the Emperor. They held the glass panes which made in the guild wards of one of the nearby cities. He was sure this tower held much importance as it was the closest to the capital and the emperor had spent vast amounts to rebuild the watch towers surrounding the island kingdom.

Telnor moved towards the pane of glass facing to the southwest, and focused his sight to the furthest point he could see in the faded light of the storm sea. The heavy grays of the murky clouds covered most everything he had hoped to find, though he was still unsure what he was looking for. Timothy had kept him here to watch the furthest reaches for a reason, and mentioned only that Telnor would know when he saw it.

Looking back to the southern pane of glass, Telnor again focused his eyes to the horizon. When he did so he caught a bit of movement in the furthest reaches of the ocean he could see. Even in the gray of the storm he could see a green patch of sail heading west. Rubbing his eyes he looked again to be sure, and this time there were more.

Far beyond the reach of human sight there was a strange vessel sailing towards him, getting closer in the late light of the day. Its sails were large and sea green with a strange rock-like tree in the bright white center of each sail. He studied the ship and saw the sails were bowed and held like large sheets across the beams. These were definitely not created by the builders in Tyrnor's shipyards.

"Telnor, you must thank Timothy for this opportunity, he has given you the chance to take credit for once." Grinning, Telnor continued to stand and watch the ship pass further from the Storm wall in the fading light. Once Timothy returned they could send word to the emperor and the garrison. Telnor noted the path of the ship and realized it was sailing quickly toward land, and some of its sails flapped free indicating it must have been damaged since its journey began. Perhaps it had sailed too close to the storm wall? Or maybe it was caught in combat as renegades from the empire? Telnor continued to watch and reflect during the coming hours as he waited for Timothy to return so they could send word of the find.

Telnor had dozed off standing up. Shaking himself he realized that is was now dark and that he heard Timothy rustling about downstairs, most likely looking for some food in the second floor pantry. Turning towards the hatchway he bellowed down to Timothy.

"Come, hairless one, I have found something for you."

Telnor heard Timothy's rummaging stop and then his footfalls across the wooden planks of the floor; evidence that his comment had the desired effect in bringing Timothy up to the lookout.

"Tell me you have more to talk about than your latest comment on my appearance?"

Motioning out to the sea where he last saw the ship, he spoke. "I saw a ship I had never seen before, with sea green sails and a high hull that is not something the empire builds."

"And you are sure? It is not of empire design?"

"Unless for the first time in my eighty years of life you have changed something about the way you pink-skins build your ships, then yes, I am sure it is not one of ours."

Timothy laughed and removed a spyglass from one of the many pockets lining the inside of his heavy black cloak. Telnor was never quite certain how many pockets and pouches were in the cloak but he knew that Timothy was never short of tools for a job.

"I am curious: how exactly do you intend to see them now? It is all but dark along the coast now."

"I intend to look for the lanterns of their ship. They have done their best to maintain their secrecy so I am hoping that they are beginning to feel safe and slip up."

"That is a slim hope Timothy."

Timothy sighed as he looked out through the glass of the watchtower. "Telnor, you know the garrison won't bring their forces on the word of a minotaur alone."

Telnor was irritated by the response but he knew it was true. "It is difficult living in two different worlds Timothy- your mother and yourself accept the presence of Minotaur's but the rest of the empire-"

"The rest of the empire thinks you are less than worthy because you all hide away." Timothy took the spyglass from his face. "The tribes stick to themselves and all the children are left with are stories from the wars."

Telnor hated the feeling of nothingness these conversations reminded him of. His people had fought for their freedom decades earlier and been saved by the emperor of Tyrnor on more than one occasion. Each of the emperors had refused the Tyrn, the people of Tyrnor, the right to destroy the minotaur and they had repaid that action with loyalty. It hadn't stopped the occasional massacre to occur on either side- but it had prevented more bloodshed then what might have otherwise occurred.

"I know what you are thinking Telnor. The emperor and my mother are close, which is probably why I learned to not fear the minotaur. Enrick has been a great friend to the minotaur during his reign as emperor."

"But not everyone knows to respect me as equal." Telnor shook his head and looked out the panes of glass, once again focusing his gaze as far as the night would let it reach. Timothy moved off towards the hatch and to the warm light from below.

"Besides Telnor, can you blame them? You are ugly as a mule!"

Telnor ignored the comment, letting the joke slide as he saw something that Timothy had been waiting for.

"Timothy, come search over here again. I found that light for you."

Timothy crossed the room; standing next to Telnor he followed his arm as it pointed to where he saw the spotted the light.

"Ah! There we go. Two lanterns, moving towards the beach it looks like. Thank the fates for a moonless night."

"It is a full moon Timothy; it's just the clouds helping us."

Telnor was beginning to let the irritation fade from their conversation earlier. He had spent too many years among the Tyrn to let their simple hatreds bother him for long. He looked at Timothy who was still focusing the spyglass toward the lights Telnor had spotted for him.

"Let's go Telnor, I want to be there with the soldiers to help capture the ship."

"Are you looking for a fight today? That is unlike your usual sneaking around, Timothy."

Timothy returned the spyglass to its pouch and moved toward the open hatch. He answered, "Just curiosity Telnor. I want to know what has become such a thorn in the emperor's side these past few weeks."

The dingy came to stop on the gravelly sand of the beach and two dark figures jumped out to pull the boat ashore. One abandoned his post and quickly walked inland, leaving his partner to struggle with the weight.

"Derrik you bastard, come help with the boat!"

"Leave it Mercurious, we will have no use for it soon enough."

Disgruntled, Mercurious dropped the boat, picking his way carefully along the shore, stepping around the pools of water formed by the surf. He came to stand next to Derrik and looked at the dark landscape opening up before them.

"Can you feel it Mercurious? Can you?" Derrik sniffed the air, letting his black hair catch on the coastal breeze. The dark cloak covering him fell loosely on his stout sailor's form; Derrik had been bred as a man of the ocean. Mercurious fondly remembered the years that he had sailed the seas as their greatest commander. With eyes the color of seafoam, Derrik had always been able to read the swells and the clouds to sail true. Stocky and carrying the tanned form of a man who spent his time in the ocean sun, Derrik stood enjoying the salty breeze off the ocean.

Mercurious pulled his much heavier cloak tight to his body. Unlike Derrik he had always been tall and lanky. His bright blue eyes were a sharp contrast to the fires he once commanded. The memory of warmer climates reminded him of the stark cold, and he pulled his cloak even tighter to avoid the chill breeze. "This is why you are the god of water Derrik; there is no reason to ever be this cold. It disgusts me."

"Ah how short sighted you are old friend, a 'God' could not have lost their power so easily as we did..."

"Lost! Easily? How were we to know we had given him so much strength?"

Derrik angrily turned to face Mercurious. "Not strength, potential. We gave him our potential and with it the keys to each of us. It is high time we made him regret not slaying us."

Derrik stomped further inland, heading northwards. Mercurious watched him for a moment before following along. Anywhere was better than being out near all this water.

Telnor and Timothy stood in the darkness on a cliff overlooking the cove that held the dingy they had seen from the watchtower. Telnor noted that both lanterns remained wide open to the night.

"Whoever came ashore didn't feel the need to stopper the lights to protect their location."

Timothy nodded. "We will have to send troops to locate those who went inland. The emperor was very clear that all of those aboard the ship were to be captured and brought to him alive."

"I wonder what harm any of them could do to us. Looking at the ship I would guess they are not here to invade."

Telnor studied the ship carefully in the darkness. The moon peeked out between the clouds overhead which gave them a little light, but not enough to expose the lookout they held over the ship.

The ship itself was a greater surprise than Telnor had expected. The bright sea green sails they had noted earlier hung from the beams and the rigging. The aft carried a flag of the same color and when it flapped with the wind he could see the white rocky tree covering its center. He wondered if the ship had taken on some sort of rot from the ocean water outside the storm wall. Stranger still, the entire ship seemed to be covered in metal beams, a great lattice work that didn't cover enough of the hull to be armor, but it appeared to be used to reinforce the wood of the hull. The metal did not look very heavy, but Telnor wondered why the lattice works were created for the ship to reach here.

"Telnor, it looks like the troops have arrived." Timothy jumped up on his horse to greet the captain of the guard coming up the road behind them. Telnor looked at the troop complement and noted they had brought ballistae with them- a sure sign they mean to ensure the ship stayed put. He turned to follow Timothy and caught up with him after he had met the captain.

The captain let his eyes rest on Telnor for a brief moment, looking back to listen to Timothy's plan. The captain had what looked to be two hundred men with him, and easily fifty of those were cavalry to ensure no one could run away. Telnor left Timothy to continue speaking while he inspected the forces. Ambling towards the back he felt a number of the silver and black clad soldiers stiffen as he passed; others ignored him, and still some smiled a little. Each of the troops wore their high helms with pride, the white horsehair plumes for the officers of each squad blaring bright against the night sky. The thick cloaks covering the plate mail of the infantry muted the shine so all he could see was the steely gray of each soldier, headed by the occasional plume of white.

The orderly rows of cavalry shone like a red sun. Unlike the silver and black of the infantry, the cavalry wore blood-red with their steel armor. Their red plumes and capes helped them stand out like strange birds in the night. Telnor noted that they were all the light cavalry, their horses were lighter war stallions, a separate breed line from the war horses of the heavy cavalry.

"Telnor, come." Timothy was waving to Telnor from the head of the line. Orders were filtering down the line of soldiers as Telnor walked over to Timothy who was back on his horse. "We are returning to the beach to watch the assault."

"Do they have a plan in place?"

"Telnor, they do. We are going to investigate the dingy left on shore once the ship has been secured."

Telnor grinned as Timothy turned his horse around and began to ride back to the beach. Telnor began to jog alongside in silence as they moved towards the beach once more. Stopping in sight of the sands, Telnor moved over to the closer of the two ballistae being set up on the beach. A long length of rope was already wound loosely on the ground, as was a second of the large ropes used for dock work.

"Is there a problem, minotaur?" one of the younger officers asked, irritated at Telnor's inspection while they worked. Telnor took his time to inspect the six stakes being hammered into the ground to hold the rope before answering the snide toned officer.

"There is none, young – man." Telnor looked the shorter officer in the eyes. Grinning as much as a minotaur could, he moved further up the beach, still keeping to the shadows offered by the clouds.

Telnor felt a vague frustration that a portion of the population still viewed the minotaur people so poorly. Some had grown accustomed to their presence but many still looked down on the minotaur. Telnor had a much greater tolerance for it than the rest of his people, though only because he had been raised in the presence of the Tyrn for most of his life. He wondered in that moment if he had more in common with his people or with the Tyrn he worked alongside.

Looking out over the small cove, the ship was still at rest, its crew seemingly unaware of the activity around them. Looking closer to shore he saw the dingy still sitting in the sand, and in the slowly expanding pool of moonlight bathing the cove he saw a broad line of disrupted sand leading away from the dingy and toward the woods surrounding the cove. Timothy was riding back toward him with the red-plumed captain of the cavalry.

"Telnor, what do you see?" Timothy inquired as he followed Telnor's gaze.

"Tell the cavalry to head north into the woods. The ones from the dingy did not return to the ship."

The cavalry captain looked at Timothy who nodded. Waving his arm back towards the cavalry, a group of twenty of them broke away and began to head north into the woods. The captain looked back at Telnor, gauging him.

"Master minotaur, how long ago did you spot the ship?"

"Three, maybe four hours at most. The ship sailed in but appeared to have some damage to its sails."

"Did you get a chance to see anyone aboard?"

"No, it was too far for my eyes to see the crew."

The captain nodded, and he had a small smile on his face. Telnor guessed from his reaction and Timothy's stance that the cavalry captain was one who didn't mind the minotaur so much.

"How long has it been since you both saw the dingy come ashore?"

Timothy quickly provided an answer though his eyes were still focused on the ship. "It has been an hour. We were very glad that you came so quickly once called."

The Cavalry captain grinned. "The emperor is very serious about this mission. He has had the army mobilized all over Tyrnor to assist the Thieves Guild in this search. He wants this done quickly and quietly and I believe thanks to your assistance we may be able to achieve that."

Telnor found the sudden surge of activity very strange. The emperor had always been slow to act, and his patience had kept the peace between the Minotaur's and the Tyrn for his rule. The sudden military mobilization was out of character for the reserved actions of the emperor that Telnor had grown accustomed to. If he had mobilized so much of the army for the capture of a single ship, Telnor was interested in finding the answer for why it had been done so swiftly.

A captain of the infantry marched up and saluted the cavalry captain. "Sir, the ballistae are ready with the grappling ropes."

"Very good, take your aim and get that ship ashore. I want that ship taken."

"Yes, Commander!" The man saluted and set off knowing that he had work to do – or he didn't want to be around Telnor. The cavalry captain called over the infantry commander as the younger officer marched away.

"I want you to reiterate to your men that as many of the crew is to be taken alive as is possible. The emperor wants prisoners – dead mean tell us nothing."

The commander nodded and marched over to his men who were preparing to jump aboard the ship. Telnor noticed a number of the first wave had already removed their cloaks and were preparing themselves for a fight. Telnor noted the first platoon also bore a tattoo of the Imperial Guard across their forearms. These were troops reserved for defending the emperor himself. Telnor had never seen any outside of the palace guard, and then he had seen only a few. One had to spend many years in training and survive many battles to earn a place in the emperor's guard.

Telnor, Timothy, and the cavalry captain all stood waiting in silence as the ballistae crew took their aims. The soldiers became silent and the crank crews stood ready to pull the mooring lines taught against the hull of the strange vessel sitting in the small natural harbor. Telnor caught the signal to fire running down the command lines out of the corner of his vision.

The ballistae both fired with a loud crack, their spear loads hitting the ship in the fore and aft, each missing the metal plating that speckled the hull. Telnor noted there was no motion from the ship itself, and the cove was filling with the noise of the empire soldiers as they worked to secure the mooring lines through the loops of the ballistae bolts. Within seconds they completed their task and the large cranks attached to each of the ropes from the ballistae began to squeal and ratchet loudly as the sound of the metal creaked across the night air. The first assault team was wading out, preparing themselves to jump aboard; one of them had swum a short distance and was already climbing up the side of the hull.

The process to get the ship close enough to land didn't take much longer, and soon the ship was swarmed with almost one hundred of the armor-clad soldiers of the emperor. The commander of the infantry seemed agitated as he stood at the shore, and the cavalry captain noted this.

"Something is amiss, either the ship is empty, or some trick has been played on us."

A cry went out from the ship, and one of the plumed officers rushed back to the edge of the ship. He quickly dropped into the shallow water and jogged up the beach, where he engaged in hasty conversation with the infantry commander. Telnor could see the commander's surprised look from a distance. He seemed to confirm something with the officer and gave a brisk order, which sent the officer slogging back to the ship to relay the orders. The commander walked up the beach towards their small trio. Timothy spoke first.

"What is it commander, what have your men found?"

"They aren't sure what to make of it sir."

"Out with it man, what did they find?" The cavalry captain spoke up eagerly.

The commander sighed, as if he was trying to tumble it around in his own mind. "The entire crew, they— they were all either unconscious or locked up somehow. Many were tied to the posts of their beds."

"Did someone get there first, and leave them for us?" The captain asked.

"It doesn't seem so sir. No trace of anything of ours was found aboard. The ship is much different than our builds, so we can confirm it is not of Tyrnor. Even the wood is nothing I have seen before."

Telnor was very surprised at the news. They had been expecting to capture the ship but to find the crew already detained? That made the tale of this strange ship somewhat more interesting than he had initially thought.

"We need to find the others who escaped. They would have the answers, and I think, they may be why the emperor is concerned about this," Telnor finished speaking and the others just stared at him.

"What? You have an entire ship's crew that has been somehow detained, at least two of them get away, and you don't think it is connected somehow?"

Telnor replied thoughtfully, "He has a point. Commander, I will send more of my horsemen to look for those that got away, and I will send messengers to the capital and other garrisons to let them know what has occurred. You get your men to take the prisoners off the ship and get them to the capital." The commander nodded and moved to comply. Telnor's statement made the commander realize the situation was likely more complicated then they all had initially thought.

The cavalry captain motioned to one of his men standing behind, and he ran off to the rest of the group who began splitting off in different directions. "Timothy, Telnor, I thank you for your help in this endeavor tonight. I think it is time you returned to the emperor though. He will have questions, and you have to help him find those answers. We will bring the ship in to the harbor as soon as we can get a tow boat here."

Timothy bowed. "Thank you for at least letting us watch captain. I will make sure the emperor knows you were very helpful."

Telnor only bowed, as the captain was already moving off to join the last small detachment of the horsemen who served as his guard. "Timothy, what do you think those men mean to the Emperor?"

"I cannot say Telnor, but I agree with the Captain. It is time for us to return and help get this to the emperor. He will tell us what we need to know."

CHAPTER 6

Timothy was walking to the side of his horse, Telnor along the other side. The bit of gravel on the stone paved road they walked was the only fixture of interest to him at the moment. He was bothered by the ship they had seized and was hoping that the emperor would have some answers. He had taken on imperial missions before, but never in his almost forty years did he have a mission as strange as the one he had completed a few days before.

He had been sent with very little information, and it was more his mother's demand then a request from the emperor that the thieves' guild look for the ship. What could have possibly been contained in a ship that came from beyond the storm wall? Was it some evil? Why were the sailors captured when they arrived? This and a thousand other questions filled his mind as they walked along the roadway.

"Timothy, your mind wanders. Your thoughts betray themselves on your face." Telnor playfully poked at Timothy as they strolled aside the steed Jintol..

Timothy looked over at Telnor, his eyes well above Timothy and the back of the horse. Telnor stood half of an imperial meter above Timothy in height and at this angle it was quite evident.

"I guess they do. The mission we were given bothers me. It was a strange discovery and the ones that escaped—" Timothy paused and sighed audibly. "I am bothered by their disappearance. What purpose do they have in Tyrnor?"

"I am also bothered by their disappearance. The empire's cavalry are after them though. If anyone can find them it would be the scouts of the empire."

Timothy nodded in agreement. He lifted his head to gaze upon the high stone entrance gates to the capital as they neared. The walls stood at least 20 meters high, their dark gray stones cut and polished smooth which gave the wall a sheen that caught the shimmering reflection of the surrounding areas. Timothy looked upon the banners of Tyrnor hanging on the walls with feelings of warm familiarity. The white banners with their black tower emblem blazed brightly in the sunlight of the day. The banners repeated down the walls and smaller versions flowed from flagpoles above the gates.

Timothy noted the crossbowmen and archers on the gate-keep and saw their nod as he entered with Telnor. Their silver and black infantry attire was in dark contrast to the white banners on the walls. The weapons in their hands were ready to keep the peace both in and out of the city walls.

Telnor had to move closer to Timothy at this point because of the bustling traffic moving in and out of the gate. As they stepped under the portcullis, the walkway opened to a courtyard filled with carts and stalls, each in trim lines and organized by the Imperial Merchant's Guild. A few stalls here and there did not carry the mark of the guild, the red scales of the official weights and measures.

Timothy lifted himself onto Jintol's back to see over the crowd around them. As they worked their way across the courtyard bazaar, Timothy took note of the crowd. Merchant's stalls here almost always bore the red scales of the official weights and measures. The Imperial Merchant's Guild organized the stalls into neat rows, and the merchants knew the importance of keeping to those lines. A stall found out of place was soon found to be without a space at all. The wares of the entire continent eventually found their way here; silks, linens, and crafts were all kept to the imperial standard of quality.

The crowd itself was not the richest the city had to offer. In the noise of the bazaar you could hear snippets of conversation from the haggling merchants trying their best to out-do each other in the sale of their merchandise. Timothy had to smile. Being a member of the guild gave him access to a far better price, though he would never make use of his discount with a proper merchant following the letter of the law.

As they neared the far edge of the bazaar, Timothy was pleased to find the mass of smells from the bazaar gave way to the fresh air of the avenue. Even in the cool and refreshing morning air the bazaar was too crowded with people and different spices and incense and perfumes to be comfortable. Perhaps he knew some of what Telnor called the "stink" of the Tyrn in that moment.

Once on the far side of the bazaar they arrived at the grand avenue leading to the palace that the eternal emperor called home. The street was lined with the houses of the lords and ladies of the court, each a small palace unto itself, with armed guards standing outside. Telnor and Timothy drew a few glances from wary looking guards. A single minotaur accompanied by a man not dressed as a commoner was a strange sight indeed.

"You would think they had not ever seen one of my kind before." Telnor said in the silence of their walk.

"They only see your kind in bondage; they know I have no hold on you Telnor. Our friendship is a challenge to the class structure that gives them their position."

"How can one be high classed when they have none?" Telnor joked.

Timothy laughed at the statement. Neither of them viewed the small palaces of these lords and ladies kindly. Their houses were held to the same codes and lines that held the bazaar from entering the rest of the city. Roads were kept clear for the movement of imperial soldiers and for the order of the populace. Timothy enjoyed the well-run sense of the city. Even in the midst of a crowd he could sense the order and took it as a comfort.

Timothy felt better as the small morning crowds began to disperse when they neared the palace in the heart of the city. Prying eyes were no longer watching; only the early morning delivery boys and merchants heading to and from the bustling bazaars were out at this early an hour. Most likely the lords and ladies were sleeping off the revelry from the night before.

Jintol paid little attention to the small boys zipping between people in the road but Timothy watched them carefully as they passed. They were paid runners, but some were also pick-pockets and he wanted to make sure that his purse stayed where he put it.

As they neared the palace, Timothy noted an increase in soldiers. Though the palace was normally heavily guarded, there were far more troops than usual. Timothy was uncomfortable with the presence of so many troops near the palace; though he was on good terms with the military it gave him a sense of insecurity to see so many troops posted near the emperor. Looking to Telnor, he saw in his friend's eyes that felt similarly about the situation.

"Telnor, why do you think all these forces are in the city? The royal quarters around the palace don't have a need for so many."

Telnor merely looked up at Timothy on the horse, but didn't respond. Timothy could guess that he also realized something was amiss in the capital and it had the emperor worried. The troops were standing at posts, but with no obvious sense of urgency except when commanders or other officers came close.

Timothy looked to the towering height of the palace. It had begun as a very large fortress but the demands to impress the people with aesthetics over the years led to the addition of a number of extra rooms and a graceful entrance to the original building. Though most were unaware of it, the fortress was built with enough capacity for food and soldiers that it could resist a siege for months if necessary.

Timothy looked at the stone exterior and felt himself wander back into his own thoughts. His mother was present in the palace and she had given him the information to start his search. Though they were some distance away yet, he began to hope the minutes would pass quickly so he could get answers to his questions from the emperor himself.

Timothy and Telnor entered the palace through the side gates. Though they maintained some status with the emperor himself; members of the thieves' guild were not given the open status of Lord which would allow them to enter through the main gate without raising questions. They more often used the side or rear gates to meet with those inside the palace that they made their business with.

The thieves' guild was one of the more secretive tools for maintaining order that the emperor employed in Tyrnor. Each part of the empire had a guild organized to manage the running of certain aspects of the lands. The merchant guild organized the commerce, and the office of official measures ensured that the imperial meter was the same through-out the land and that the public had a standard to gauge the prices and amounts of goods they were purchasing. To his recollection, Timothy was sure there were dozens of guilds, but it was his own that he had devoted his life to.

Though called "thieves," his guild was more of a way for the emperor to have eyes and ears to rely upon other than his own royal house. They dealt in information first and foremost, though Timothy knew that they were to some degree outside the word of the laws. If the emperor needed something done surreptitiously, the thieves guild would be called upon to assist, and the thieves rarely acted without assistance from the imperial army. Their guild would not normally have enjoyed prominence, but their special place was attributed to his mother's close work with the emperor. Her place as the leader of the guild and as a confidant of the emperor gave the guild great power.

The guards at the gate recognized the two, and even though only a couple hundred minotaur were known in the capital Telnor was easily allowed entry. They were escorted deeper into the palace and Timothy admired the white stone that covered the deeper fortress underneath. After leaving the guard house they walked through a series of courtyards, filled with carefully trimmed shrubs and small trees. A couple areas even had fountains with exotic birds called their waters home. Many of the lords and ladies would spend time in the courtyards observing and feeding them by hand as they were so docile.

Coming to the final courtyard the guard stopped, motioning for them to continue on.

"I am to bring you here today, and go no further. Lady Galana will be seeing you both here. Good day to you both; Master Timothy, Master Telnor." The guard nodded and strolled off.

Timothy and Telnor stepped into the courtyard, the walkways surrounding it enclosed by pillars that held up the rooms and walls that carried the palace walls above them. Timothy scanned the higher reaches and saw the walls were still smooth and seamless, still coated in the stonework of masons long dead. Lost in appreciation of the craftsmanship, he didn't notice for a few moments that Telnor had strolled off and was speaking to a woman sitting near a fountain in the courtyard.

Looking across to the new arrival, Timothy admired at the deep wine colored dress with silk lace at the cuffs and collar. She wore a black shawl to cover her shoulders and her chestnut hair was worn high and showcased its regal streaks of silver. Timothy smiled as she rubbed Telnor's lowered head in greeting. He walked over to join them and felt his feelings of adoration for his mother rise in his chest.

"Mother, I see you are doing well today. How are you?"

She smiled; her sharp features were as strong as he had ever known them, lending a sense of royal beauty to how she carried herself. She came over to give Timothy a close hug, he leaned down a little to allow her arms to go around his neck and kiss his cheek. "My dear son I am glad to see you made it back. I heard the mission was a success?"

"Yes it was. We had only one failure in the whole plan and the search didn't last anywhere near as long as the emperor expected."

Timothy's mother looked concerned. "What do you mean you had one failure?"

Telnor spoke first. "We were only able to take notice of the ship because at least two of those aboard came ashore at night with lamps lit. They left their boat on the shoreline and moved inland."

"And you were not able to capture them before they made it further inland?" Galana looked concerned but was beginning to regain her composure.

"No mother. The imperial cavalry were sent after them but last I knew we had not heard anything more of the fate of those men."

Galana sat back down on the bench, clearly thinking about the situation more than Timothy and Telnor could with their limited knowledge of what was going on.

"Mother, if we knew more perhaps we could be of more assistance to you? I can't help solve a puzzle if I am in the dark."

"He is right my lady. Timothy and I are more useful if we know what we are dealing with in this situation." Telnor looked down at Galana while Timothy sat next to her. Though she carried herself with the prestige required of a lady of the court, he could see that she was worried about something deeper and was attempting to keep it hidden. Timothy put his arm around her and pulled her close; he had never been too shy to show his mother he cared.

"Oh Timothy I wish I could say more, but the emperor has bound me to silence. If he wants you to know more I will share, but not before he gives the word." Galana looked her son in the eyes, their deep brown depths filled with a sadness that Timothy could not quite understand.

"That is alright, but are we still to deliver the report to the emperor? That is why were told to return here is it not?"

Galana stood . The emotions and thoughts she had struggled with disappeared quickly and were replaced with a regal visage. Timothy knew this was the face that his mother had to maintain to keep up her image in the court. The lords and ladies may have to bow to the emperor's rule and command, but it was they who controlled the guilds that conducted the emperor's bidding. Any emotion she showed would be seen as a weakness and could be exploited to turn control of the emperor to their will. Standing, he took his position next to Telnor, who stood with his arms crossed watching the walkway and windows around the garden.

"Come. I will take you to the emperor so you can give your reports. The fort commander who helped with the capture is here also, so you will all get to speak of what happened at the same time."

Timothy and Telnor followed Galana back to the covered walk leading to a set of double doors stained a deep oak brown. Telnor stepped ahead and pulled open the door for Galana and Timothy before following behind them. Timothy made sure to give his mother the proper three step lead for a man following a noblewoman. His mother or not, Timothy was bound to not let those connections show in front of the court. He didn't always like to hide his connection to the court, but as long as he was suspected of being a member of the thieves' guild his mother would have to remain a stranger to him in the eyes of the ruling elite.

The low stone hall they walked was clear aside from the torches on the walls that provided a ruddy light. These were walls that were part of the original keep as they were not smoothed or polished, and the mortar between the stones showed their age.

Though they were well kept, after hundreds of years everything would start to show its age.

Coming to a small set of steps leading upward, Timothy saw the commander ahead in a larger room. Galana reached it first, slowing a bit in the natural sunlight filtering into the room from the windows on the eastern side. Timothy and Telnor followed shortly after, Telnor stretching himself out a bit. Timothy realized that Telnor had been stooping to enter the hall through this route.

"My Lady, it is a pleasure to see you again. You are as beautiful as ever." The commander was dressed in the uniform Timothy remembered from the night at the beach. He was clean-shaven and carried his plumed helmet under his arm. With his other he reached for Galana's hand to kiss it. Timothy realized he had not picked up his name the other night in the darkness. Thankfully his mother addressed him directly.

"You are too kind Donovon. I hope your ride to the capital was pleasant and you come bearing good news for the emperor?" Galana smiled sweetly towards Donovon and his cheeks pinked at the attention.

"Well, I have some good news. Thanks to the sharp eyes of Telnor, we were able to spot the ship and set up a trap to capture it."

Galana laughed as if she was entertained by a joke. "Come now Donovon, save the war stories for the emperor." She lightly placed a hand on his shoulder with the last statement, keeping the same sweet smile trained on him. She turned to and moved toward the double doors on the far side of the hall that led to the throne room. She said to the trio, "I will advise the emperor that you are here gentlemen. Make yourselves comfortable."

Telnor snorted as she exited the hall. "Gentlemen? I am not soft-fleshed like you, Timothy."

Timothy smiled at Telnor's joke and looked about. This reception hall was part of the original keep, but had been refinished to look much nicer than the other old parts of the palace. At the center of each wall was an almost two story tall tabard of the symbol of Tyrnor. On the wall opposite the windows was the door that his mother had exited through and it carried a mix of the symbols and banners of the old clans of Tyrnor, the ancient families that helped govern the different provinces. Some of them had gone on to found the guilds and he recognized their symbols.

"Timothy, did you want to hear the bad news before I deliver it to the emperor?"

Timothy looked over to Donovon at the same time as Telnor, who had by this time moved to stand by the window. It was his preferred spot to admire the heights of the city.

"There was bad news? You retrieved the ship, did you not?"

Donovon nodded. "Yes, we did, but the two seamen who escaped us? Well my cavalry did not return with them."

"Your men came back empty handed?" Telnor asked gruffly.

"No, they did not come back at all. Twenty of the emperor's best light cavalry and scouts did not return. One of my officers found some of them a day before I left for here. They found them by following the buzzards in the air above their bodies."

Timothy could only stare. The thought of what could have taken on such a large detachment and leave no survivors struck him speechless. Though trained to fight to the death, imperial soldiers would never let their lives go to waste if some word must be returned. One of them should have come back.

"So we are dealing with a force of some size then. Where else could they have landed to give our men such a challenge?" Donovon looked at Telnor as he spoke, thinking of his response.

"There is no other spot. Every watchtower in the kingdom is still reporting all normal activity, no outposts have been attacked."

The men were interrupted by movement at the doorway; a servant threw the doors open firmly but not angrily. "Commander Donovan, Masters Timothy and Telnor, your audience is received by the emperor. Come and you may speak."

The servant turned just as quickly as he had entered and bowed with his arm motioning towards the doorway beyond. The doors opened directly into the vaulted chamber that belonged to the emperor of Tyrnor.

Timothy always marveled at the natural beauty of the throne room. The light grey stone seemed to flow into pillars that rose to the ceiling many meters above them. The stone branched outward in smooth arcs to support the high vaults. Broken only by smaller domes further above them, the room was kept bright by a system of mirrors bringing light down from the high towers of the palace, and the small side halls filled with tall windows of worked glass.

Running about half the length of the keep the room had space for hundreds of courtiers to be present but rarely did it have more than a handful. Few without direct business with the emperor stayed in the palace; he did not value a man who dallied or got behind in completing his work and he made sure all the families in the territories knew it.

Timothy and Telnor let Donovon go first. With his back straight as a military pike he marched to the center of the steps as the emperor motioned them forward. Timothy avoided making too much eye contact with his mother who sat on a low black cushioned chair fringed with white next to the emperor.

As for the emperor, he sat on the black stone throne. It was covered in plush red cushions to keep him comfortable during the long hours of receiving visitors. The clothes he wore were a soft white linen shirt made by the imperial weavers, covered by a similar coat of black. His pants were also black and his hands carried but a single ring of opal and silver with the sigil of the tower etched into it. He watched them all closely as they approached, giving each a moment of his attention in turn.

Once all three were kneeling in front of him, the emperor spoke.

"To you three I have entrusted a mission of great importance. I have heard that it was met with success. Is this true?"

Timothy looked up at the emperor as he spoke. The emperor was almost to his middle years. If Timothy remembered correctly, he was just past his 75th year, and could easily expect another 75. He had steel gray at his temples but his hair was still a deep brown everywhere else. His face was firm but handsome, and the emperor once had more than just Timothy's mother at his side.

"My liege," Donovon spoke. "It is true that we met with some success, but we did have some failures with the mission."

The emperor waived to a servant off to the side to have the few stragglers in the hall removed. He leaned forward a little and motioned the three to stand.

"What failures did you have with your mission?" His voice was concerned, but not angry. It was a tone that Timothy had never heard in the emperor.

"Once the ship had been spotted, thanks to Master Telnor, we sent scouts and our troops to the location they noted. A small boat had come ashore and we believe two of those aboard landed and moved inland."

"And did you send anyone after them?"

Donovon nodded. "Yes, we immediately sent two detachments of light cavalry to track their path. One of those detachments was found completely decimated, all men and animals were killed." Donovon stiffened as he described it. Timothy was still stunned at the loss of the unit. The emperor leaned back again thinking on the revelation.

Donovon spoke up. "That is not all, liege. The sailors aboard the vessel were themselves captured or detained somehow. We found them in the ship's brig or tied to various parts of the ship. It was if those who left wanted us to find the ship and capture the crew.

"The entire crew was detained?" The emperor looked confused at the news that the ship had been found in such a state.

"Yes liege." Donovon bowed his head. Timothy could tell he felt shame from his inability to bring the two mysterious men back to the emperor.

"Commander, if you have nothing else to tell me you may be dismissed. I know you have much to do with the bringing news of the death of your men to their loved ones."

Donovon bowed again and stood, he turned but did not take any further steps. "My liege, what shall I do for their families? Were their deaths honorable?"

The emperor nodded. "Have them given full rights of honor. Make sure their families do not want for the rest of their days."

Donovon bowed, relieved that the families would not go without aid. Timothy knew a soldier's salary was modest, but still a nice amount of money for a family to live off of. Having the soldiers given full honors meant the families would keep receiving the salary of their loved one. Donovon through the same door that had born them entrance, and the servants closed the doors behind him.

Turning back to face the emperor Timothy prepared himself for the difficult questions he expected.

"Master guildsman, tell me of the sighting of the ship."

"The ship was spotted by my companion, Telnor. The ship location was confirmed later at night with myself present when the escapees went ashore and left the lanterns lit on their skiff. I immediately sent word for the local garrison to send a force to assist us with the capture."

"Did you see those that came ashore?" The emperor held his head on his hand, his gaze looking deep into Timothy's eyes. You could tell he was evaluating everything he said with care.

"I did not, liege. Telnor and I counted the sets of footsteps that left the shoreline and saw that it was two persons, though I cannot say whether it was man or woman."

The emperor nodded at this and seemed to weigh the situation in his mind. He sat in silence, and drew his eyes from Timothy to Telnor. "Do you agree with his words Master Telnor?"

"I do sir. Though if I might ask, what is the importance of a single ship coming to our shores?"

The Emperor smiled, he had always been entertained by the forthright nature of Telnor as Timothy had heard him say in the past. "My good Minotaur, those are state secrets, but I promise you will know in time."

"Time, my liege?" Timothy jumped in.

"Yes, time. I am not done with you two yet, I have another mission that is directly related to your finding."

Timothy and Telnor looked at each other confused.

"Liege, I thought the mission was locating the ship. Surely two people wandering around the countryside-"

"Silence Timothy." The emperor looked irritated. "The mistakes that allowed them to escape is something that we cannot make up for now." The Emperor stood and came down the steps towards Timothy and Telnor. He motioned for Timothy to walk with him on the open floor.

"The Empire needs you in ways that I am not able to explain yet. While I trusted you two to locate the vessel, I was not counting on the timing and the darkness. There was simply too much coast for us to watch."

"I understand that, but I don't know why the concern, it is one ship—"

The Emperor shook his head, which silenced Timothy. "It is not just one ship; it is a ship from outside our borders, outside the storm wall that has kept us separate from all of Theron. There is a reason that was done and we have no idea what could be coming in. Timothy, it is for that reason I have to send you out on another mission, though this one could just be a leisurely walk through the countryside."

Timothy looked back at Telnor and his mother who had been following them. He knew they had been listening but this conversation concerned them all in one way or another. Looking back at the emperor he met his eyes and Timothy couldn't help but nod to him. He felt somewhat blind, but if he was to serve the emperor and keep the thieves' guild in good standing, he would have to accept.

"Very good Timothy, this next task is simple. I am sending you both to the temple of the first emperor." The emperor motioned towards Timothy and Telnor for added emphasis.

Telnor made an audible snort of disbelief, Timothy and the emperor both looked over, but Telnor had regained his composure. Timothy's mother maintained her mask of unconcerned disinterest.

"You are sending me to ground where only the blood of the royal line can tread liege. How are Telnor and I going to get in?"

The Emperor smiled at Timothy as he stated the facts as he knew them. "That is merely legend that was created to keep away grave robbers and those who would have less then respectable intentions. It is, however, guarded by a force of some five hundred men, which ensures that those coming uninvited are not allowed entry."

Timothy looked at the emperor again, his mind trying to wrap itself around the implications of what he was being asked to do, the strangeness of it all and what it could mean to him in the end.

"Excuse me for asking liege, but what is there that requires that many men to guard?"

"You will find out when you get there. Once I heard the official reports come in I prepared a letter to be sent with you, here." He reached into the vest he wore and handed Timothy a sealed envelope bearing the sigil of Tyrnor. He placed it in the most secure jacket pocket located close to his heart and then Timothy gazed at the emperor for further direction.

"Once at the temple, go to the lowest level, and have the guards there assist you. Underneath the casket in the tomb you will find a stairwell that leads even further down into the temple, into the old under-workings. Once there if everything is still secure, exit and seal the tomb again. What is located there is not to be disturbed, is that understood?" The foreboding look in his eyes made sure Timothy understood his meaning.

"Of course my liege. Is there anything else we are to do?"

"Yes, do not let any of the soldiers go down with you, and if any try to, you have my clearance to kill them. If any man there attempts to go past the stairwell threshold, his life is forfeit."

Timothy bowed, and stood solemnly. The emperor took a few steps back and looked at him again, shaking his head.

"If only you could stay longer this time, I am sorry; perhaps when you return we can speak more." Turning away quickly, the emperor walked towards Galana and took her arm in his own, and they continued to walk towards the thrones located at the far end of the hall. Telnor came closer to Timothy so they could speak.

Timothy felt a pang of sadness for his mother in that moment. A single mother forced to hide herself in plain sight with the risk of dishonor. She risked much for the guild by being so exposed to the nobility and the rival guilds they shared. No guild would be allowed to gain too much prominence if the other guilds could help prevent it, which made his mother a prime target if ever discovered. If the other guilds knew that his mother and leader of the thieves' guild was on the arm of the emperor, the guilds would create chaos.

"Did I hear those orders correctly? Kill anyone who crosses the threshold?" Telnor asked him as he approached.

Timothy pulled the letter from his pocket and sighed, wondering what was truly going on with the missions the emperor had given them. "Apparently so, Telnor. At least we might be able to figure out what is making him so paranoid when we get there."

"Very true, or we may find more questions than answers. Being granted access to the most sacred location in Tyrnor is not a normal occurrence."

Timothy shook his head, the confusion mounting about the strange missions he was performing. He headed back towards the rear entrance, his footsteps echoing in the large empty hall. "Come Telnor, let us go prepare for our trip."

Mercurious had been following Derrik as they picked their way through the hills of the landscape. Mercurious had few memories of Tyrnor, as he had come here very rarely before the war broke out, and when he did he wouldn't have been walking. The chill of the northern sea was too much for him, and he knew it. He much preferred the deserts and the jungles of the regions further south.

Mercurious saw Derrik pause atop the hill, his sea-green cloak flapping in another chill breeze that brushed across the hilly plains. His skin was the dark color of a tan earned at sea, and his face bore the look of the farsight needed on the ocean. As Mercurious crested the hill he took a moment to pull his thick black cloak closer.

Mercurious was like a black pock on the landscape. His cloak was probably visible for miles, and his long shock of white hair would have given him away immediately. Mercurious knew that Derrik would not be so out of place and was jealous for a moment for the chance to not feel so cold.

Derrik stopped at the top of a hill, and Mercurious came to halt next to. The trees had been cleared to allow for an unobstructed view of the landscape for miles around. Looking out into the, Mercurious searched for familiar landmarks. The trees and hills looked too different to remember, but the northern mountains on the continent stood true. Snowcapped and blue-grey, they ran the length of the land. Inside them though, Mercurious knew something he longed for was hidden.

"Derrik, do you have any idea where we need to go?"

Derrik stood silent, looking out to the north a few moments before responding. "I think as we get closer to the mountains we will catch a glimpse of the old road leading to Somersund. If Kal was going to try and defend this land from us getting in, then the seat of the black tower would be my first guess."

"And if you are wrong? It could still be a trap."

Derrik laughed at Mercurious's statement. "A trap laid for how many centuries? For how long could any simple human—" Derrik spat the words with visible distaste, "wait to fulfill such a plan. They are short lived and weak, Mercurious."

Derrik was visibly disgusted at the absurd notion of humans being able to best him and turned toward the path. Mercurious knew it was that trait that had let Kal's people overwhelm him and imprison him without his stone, something Derrik would have never admitted without great displeasure. As Mercurious turned to follow Derrik north, he thought deeply on the idea of the trap. In his heart he hoped there truly was nothing, and that Derrik was not just filled with pride.

The emperor sat on the stone bench facing the watery wall in front of him. Though he knew it was not water that created the barrier it was the closest comparison he could come up with. All he knew was that since his birth he had been told that the future of Tyrnor depended on this barrier never coming down. His childlike curiosity had tested the wall, and each time he had been thrown back and even once nearly broke his arm. Now he spent his time gazing at it, hoping that during his reign it would not fall.

Behind it he could see a room containing two pedestals, each holding a weapon. On the left pedestal stood a sword slowly turning in the air above the stones. Its surface was etched with red, false flames giving the sword a cruel and jagged look. From the right pedestal hung a large war hammer, though he could never get a clear look. Through the shimmering wall it looked porous, as if it would hold water.

"Enrick my love, are you gazing at those old relics again?" Galana stepped up the small steps into the circular room he sat in.

Enrick gazed at her, a glint in his eye. Even after all the secret years they had been together he still found her to be the most beautiful woman in all Tyrnor.

"My dear lady, I must safeguard the kingdom. You know that is the only fear I truly have."

Galana smiled and leaned against Enrick on the stone bench. He closed his eyes and nestled into her side as she placed her arms around him. He was concerned but in that moment he could let it all slip away and enjoy having her close.

"I see the gateway is still active?" Galana stated as she too looked through the shimmering wall dividing the circular room.

Enrick studied it, the depths of its arch made him ill. It seemed made of the same force that created the wall blocking him from the weapons in the room.

"It is. Ever since the ship landed it has been open." Enrick looked up at Galana, her eyes still trained on the hovering weapons.

"Then they are close then. Are you sure this will work?"

Enrick closed his eyes and squeezed her close. "It must, for if they don't, then all of Tyrnor and Theron will be lost."

CHAPTER 7

To the South of the Kingdom of Yulan lies the large jungle island of Brodesia. A harsh place, it is filled with stone cities constantly fighting the jungle for place on the island. The jungles are deep and filled with savage beasts that make even the smallest child aware of its choices for survival. The trees and vines, and the passing of time, have ensured that the cities and people who did not heed their strength were erased from history. On the eastern coast lies a huge ridge in the mountains, spewing forth sulfur and ash from its volcanic heart to fill the jungle below with an acrid mist, blinding prey and covering the approach of predators.

It is in this land we find the fearful young man Mesieve. Living outside the city of Gran Al'Hadir with his family, he has done his best to help his family farm their lands. He has spent his days living in fear of the jungle, and his one wish is to move from the farmlands of his family to the city to be further from the beasts that fill his nightmares.

The farm was quiet. Never in his forty years of farming had Bartellok ever heard such silence from the land. Leaning on the hoe he had been using, he took a moment to look out into the deep green of the wild he fought with daily to keep his farm. Bartellok stood almost six feet tall and had the wide sturdy frame that a lifetime of farming had given him. His hair had thinned some, but was still long and covered his head and neck, and his skin had leathered in the sunny decades of hard work.

He stood in his field, the nearly mature stalks of the beets under the soil swaying gently in the occasional breeze. Bartellok wiped his brow and used the collar of his brown linen tunic to dab his neck. His pants were of a darker hue, and he was thankful for the breeze finding its way through the threads when it came.

He squinted to look deeper into the trees that bordered his land, but saw nothing. He turned back toward home, seeing his young daughters playing near the log and stone home that he had built as the place to raise his family. Each of the three had his dark hair and bronzed skin, their blue clothing the only smatterings of color on the ruddy brown farm. Bartellok himself had been born on this land, as had his father, and as far as he knew, everyone that mattered to him personally had been born here as well.

"You look concerned my dear, what is it? Is something wrong with the beets in the fields?" Bartellok's wonderful Tyana, wife of twenty-three years, asked of him. Her dark hair was pulled back in a tight knot and her sky blue dress fit loosely on her figure. She was as beautiful to him as the day he met her, and his most trusted confidant. Tyana was motherly through to the bone, and her expressions rarely seemed angry, though Bartellok knew his wife's temper to be more fierce than the beasts of the jungles surrounding their farming community.

"I think it's something that we will have to speak of later, nothing to frighten the children with." As he said it he looked over and saw their eldest child, Mesieve, look up at him. Bartellok knew Mesieve would never be meant to take over the farm, nor be a warrior for the king. He was small for his fifteen years with blond hair that was rare in Bartellok's family, and he cared more for reading the few books that his family owned than for caring for the farm. All those things added to the fact he had always been haunted by nightmares of the beasts that lived in the jungle. Of the children he was the most clean; he was very particular about being dirty. The only time he came home in a mess was when he felt daring enough to climb, the one boyish activity in which his son partook.

Tyana followed his gaze to Mesieve and looked back at her husband with a tinge of sadness. He was their only son and his fear of the jungle had meant many sad nights for her husband. "We can speak of it in private then. Let's go inside for a drink." Tyana motioned towards the open door of the stone home, and followed her husband inside. As she came in she removed the clamp from the fan ropes, and air began moving around the room again.

Bartellok took his seat and gazed at the old contraption. Its weighted rope attached to a large gear system, and he had only learned enough about it to keep it repaired. The slow moving larger gear drove the shaft that had two fans in the room attached to it, and a few smaller ones in his the family's sleeping rooms. Feeling the cool breeze across his arms and brow helped him to relax some; a respite of wind was required to make living in the jungle survivable.

The stone walls were smoother inside than out, the result of a long history of bumped walls and moving through the home had worn the edges of the stone smooth. The windows were open, with shutters on the outside to help keep out the rains that came almost daily in the jungle. It was a luxury that their floor was stone as well. It had been supplied from a surprise cache of worked stone from the first building of the home Bartellok found while tilling a new field. The wood tiles of the roof kept the rest of the rain out and his family dry, so he felt the home would serve them for years to come.

"Are the children playing away from the house?" Bartellok asked.

Tyana went to the window to look. The glass was just clear enough to see through, a rare commodity they had paid for years earlier, purchased with money from their wedding as a gift from Bartellok's father. "I see the girls, and Mesieve is not in his loft, so we can assume he is in the tree near the barn."

Bartellok wasn't entirely pleased with the answer, but it was good enough for the moment. "I hope he stays away from the horses in the barn."

"You know better than that. Mesieve would have to get dirty to go near the horses." Tyana looked over at her husband as he sat at the table. "Mesieve is not the reason we came inside to speak though is it?"

Bartellok took a moment to compose his thoughts. "I am worried about the jungle. It has been getting steadily quieter the past few weeks. Then today it was deathly silent. I barely even heard bugs on the edge. I don't like it."

Tyana sat and placed a hand on her husband's arm, her skin lighter than his but still tanned from the tropical sun. "My dear, there are plenty of reasons for the jungle to get quiet. I am sure it's nothing to be worried about."

"Tyana, I have been living on this farm for most of my life, and there has never been a time I have heard such silence from the jungle. It is as if every animal has left in fear of some unknown beast. I have seen some of the large beasts that we warned our children about and even in their approach the jungle alerted us with noise. It knows that sort of creature."

"So you are thinking that some new thing is out there?" Tyana laughed a little at her husband. "You are starting to sound like Mesieve now. You can't be serious."

Bartellok put his glass down on the table growing irritated with his wife for not taking him as seriously as he felt about this. "Forty years Tyana. That is how long I have had to learn and know how the jungle works. I am sure something is not right. I can't name what or how, but I know something is not right."

Bartellok looked at his wife, his eyes filled with a rare earnest concern reserved for the most troubled times of his life. It was a look that Tyana had always taken to heart, and in that moment she felt the concern her husband was feeling for their family. She squeezed his hand, and tried smiling at him. He relaxed some, but the concern showed as a furrowed line on his brow.

"I know it is not the best idea, but perhaps you can take our children to the city for a time."

Tyana looked down at the table; she was lost in indecision about whether or not she could help her family survive in the city. Doubtless she had weaving skills, but there would be little need for her in the city.

"How long will we have to stay away? I don't know how to support our children in Gran Al'Hadir."

Bartellok lifted his wife's chin to look her in the eyes and leaned forward for a gentle kiss. "I don't know my love, but I fear that it is not safe here for our children. If I am proven wrong, and the jungle returns to normal, then so be it."

Cries of surprise from their children outside snapped Bartellok's attention from his wife. He stood rapidly, grabbing the spear he kept over the door of his home as he exited. Its red hooked blade was kept sharp, and the wood polished to a deep mahogany shine. As he exited into the light of the sun it captured and shone with a blaze of fire on the blade. He felt a deep relief when he saw that his children were not screaming in fear, but laughing with glee as one of the neighboring farmers came up the lane with his wife and children.

Their farm was located on the edge of a swath of farmland stretching in a circle around the city of Gran Al'Hadir. Each farm was a home unto itself, though some chose to live in a closer community farm for companionship. Bartellok and his family were one of the oldest farms, and had stayed near the edge of the farming regions instead of near the center. While those closer to the city had their farms closer together, they did not have the amount of land that he did. He had rarely gone to the edge of his family land, as it sat deeper in the jungle than he felt comfortable being in, near a series of cliffs overlooking a rapids and waterfalls.

The family he saw now was a newer farming family that had moved into the home of an older farmer. Kelneth was his name, and Bartellok had known his father many years. They had more money than that which farming brought, as Kelneth had some inns he supplied with ale in the city.

As the small crowd of little arms and legs moved out of the way Bartellok approached his friend. Kelneth's stocky form was wider even than Bartellok's, as Kelneth was still bristling with the muscles of his youth. His light brown hair was kept cut short to the scalp of his head. He was quieter thean most his age, though having a child early had probably helped mature him before his time. Bartellok shifted the spear to his left arm to shake Kelneth's hand with his right.

"It has been some time Bartellok. Hopefully I find you in good spirits?" Kelneth's eyes were obviously drawn to the spear and the appearance of flame on its tip.

Bartellok felt a little awkward at having the weapon in his hands. Motioning towards the doorway of the stone house where his wife was standing, he spoke clearly.

"Let's leave the children here to play, your wife and you should come into the house to have a drink and talk since it has been so long." Bartellok kept his best smile on the whole time, covering the concern he had been feeling just before the arrival of his neighbors. The young couple left their three blond haired children by the barn with Bartellok's daughters. He looked over at the barn and noticed that Mesieve was not among the children. The dark hair of his sisters was plainly seen but his bright hair was not to be found in the space between the buildings. Turning back, he joined the adults moving into the house.

Mesieve was concentrating on the voices of his parents below his bedroom loft. He had been trying to find out what had set his father so ill at ease with the jungle, and hoped it had nothing to do with him. Mesieve breathed slowly, thankful that his parents turned on the fans when they had come inside. Hearing them finally sit down, he tried to keep pace with the words he heard coming from below.

"They found something at Lobrock's old farm." It must have been Kelneth's voice Mesieve noted. What could have been found?

"Your father is always finding something! He claims to be living on top of one of the old cities!" Mesieve stifled a laugh at his father's joke. He remembered the tales the old man had shared during their festivals in the fall.

"This is different. This story isn't coming from him, but from his neighbors. Lobrock is nowhere to be found." Kelneth's wife sobbed at his telling of the story. Kelneth himself tried to appear unmoved but Mesieve could imagine the tears coming to his eyes, as his voice was thick with emotion.

"I am sorry to hear that. Does it have something to do with what was found?" Tyana asked gently. Mesieve could picture her sitting down at the table as she tried to console their guests..

"They found some sort of beast, and it was nothing like any of them had seen! It was like a great lizard, in the shape of a man, but a full head higher than any man I have seen."

"Then you have seen it?"

Kelneth replied, "I saw what was left after the birds had their way with it. It had my father's spear in its chest, but my father was gone. The others near us are working to track the beasts, as they found more than one set of its tracks."

Mesieve heard the gasps of his parents at the table. Clearly he knew there was something to be feared in their words. He had feared the jungle most of his life, ever since his dreams had begun. Knowing that there was a beast his father feared but did not know gripped Mesieve with more icy terror than anything he could have seen in his own overactive mind.

"I know we live closer to town Bartellok, but Anase and I feel uneasy being this close to the jungle right now." Kelneth indeed sounded troubled to Mesieve.

"It is good that you came today Kelneth. Tyana and I were discussing the idea of sending her and the children to Gran Al'Hadir until it was safe here again. I was only worried about the silence of the trees but now with this, I think we will move forward with our idea."

"Bartellok, I know you don't have much gold, and my father left me much to care for our children." Mesieve could guess where he was going with this. "If I helped by giving you gold, could my Anase and the kids go with Tyana?"

"Oh Kelneth, you should know that Bartellok and I couldn't take your money, and that we would welcome them along." Mesieve's mother said.

"What is it my dear?" Mesieve remembered then why he had not heard anything from Anase; she was mute. She had lost her voice early in childhood. No doubt the silence was Kelneth interpreting her signing to him. "She says you have no choice but to take the gold Tyana. You have your children to think of."

Mesieve at this point got lost in his own thoughts. Though he lived in fear of the jungle, he was also afraid of leaving his father's side. He had always felt somehow separate from his family, but he trusted in the strength of his father more than anything. If his father wished him to go to the city he would go, but he was afraid of leaving the safety of a home that he had known his entire life.

What was Gran Al'Hadir like? Mesieve eyed the few books his family owned, one of which had been given to him by his grandfather before he passed on to the other world. His grandfather had always said it was special somehow, something that Mesieve would one day understand the need for. Once he was old enough to read it, he had begun to memorize the symbols of the book, reading it from leather cover to leather cover so many times that he could probably recite the book from memory by now. It had been almost seven years, and still the book had no greater meaning to him than when he had first read it. Perhaps in the city he could find more books to read! Perhaps one of them would give him the knowledge he needed to finally understand why this book had been passed on to him.

Mesieve thought on his grandfather, whose wizened hunched form came to mind readily. Though he had been gone for a few years now, Mesieve always felt he could remember his grandfather clearly when he really tried. It was as if he wasn't really gone at all, so long as he remembered him. He had taught Mesieve how to read, and how to wake up from his dreams when the nightmares came. While his parents thought that Mesieve enjoyed sleeping longer than his sisters, it was actually that he needed his rest after spending the night constantly waking himself up to avoid the nightmares.

"I think we can all stay here this evening to let the children rest. If we are going to send them to the city then we must take care to prepare for a proper trip." Kelneth spoke again. Mesieve could only imagine his father's response to someone else coming in and offering this much help to them as a family. Though Kelneth and his wife were almost second parents to Mesieve, his father's pride rarely allowed them to accept help.

Mesieve heard his mother whispering to his father, and while he was curious what had been said it was quickly revealed.

"I am forced to accept, Kelneth, for the safety of my family. There is nothing I can do for them if I let my pride get in the way of protecting them."

"Good! I am glad you accepted." Kelneth was obviously pleased from the noise he was making. "I do not have to worry about my own children and wife now. Tyana can sign enough to help Anase and the girls."

There was a shuffling as the adults moved around, the chairs legs skidding on the floor. Mesieve looked up at the fan blowing down on him, his spot on the rug of his sleeping was warm but comfortable with the fan continually blowing on him. A trip to the city! Even though there was now a true monster to fear in the jungle, Mesieve could not help but feel excited about being able to go to Gran Al'Hadir. People rarely went to the city, so knowing they were going to be there for a lengthy time brought ideas and possibilities into focus. Mesieve was excited for his first trip outside of the farmlands.

"We will wait to tell the children until after dinner. It will give us time to work out the details while they pack their things for the road." Mesieve heard Tyana speak.

"Are you and your wife ready Kelneth?"

"Yes Bartellok. We brought everything in our cart that we may need while we are away. I will get my things and set up in here with you while the children get their things loaded."

Mesieve stared at the ceiling, the details of the conversation fading as he turned his thoughts inward. His parents were worried, and the mention of the beast did strike at him now that the excitement of going to the city had faded. He knew that if his family was going to send him and his sisters to the city then there really was a reason to be afraid. It was no more just his parents telling him it was his imagination; this time his fear was manifest.

Trellax crouched on the branch of one of the great jungle trees, his yellow eyes peering into the darkness that spread over the small farm his troop was watching. They had been picking small farmhouses and razing them all. With each farm they destroyed, the got closer and closer to the human cities. The soft hides of these 'hewmons' did nothing to protect them thus far, and none had provided Trellax with the sport he had been promised by his master Malakia.

Rubbing the bright orange plumage bridging his skull, Trellax shifted his weight to begin his climb down to the jungle floor. As he did so, he could hear the growls and the fighting of his less intelligent troop mates below. Malakia picked her troop commanders based on awareness and intelligence, something that most Larathi had in what she could call very 'moderate' amounts. With his feet on the ground, many of those around Trellax turned to face him, wearing a mixture of fear and respect. Their skins filled the spectrum of the rainbow: red, blue, yellow and green – and all with yellow eyes that glowed in the fading light.

"Brothers," Trellax hissed, "As the last ray of light dies upon the horizon, we attack this hewmon farm."

Growls and hisses of joy greeted this comment. The troops enjoyed the mindless slaughter unlike their plumed commanders.

"Kill them, and let none escape our grasp – our master commands it! Prepare to make them die like the animals they are." Trellax grinned as the group of his simple brethren prepared in their various ways for the battle ahead. A few of the Kanji-Larathi reds kept quiet, waxing their bows, while the Polgoth blues and Milshan greens prepared themselves and their twisted swords and spears. Trellax stepped over to one that looked particularly cruel alongside his spear.

"Can I see your weapon?"

The Polgoth obliged, offering the center haft of the spear to his plumed commander. Trellax took the weapon, looked closely at the blackened steel edges, hooked and serrated to cause more tearing and rending of the Polgoth's opponents.

"Which of your weapons is this? Is this the first you have made?" Trellax inquired. Each of the soldiers was required to make their weapon. The more adept would be granted a position as a smith for the Larathi cities – a much better position than the front lines for the military. If a soldier was found to be gifted with metalworking ability, they were to be protected. If their weapons were clumsy and not much more than a stick – then they were sent to be used as troops in the army.

"It is, commander. I have had it with me since I was able to carry a weapon."

Trellax smiled as he handed the weapon back to the blue. "Take it and head back to our base and show it to our smiths. If you are lucky you may be joining them soon."

The Polgoth bowed silently and retreated towards the base camp they had left a few days ago. The others watched him go, murmuring and hissing among themselves at a smith being found among them. Trellax growled at the nearest to him, a Vestai yellow, and when he cowered in submission, Trellax removed himself to the edge of the jungle to watch the sun fall.

Trellax thought on his work as the sunlight dipped further. This was only a small farm, mostly women and children. His orders were to kill everyone, and at times he pondered why. All these creatures looked similar to the dark and soft skin of his master, but none had such strength as she. He was very curious what they possessed that caused so much hatred from his master to be manifested in such a cruel way. Though his troops enjoyed the slaughter as any Larathi would, Trellax was allowed to have thoughts on why they killed the hewmons – so long as he kept them to himself.

The line of Larathi on either side of him had become anxious and were growling and snapping their jaws. The sun had fallen. Trellax knew he would have to let their bloodlust be sated soon.

Trellax took his place in front of the troops and turned to face the small force. His voice bellowed across the open field, "Take no prisoners. Allow none to escape!"

The clearing was filled with the roars and growls of the Larathi warriors. The colors of the rainbow flowed from the jungle and ran across the field, thrashing plants and fencing out of their path.

Trellax stayed behind, slowly walking across the field, watching as panic struck the house. Two hewmon males came out and a few of his warriors fell. Apparently the hewmons carried crossbows. Some of the Larathi charging the house broke away from the pack to check the stables and see if any other ambushes awaited them.

Trellax continued to march forward, watching his forces fight at the doorway to the small home. Two long spears held them off from entering. A couple of Kanji hissed and spat as they attempted to fire into the home at those holding the spears, but the closer warriors had lost themselves trying to get in.

Counting the bodies, Trellax noticed he had lost six of the twenty he sent after the small farm. A grim bellow from the house caught his attention as he saw that a Milshan had thrown the body of a fallen Vestai into the spears and charged into the home. Trellax heard the shouts and screams from inside, and as he watched it looked as though a horse drawn cart was leaving at the back of the home. Waving his sword towards the stables he bellowed orders to the Larathi inside.

"After the cart, allow none to escape!" Trellax saw a few sprint off, quickly cutting the distance to their prey. One jumped on the horse drawing the cart and tossed it to its side, which pulled the cart over with it. The trunks and people inside spilled out onto the trail leading from the farmhouse. Trellax watched as the children scrambled, and a pale blond haired child made a mad dash for the road, his white linen clothes a glaring marker of his path.

Trellax observed two of the Larathi start to follow him, only to stop in their tracks. Small flashes of light opened up in the darkness and he saw the struggling Larathi bodies fall to the ground lifeless. The lights stayed hanging in the air for just a moment, before he saw them split and charge the nearest of his warriors.

Feeling the terror and the surprise of his men, Trellax paused to gauge the scene before coming any closer. The orbs of light were striking at the remaining three of his men that had attacked the cart, two of whom were already struggling with the strange, formless foe. The third was bounding back to the others in the farmhouse, growling and spitting in rage and fear.

Trellax watched as the struggling of his men ceased and the lights holding their forms faded like a mist caught in a breeze. The hewmons that were in the cart were gone, fled into the forest for the moment.

Trellax knew he could send more men after the women and children later but for now he had to return to camp after the burning of this farm. He had some questions for Malakia about these lights and what they meant for the Larathi advance on the Brodesian capital.

CHAPTER 8

Mesieve ran. Never in his 15 years had he run with such determination as the fear for his life had given him now. He had left the only home he had ever known, and abandoned the overturned cart that had carried his mother and siblings down the dirt road. He ran with all his might. The night sky continued to deepen, and as the stars appeared he felt exhaustion hit. Mesieve staggered to a stop against a tall tree and struggled for air.

As he collapsed to his knees, Mesieve felt the bitter loneliness of the night. He had not even tried to help his sisters or his mother. He had hit the ground and immediately ran as far away as he could without a thought for his family. The strange colored monsters had attacked, and he had run into the night.

Mesieve buried his face in his hands, sobbing at his shame and what he imagined the horrible creatures did to his family after he ran. Their teeth and eyes burned in his mind with a clarity he could not shake. He looked beyond the trees to the stars in the night sky. His nose ran from all the crying so he wiped it on his sleeve and fought through exhaustion to stand; he could not stay here tonight. Mesieve stepped hesitantly on the road and began to walk further away from his home, painful step after painful step.

Mesieve woke with a mouthful of sand. Rolling over, he looked at the bright light of the sun above him and in that moment he knew the night before had not been a nightmare, but had become the horrifying reality he feared.

Mesieve sat up with no memory of having laid down. He woke to the stinging of the cuts and bruises on his arms and knees suggesting he had collapsed through brambles the night before. Pulling himself to his feet, he dusted the dirt from his clothes as best he could.

He examined his surroundings and realized he stood quite literally at a crossroads. To the south was the path he had come from; his footprints were in the sand stopped where he now stood. To the west was a path he knew led to the cities of the coast. He did not know their names except that of Ygdrosen, the capital of Brodesia.

He turned to the northeast Mesieve and had to cover his mouth. A short distance along that path, the road was littered with refuse and forms being pecked at by buzzards. Stepping back Mesieve realized that the path to Gran Al-Hadir was filled with the dead. He could not think the city to be safe now; monsters must have attacked the city last night as they had attacked his family.

With no other option, Mesieve turned and ran down the road, away from Gran Al'Hadir and —hopefully — the beasts that attacked it.

Mesieve had been wandering for days, the leather soles of his sandals wearing down to leave his feet open to the stones of the road. Mile after mile of jungle wore on. Occasionally he would see a form by the side of the old stone road he now followed, buzzards pecking at it, eyeing him hungrily. Each time he took care to stay to the far side of the road and walked a thin line between the large buzzards feasting on the corpses, and the jungle that he knew contained more of the creatures he feared.

Mesieve woke on the fifth day in the dust of the road, the sour smell of rotten bodies hanging in the air around him. He lifted himself up yet again to observe his surroundings, painfully aware of the bits of gravel in the gashes on his knees. He picked at his wounds and felt eyes on his back; a large buzzard stared at him. It cocked its head to the side, sizing up Mesieve to see if he was close enough to death to eat him.

"Go away, shoo!" Mesieve threw a handful of dust and rocks at the black bird and continued to walk on. Day after day he had walked, and he was beginning to wonder if it would rain again. The rains had come daily before he had left his farm and now the jungle was starting to dry. One dry turn after another greeted him and he was also forced to wonder if he was wrong about where the road was leading.

He had not walked much further when he came to a crossing of the roads littered with overturned carts and dark stains on the ground. He stopped far enough away that he could size up the clearing. Mesieve found it strange that with so much blood dried into the stones he could see no corpses.

Stepping in, he peered around, hoping to see something he could eat or drink to salve his parched throat and burning stomach. As Mesieve entered the clearing he also looked around at the options for the roads here. To the north, there was eventually a coast but what else he did not know. To the south he saw a large mound, dozens of the hungry buzzards floating in the air around it. It did not take much effort to choose another path. Looking again to the west he started tottering down the path he hoped would lead to help.

The thunder of a coming storm rolled across the treetops of the jungle. Mesieve gazed up at the clouds as he stumbled along, seeing the fast moving jungle storm rolling in across the skyline. He continued to walk as the rain started, barely feeling the moisture on his skin. He took a few moments to stand with his mouth open to the sky, feeling the heavy drops hit his tongue, their refreshing coolness stopping the parch and cooling the burning of the hunger in his stomach, at least for a while.

He trudged through more mud on the side of the road and saw an overturned cart ahead, the unmistakable splash of colors surrounding it suggesting it was a cart from a fruit farmer. Seeing no bodies around, Mesieve moved under the overhanging boards from the frame of the cart. The ground was still muddy underneath but it kept him from being pelted by painful drops as the storm picked up. The cart had been filled with a harvest, and Mesieve found he was sitting in the middle of a pile of oranges, lemons and a few bananas. Grabbing an orange, he let it be rinsed in the rain as he held it out past the covering, and then bit into it.

He spit out the peel and bit into the soft inner fruit, tart juice coating his chin as it dripped from his mouth. He continued to pull more of the peel free as he savored the first bite and was already starting on another. The same juice filled his stomach and quenched the hunger pangs he had battled for days. Quickly finishing, he grabbed a banana this time, peeled, and consumed it. It was not until he was grabbing the third piece of fruit that the sick feeling started to fill his stomach. Choking on a piece of banana still in his mouth Mesieve felt his stomach squeeze and revolt against him; as much as he tried not to he found himself retching and the fruit he had just eaten came back up.

On his hands and knees Mesieve looked at what he had done and began to cry, the deep sobs of a child's sorrow, confusion, and pain. He was so deep in this moment of release, with the rain coming down on him, that he did not hear the approach of the horseman that was now behind him.

"Come lad, why are you crying?"

Mesieve jumped at the man's voice ringing out over the sound of the heavy rain. Filled with terror he dove back under the cart, saying a prayer under his breath that the horseman would just go away. He could see the legs of the horse from under the cart and saw the polished boots of the man splash down into the mud as he dismounted. From under the cart Mesieve stared at the legs of the man coming closer. Mesieve pulled his knees to his chest and held his breath as the man kneeled at the end of the cart, bringing his face down to ground level.

"Easy, I am not here to hurt ya." The man kept a keen smile on his bearded face, the brown hair hung out past the edged of the hood of his polished cloak. Mesieve watched the rain run off the fabric, the treated leather not letting any of the heavy rain inside. Mesieve made no move or said a word as the man made himself comfortable under the edge of the boards of the cart. He dropped his hood back to let the curled hair of his head move about, and sat looking out at the rain covering the jungle.

Mesieve was curious about this man, how had he survived this part of the jungle? After all the days of seeing nothing but dust and corpses, seeing another living breathing human was a difficult image to process.

"Since you are sitting in all of it, mind that you could hand me a ripe banana? All I have had is jerky for days." The man held his hand out and Mesieve inspected it, staring as if it were another strange creature of the night. "I assure you I am safe. I would just appreciate something sweet to chase the dust of the road."

Mesieve slowly reached into the pile of fruit and grabbed a yellow-green banana from the pile. He held on to the furthest point he could as he dropped it into the hand of the strange man looking at him.

"Thank you. Not so bad, was it?" Turning back to face the rain that was starting to slacken, the man spoke, somewhat to himself, but mostly to Mesieve.

"Nothing to be done out here I guess. The bodies explain the lack of refugees. I am guessing that you are from one of the farms in the outliers, the edges at the confluence of the cities. Am I right?" He looked over at Mesieve who silently nodded. "Well then, I would guess that you have been running for the past week. No food, little water, and a lifetime of memories that won't ever go away now. Tell me, what is your name?"

"My name is Mesieve."

"Mesieve," the man nodded as if weighing the name in his mind. "A good solid name, though your voice sounds much older then you look."

"I am small for my age."

The mysterious man smiled, Mesieve could see kindness in his brown eyes. His skin was the dark tone of someone from the cities, closer to his father's dark skin than his own. Under the cloak Mesieve could make out a ruddy brown shirt, and the gold chain of a necklace around his neck.

The man began to adjust his cloak hood and looked like he was getting ready to move back into the rain. He stepped out from underneath the low cart and stood, and Mesieve crawled towards the edge to see him. He was a full height, at least a head and a half above Mesieve if he had been standing as well.

"Where are you going?" Mesieve tried to keep the fear of being alone again out of his voice.

"Ygdrosen, near the coast, someone has to report what has happened to the cities in the jungle's heart. Care to come along, lad?"

Mesieve looked underneath the cart and then back at the man. His mind made up, he decided he would not stay any closer to this jungle than he would have to ever again. It had taken everything important from him.

"I will come along, but what is your name?"

Holding his hand out to help Mesieve up on to the horse, the man answered with a grin, "Vandahar Gates."

Mesieve and Vandahar traveled for days, repeating the process of searching for food and finding shelter from the jungle rains. Mesieve was thankful to at least have company now as he traveled. Each time they passed another of the piles of bodies he would bury his face in Vandahar's back to keep any more of the images from his mind. They didn't encounter any of the creatures on their way to the city and Mesieve and Vandahar both were worried about this, it was something that Vandahar was very vocal about as they traveled.

Vandahar spent time talking of the capital as they rode along, stories of the towers of the Queen and the King, and the temples to the Duchess of the Moon, the goddess that had once protected Brodesia. Mesieve listened intently, thankful for the distraction. Vandahar seemed to have traveled to every corner of land at one time or another. As a royal commander, he was one of the guardians of the people.

Mesieve felt safer knowing that one of them had found him, and not just a simple soldier. The royal commanders were almost a rulership unto themselves; while they pledged fealty to the royal family, they also swore to put the people first. Where Mesieve had been raised they were almost a myth, more legend then reality.

By the time they had come to the outskirts of a city, they found it under siege. Though the road was clear in the early morning light they arrived in, the walls were surrounded by the corpses of men, women, and children that were unable to escape the tide of monsters coming towards the city. And then they came upon the monsters themselves.

Mesieve looked at them with the same fear he had when they attacked his home. The colors of the corpses were more mixed and bright than any rainbow Mesieve had seen. Masses of blues and red, with greens mixed in and different colors on each of those seemed to be almost silly compared to the dark red stains of slain men on the fields.

Mesieve turned his eyes forward, around Vandahar, to inspect the city gates. Marks in the dirt suggested that bodies had been cleared from the road, and a single man stood at a doorway that opened through the larger wooden gates.

"Vandahar, you returned!" The man was excited but wary as he watched the jungle behind Mesieve and Vandahar.

"Was there any doubt of my return? You think a silly monster invasion will keep me from the city!" Mesieve listened to

Vandahar and it seemed like even through all the horrors he had seen on the road, a man like Vandahar was unfazed by it. For a man like him, dying was unheard of; living was the only option.

The man at the gateway reached in and knocked on the inner door with his spear. Looking back he noticed Mesieve behind Vandahar on the horse, and stared warily at him.

"And the child, Vandahar? Where did you find him?"

"This one was wandering the roads generally heading this way. I will keep him with me, he will not bother you."

The gate keeper nodded at this statement, the gate had opened while Vandahar had been speaking and now stood wide. The city inside looked deserted, the buildings at first glance looked either burned or crumbling through the slit of the gate that opened to let them ride though. As they entered the city Mesieve began to take in the devastation there in greater detail.

Almost everything was coated in a layer of ash, and where there was not ash, there was mud. The buildings had been scoured by fire, many of them in different states of collapse, and the blackened beams and stones of their walls crumbled in on themselves.

Mesieve watched as a cart drawn by a haggard pair of old men rolled around a corner from the passage near the city walls. They struggled under the load, each of them had mud over their legs and hands, and as he watched one of them fell to his knees, splashing in a puddle filled with soot and refuse. Their load looked bundled and muddy with splashes of black, and as they passed behind them Mesieve saw that is was the corpses of soldiers clad like the few at the gate had been. The stench was pungent though Mesieve could tell that the ash in the air dampened the scent of the dead.

Looking ahead and forcing down a shudder, he noted that the buildings nearest the walls were not filled with their normal merchants, but inside each were the soldiers and guards of the city. Either wounded, or resting, the broken glass of their windows showed dozens of men stuffed into the small rooms that were once shops and inns. Mesieve felt a grim mood had latched on to the city. While some of the men were pleased to see Vandahar and grew bright, even the royal commander was not enough to lift the pall over the soldiers.

"I would pay attention lad, this is the place we have been driven to."

"Is this the Ygdrosen I was told of? This is our capital?" Mesieve looked at his surroundings with surprise – it was nothing like what Vandahar had described.

Vandahar shook his head and snickered a little under his breath. "No lad, thankfully not. Ygdrosen lies some distance down the coast, about three and a half days in fact. This is the town of Calril, once the trade junction for the cities heading to the capital."

Mesieve felt somewhat better that it wasn't the capital that was reduced so far. It still concerned him though that he was heading further into a city that carried the burden of being hunted. He had seen the monsters and he knew there was something in the jungle to be afraid of. He buried his face in the back of Vandahar once more, trying to block out the painful memories that were coming back to his mind.

He couldn't see it, nor would ever learn of it, but as they rode towards the center of the small city, Vandahar cried.

"Come lad, it's time to wake up."

Mesieve opened his eyes slowly, feeling a knot in his neck from the strange position he had found himself sleeping in. His eyes slowly adjusted, and he saw that Vandahar was dismounting the horse carefully, so as not to knock him to the ground.

Stone columns surrounding them stood almost fifty feet into the air, and Mesieve saw at their top they held a domed marble roof. At its top was a statue of a woman, robed and with long hair carved into the stone she was made of. Vandahar saw where Mesieve had directed his eyes and looked above them as well.

"That is the Duchess of the Moon. Do you know of her?"

Mesieve nodded. "My mother spoke of her in our bedtime stories. She is one of the guides of this world, the goddess who protected Brodesia is she not?"

Vandahar smiled. "Yes you could say that. She was lost to us hundreds of years ago though; none know what became of her. Come though, there are people here I want you to meet."

Mesieve walked beside Vandahar, keeping close, and away from the prying eyes of the guards standing near the entrance to the temple. Their gaze was a mixture of exhaustion and bitterness as Vandahar approached, but they did not stop the pair from entering.

As they stepped through the white marble archway, Mesieve was surprised at how light it stayed. He peered upward and saw that a large ring of light was being reflected back towards the ceiling, its flickering lines suggesting that water was somehow involved. Ahead, rows of benches led his eyes to a raised platform at the center of the room, a group of men standing around it and pointing at what he assumed was a map because of the way they moved their arms.

"Lords, I return. What news do you have for the city?"

The lords looked up at Vandahar, some of them glad to see him, and a few remained neutral to his arrival. Only one paid attention to Mesieve. The older fellow was clad in robes, unlike the armor of the others present. His wispy beard covered his Yulanese face and the white robes hid what looked to be a firm frame given his age, based on the hands Mesieve saw protruding from the sleeves. There was strength to him though; his hair was trimmed almost to the scalp and his face was impassive though interested in Mesieve. He was suddenly aware of how dirty he was, his clothes torn and muddied from the road.

"Captain, I take it that since you return with nothing but a boy, that the inner cities are lost to us?" A tall fellow with a shock of fire red hair braided down his back asked of Vandahar. He seemed curt, but not rude to Vandahar. His skin was very dark, and his face looked like it had seen combat before. His eyes were hard and a scar marked his chin.

"They are lost to us for now Siegfried. Activity in the jungle seems to be very limited; I saw none of the lizardmen while I rode to check the cities."

"Captain," asked the Yulanese gentlemen that had looked at Mesieve, "Where did you find this boy?"

Vanadahar looked over at Mesieve. "I found him wandering the roads. I picked him up since he was the only living being I found during my journey." Vandahar turned back to the lords around the table, "There will be no reinforcements from the other cities."

The old man went back to studying Mesieve, while the four armored men and Vandahar stood around the table studying the map. Mesieve stepped off the platform and sat on one of the benches to listen to the older men speak about the state of the city. He learned that the city had been attacked a few times by skirmish forces of the lizardmen, and that the same thing had been occurring to other cities further in the deep jungle.

He also learned that the suddenness of the attack had taken most garrisons off guard and all available people and armies were being pulled back to the capital. It made sense to him now since he had seen so many corpses in the road as he headed this way. They must have all been killed by the lizardmen. It also explained why the city was abandoned and empty aside from the garrison and a few older merchants left to assist with defenses.

"How many men does the capital have to defend itself Siegfried?" Vandahar asked the man with the red hair again. Mesieve was surprised at how dark his skin looked with the fire red hair against it. He was curious how the unnatural color was achieved.

"They should have at least seventy-five thousand men at their disposal with the conscripts and the garrisons surrounding the city. The military always keeps its main force there because of the unpredictability of Iliana."

Vandahar nodded, looking again at the map. The old man spoke up.

"I think it is safe to assume now gentlemen that the inner cities are either lost or are on their own. It is time to abandon Calril and move to the capital ourselves." The old scholar stood and walked to the platform. Mesieve was curious why he was able to speak so freely to the lord and to Vandahar.

"I agree with the scholar from Yulan," Vandahar said.

"The name is Sao Len."

Vandahar smiled and continued speaking again, "My apologies Sao Len. Either way, it is time we moved from this place. How many men are left in the city?"

"Maybe a couple hundred, though we have wounded," one of the officers stated as Vandahar raised his hand to cut him short.

"I am aware we have wounded, but the city is no longer worth holding for us. Get all the carts and horses we can and get the wounded out within the hour. We must leave the city by nightfall."

The men at the table knew that the city was lost, but Mesieve felt that this defeat was no less biting then any other. Even against overwhelming odds, a loss was still painful to bear. He caught himself thinking of his family and fighting back tears. He rubbed the tears from his eyes and held his knees to his chest. When he opened his eyes he found the scholar from Yulan standing in front of him, staring.

"What do you need sir?" Mesieve asked.

"Nothing child, but I am curious what you need." Sao Len sat down next to him, and gathered his robes around himself. Mesieve looked at him closely but didn't feel threatened by his proximity. The men at the table continued to talk as if neither of them were there.

"I ask again young man, what is it you need?"

"I don't think I understand sir."

"I see death very close to you, but not your own. It is as if the spirit realm and our realm are thin and stretched around you."

Mesieve thought he was joking at first but Sao Len looked quite seriously at Mesieve while he spoke.

"If you are trying to frighten me then I want you to know I do not appreciate it. I have lost my family, and…"

Sao Len raised his hand to cut him off. Bowing he spoke. "I am sorry young man. I was only telling you what I see around you."

"My name is Mesieve."

"Mesieve?"

"Yes Mesieve."

"Well Mesieve I just want to reiterate that I meant no harm. My people have ways of seeing and feeling the world around them better than most and I wanted to share what I saw around you."

Mesieve nodded, but was beginning to grow curious about what else the man had to say and what he could see. How could someone see more than any other? He knew his elders' vision always faded, but what else could he mean? "What can you see and feel?"

Sao Len smiled. "All of life. We can see the energy that lies underneath, driving the world around us. Each thing in this world has an energy to it, from the rocks and dirt of the ground to the trees of the jungle."

"You are telling me that a rock and dirt has energy to it? And you can see that? That seems a little strange to me."

"Strange? Does it not also seem strange that you are the lone survivor that we have found from the inland regions?"

Mesieve looked at Sao Len; he had assumed that others could have made it out if he had. He just thought he was the last of them.

"What do you mean I am the only one?"

"Vandahar was gone for some time. I arrived here to help while he was gone. He went looking for help and to see how bad the attack was, and if we could expect more. In that whole time, only you were found alive. If I am strange because I can sense the energy of the world, then you need to explain how it was that you were able to stay alive for so long when not even the army garrisons made it here."

Mesieve looked at the floor. He was the only one? How could that be? He knew enough of the geography of his homeland to know that there were thousands of people living in the cities. One young boy out of thousands would leave much to be explained, and it would explain why Vandahar had taken him in. He was an anomaly in a time when hope had been lost.

"Now, Mesieve, you can see why you are the only person who is not a military leader, who is present at this meeting. I see something in you, a great importance for us, and if you like I can teach you how to see what I do after the evacuation to Ygdrosen."

Mesieve looked at Sao Len again; he met his eyes and couldn't help but think that the scholar from Yulan was right. There was an honesty in his eyes that he was comforted by, no matter the strangeness of his ideas. Besides, if the boundary dividing the realms he spoke about was thin around him, maybe one day he could, in some way, see his parents again.

"I will let you teach me this ability you speak about, but I want something before we do."

Sao Len looked concerned but nodded. "Agreed, name your price."

Mesieve lifted his foot from underneath him, the holes in the soles of his feet gaping and showing dirty calluses from walking the rough road. "Can I get some new shoes? If we are evacuating I need to be able to walk."

Sao Len looked at the foot on the bench in front of him, and began to chuckle. Looking over at the table where the group was still talking about the map he called out. "Captain Vandahar, I have a request."

Vandahar stopped what he was saying to look over at Sao Len and Mesieve.

"What is it I can help you with scholar?"

"Is it alright if I take this young man of yours for some shoes and a good bath? We can't have him arriving in the capital with you in nothing but rags, mud, and holey shoes."

Vandahar nodded and smiled. "Make sure to have him get something for clothes other than those he has on. Mesieve, before we evacuate I will come for you, alright?"

Mesieve nodded as stood up. Sao Len was already motioning for Mesieve to follow him deeper into the temple. They walked away from the entrance towards another archway in the back of the great rounded temple room. As they passed from the main room he noticed that the material of the walls changed, the marble faded away and was replaced by a very smooth and seamless stone. Mesieve reached out to touch it with his hands and noticed it felt that same as the shells he had seen on the beaches his family had taken him to.

"This part of the temple was not built by your people; this has been here much longer." Sao Len stated while walking.

"How do you know that Sao Len?"

"I see it, and I read some of the history of this temple complex. It was partially destroyed during something called the "Council Wars" years ago. The Duchess of the Moon, who this temple is dedicated to, disappeared at that time."

They came to a set of stairs that dropped them down a few feet, and the hall curved around a bend. They continued, but there was a door in the corner that Sao Len walked towards. They stopped at the door to allow Sao Len to pull some keys from his robes and unlock the door. Mesieve noticed that where the hallway continued he could see another grand stairwell with a darkened room behind it.

"Sao Len, what is that room for?"

Sao Len followed Mesieve's pointing arm to gaze at the dark cavern beyond. "That is the old temple. It is unused, and it is off limits to most. To be honest, I do not know of anyone who is allowed in those areas. Come though," Sao Len held open the door. "Let us get you bathed and into some clean clothes. We may have a chance to get a lesson in before the captain begins the evacuation."

Mesieve stepped in and Sao Len closed the door behind them. The room he was in was very bare, and Mesieve was struck with the number of books in the room. It seemed that all that was there was a bed, a small writing table close to the ground with a cushion instead of a chair, and shelves of books. There were even books in piles in front of the shelves.

There was a single door in the back of the room that led to a warmly lit room. Next to the small writing table was a trunk that was made of dark ebony wood with polished steel seams and edging. The table had an ink pot and quills, and the paper on it seemed to bear a few different languages though Mesieve recognized none of them.

Sao Len let Mesieve search about while he walked into the room further back. "Feel free to look around. I will draw a bath for you."

Mesieve was already engrossed in the books on the writing table, and the strange notes in all the different languages on the pages. He heard the water begin to fill a basin, and looked at a book that bore his own language, with a series of pictures next to each series of words.

Sao Len came out from the side room and noticed the book that had captured Mesieve's attention.

"I see you have taken an interest in a very rare piece."

Mesieve looked up at Sao Len. "What do you mean rare?" Mesieve recognized the symbols from the book his grandfather had given him

"This is the only copy I known of the hieroglyphs of the Zephyren that founded Brodesia. These glyphs are what the first

Brodesians used to tell the tale of how the Duchess of the Moon and the Dragon King revealed themselves to the world and the story of their lives during the council war."

Mesieve was confused, he had never heard of the Dragon King that Sao Len spoke of. "Who is the Dragon King?"

Sao Len smiled. "I will tell you about him while we travel to Ygdrosen. The water should be warm, I put some of the coals from the fire under the basin to keep the water warmer. Come."

Mesieve followed Sao Len into the other room, shutting the cover of the book as he moved away from the desk. He noticed how much time Sao Len must have spent making the bathing room a welcoming place. Mesieve appreciated the amount of devotion to a room meant for cleanliness, once again aware of his own grime.

There was a brass basin surrounded by stones that had been cut and formed to make an outer wall for the basin. There was a small door with a vent in it that was smoking gently, with an incense Mesieve didn't recognize. The inside of the tub was filled with water, and soapy foam covered the top hiding its depth.

"I have found a set of student clothes that will fit you. They are simple but I think they will do."

"Thank you, Sao Len."

Sao Len bowed as he prepared to exit the room. The clothes in his arms were set down on a bench next to the tub, which already had a white towel folded crisply on it.

"I will close the screen while you bathe. When you are done I will give you a lesson in meditation."

Mesieve stripped down, the rags that used to be his clothing fell into a small, dirt-caked pile at his feet. He stepped gingerly into the warm waters, and felt his skin tingle at the warm sensation of the water. Easing himself into the tub he slowly relaxed, letting the scented waters soak into him.

He thought on how long it was since he had been clean, almost feeling the dirt fall from his skin as he laid back. He remembered his family, feeling a pang of disbelief and sorrow all mixed into one. He had no idea what a life without his parents meant. He rested his head on the tub, letting his eyes lose focus on the lines of the beams in the ceiling above him. He did not want to think of his family being gone today.

Before he knew what was happening he found the world fading from view. When Sao Len came to check on him, Mesieve was deep asleep, with lines drawn on his muddy cheeks by his tears.

CHAPTER 9

Cael and Herth followed the footsteps of Qonos as he marched through the woods. Though he was covered in plate mail from head to foot, the elven king moved quickly and quietly, rarely making more than a few trace sounds of his armor ringing against itself.

They walked deeper into the wood, and the ground began to slope upwards. Cael began to catch the scent of pine as it wafted through the trees. They strode along and sometimes climbed over what appeared to be the side of a mountain, with trees still growing straight up towards the sky in defiance of the uneven ground. Looking ahead up the hill, Cael could see a ridge nearby, and Qonos waiting atop it looking out at something still hidden from Cael's eyes.

As Cael crested the ridge, he realized why a king would stand here and wait. The ridge opened into a valley before them with massive pines the likes of which Cael had never seen. They were easily hundreds of feet tall from the ground to their tops, with branches stretching out to bridge the gap from their trunks to the smaller trees on the edges of the wide valley. In the dimming light of the day, Cael saw white-blue lights beginning to brighten across the great trees, illuminating and outlining all the pathways connecting the massive boughs.

"Cael, Herth, I welcome you to my capital, Galtania, the city of the first born elves." Smiling, Qonos walked back down the ridge, towards what appeared to be a large wooden bridge connecting the steep valley wall to one of the immense branches growing in its center. Cael barely caught the sudden appearance of elves armored similarly to Qonos. Their armor had the browns and greens of the forest decorating them; the plate bore the natural lines and color of the pine bark, but Cael could see that it was steel. The leather padding they wore beneath was green, patchy and natural like leaves would appear on a tree. They did not glow with light as the armor of their king did, which allowed them to fade into the woods around them.

Qonos waved the elves back to their posts as the trio continued onto the bridge and towards the city. As quickly as they had appeared, the elven guardsmen were gone again, but not without sounding a call that alerted the city that they were coming. Cael knew it to be one of the birds he had heard as they rode through the forest though much louder and clearer. Across the valley a few isolated calls echoed back through the vast distance from the bridge to the city, obviously bearing tidings of Qonos returning to Galtania.

Cael felt Herth become tense behind him as they walked on the bridge. He looked forward, carefully making sure he kept his feet on the wood beneath his feet. There were no lines for separate boards, only the woody lines of the trees and vines wrappings against each other, closing all the gaps for a smooth walkway. Cael felt that whatever they were, these elves seemed to be able to grow the trees into forms they could use to live in. He let his hands run along the railings on each side and could almost feel the wood vibrating with life and energy, and it left him with a warm sensation in his heart.

Cael nervously looked over the edge and saw they had already come to a point at least a hundred feet in the air, and the ground was still dropping out from underneath them as they continued along. Cael realized then that the wooden bridge that they were walking on appeared to be suspended from the trees around them by nothing more than an occasional thin branch or vine growth. Nothing gave the impression of the stone strength he felt himself walking on. Cael caught Herth cursing behind him.

"Herth, don't tell me you are afraid of heights?" Cael joked. "You come from the tallest mountains known to exist."

"The mountains underneath my feet are entirely different from walking upon twigs suspended above the ground."

"Come barbarian, it is not much further." Qonos said. Cael would swear he had seen him smile as he turned away to lead them along the suspended walkway.

Cael looked beyond him and the side of one of the mammoth trees was nearby. He saw the pathways growing out of the sides of the trees. Their forms obviously did not grow this way naturally, but they did have a sense of growing willingly. No piece of the bark he saw bore the mark of a chopped or sawn edge.

He quickly followed close behind Qonos and occasionally looked back to check on Herth and his progress. Cael reached the solid body of the walkway and saw the source of one of the lights. Looking closer at it, he was surprised at the beauty of the glowing, flowering orb. Cael peered behind it to see how it was attached to the side of the tree and saw a vine squirming through the raised edges of the bark. Ending at the flower, the vine was blooming from the side of the vine as it wound its way along the bark and branches of the tree.

Herth finally reached the end of the walkway as Cael finished studying the light from the bloom. He stumbled onto the walkway and looked back at the raised bridge with bitterness. Turning back to where Qonos and Cael stood on the walkway, Herth nodded and waved Qonos along to continue.

Qonos turned to walk along the side of the tree, mindful of the edge of the abyss a few feet. Cael followed, keeping his hand on the tree to his left and following the sure steps of the elven king.

"My lord, how exactly did you come to have the trees as your home? I have never seen such a sight before." Cael asked.

"Firestorm, your answers will be forthcoming but for now we have to continue inside. The forest gets cold here at night and I doubt you wish to brave the icy nights of my kingdom without a warm place to stay." Qonos motioned toward a nearby arch in the side of the tree. Herth stepped off the walkway and was already moving in the direction where Qonos was pointing. As he walked, Cael noticed his friend regain some of the composure he had lost.

Qonos also watched Herth closely, following him inside after he had passed through the entryway. Cael, left on the side of the tree, took a moment to look over the city as night fell. The mammoth trees were interspersed with smaller trees, which created the spots for bridges to cross the wide gaps. Cael looked out into the vastness below and saw that the walkways continued downward, giving the tree a sense of a hive. Layers upon layers of ordered growth housed what Qonos called the elves of Pentath.

He tried for a moment to guess at how many called this place home, but quickly realized the futility of it. He could easily see there were several thousand of the glowing flowers lighting the trees, and doubtless more beyond the branches and trunks of the trees.

"My lord, Qonos awaits you"

Cael turned to see another elve standing in the entryway that the others had passed through. He was wearing a silk robe colored a deep blue across his chest, but the sleeves were a bright yellow matching the belt tied at his waist.

"My apologies, I was just appreciating the view"

The elve nodded, stepping aside and motioning for him to enter.

Cael ducked through the arch and into the hallway, passing a large wooden door that swung on what appeared to be two intertwined branches of the tree. As it shut behind him, he saw he was in a warmly lit room, and caught the scent of the same fresh mountain pine that he had been breathing for hours, but this time it was tinged with a sweet hint of what he thought to be wild berries.

Qonos and Herth were seating themselves and Cael noted several elves in the room. Most were dressed similarly to the robed servant that had fetched Cael outside. Only Qonos and one other were attired differently from the rest. The other elve was dressed lightly in green-gray tights and a low cut top with white hair, and was fixing him with a glance that could only be described as distaste. Cael was awed by how beautiful she looked, even when frowning with such great displeasure.

Cael diverted his attention with slight embarrassment at thinking of her in such a way. He turned to the others who seemed either neutral to his presence in the room, though a few appeared curious and pleased at the sight of Cael and Herth. They were all seated in a lowered seating area, so Cael stepped down to join them and squeezed between Herth's booted feet and the table in the center. He made himself comfortable on a fluffy cushion on the long couch next to Herth and looked around the room. The tabards on the wall were a deep green and held a single white sword with sunbeams coming off of it.

"That is the symbol for Pentath, Cael. The white sword lights the path of our people."

"I can't say I am familiar with the white sword Qonos, nor your banner," Cael said as politely as he could. A servant came bearing a tray of steaming mugs. Herth took two handing one to Cael sitting next to him.

"The white sword is the sword I carry, given to me when I awoke in this world. It is a symbol of the order of elven paladins I lead. The paladins are responsible for maintaining the sanctity of the forest and bringing order to Pentath."

"So they are your army?" Cael asked.

Qonos smiled and took a mug of the steaming berry solution from a servant offering him the tray. "Not quite. The paladins are not the army; they are guardians and too few in number. They choose to chase darkness and cleanse it, like the beasts you slayed in the woods."

Cael noticed Herth drinking deeply as Qonos did, and sipped carefully from his hot mug. The liquid was scalding but tasted very sweet. He was unsure how his companions were able to gulp such a hot beverage.

"Now that we are here, I want to apologize for your rough handling. It is not often we get anyone coming through the wood who is trying to do no more than just pass through." Qonos motioned to one of the elven servants who brought over a platter covered in berries and nuts, many of which Cael had never seen before. He could recognize the raspberries and blackberries, but some of the others he had never seen before.

"My lord, do you often have orcs in your lands?" Cael picked up a wine-colored berry by its stem and studied it.

Qonos sighed. "We have had an increase in what you call orcs over the past year or so, but nothing more than a nuisance. None who see us are allowed to leave the forest so they do not know we are here; I presume they are scouts for some other purpose."

"I didn't even know you were here." Herth spoke up quickly, and continued to drink his tea in long gulps. Cael had a passing thought about whether or not he really tasted his food when he ate.

"The First Born have maintained their anonymity for as long as they could. It is only now that we have broken it to speak with you." Qonos explained. "We were told long ago by our guide to do so, to keep silent about our existence."

"Your guide? As in your god?" Cael was surprised Qonos could speak as if he knew his own maker.

"He would not want us to think of him in such a way, though he was there when I awoke in this world, and was the first person my eyes fell upon." Cael eyed Qonos carefully. Speaking of seeing his 'guide,' as he put it, made Qonos seem crazed. However, Qonos spoke with a calm lucid confidence that had Cael believing the elven king had indeed met his maker.

"You seem surprised Firestorm, have you not met your guide yet?"

"I cannot say that I have, the closest figure to what you could call my guide would be my father. I know of no one else as my 'guide' as you would put it. I am even more curious to know where exactly you came from and why you keep yourself hidden away."

Qonos took a sip of his tea, glancing momentarily at Herth who was starting his third mug. "Unlike the humans, the elves are a young race; our guide saw a need for us to exist and made it so. We were given a task to help maintain the balance of Theron in the absence of the older powers once charged with protecting this world." Setting his cup dow,n he continued. "It was our guide who gave to me the white sword and gave me sovereignty over the elves."

"What are you protecting the world from? The orcs have been kept in check by humans for centuries. My family has fought them for as long as we recall."

"Surely you know the stories of the first humans, a group I was told to call 'The Zephyren'. After they fell from their towers of the world, humans grew weaker and were no longer capable of the same feats they once were. We were created to fill that power gap."

"You know of the tower wars and the stones of power then?" Cael looked over to see Herth beginning to nod off. The fourth round of his tea sat half-finished in the mug in his hand.

"We do. Our guide made sure I was very clear on what had happened during that time of strife. In the creation of Theron, my guide had a pair, and both were trusted with the safekeeping of our world. One chose to take the form of a man, and the other a woman. They were sibling beings charged with making Theron something for the gods to love when they returned. During the Council Wars, the two were separated and the female half, the Duchess of the Moon, was kidnapped by the orcs. The male half continued to help the men in their wars against the Council and the Zephyren that still supported them. He eventually learned the fate of his sister but he was too late, unable to save her before the orcs spirited her away. She is lost from history at that point."

"So you are you saying you were created by the male half of these guides?" Cael asked incredulously. "And what are you maintaining the balance against?"

"I am not sure 'created' is the right word. We were left with a guide that has been directing and helping us since I first awoke in this world. We maintain balance because the orcs used the Duchess for evil, and they have increased their strength and numbers faster than man has." Qonos took a long drink from his glass, measuring it in his mouth and weighing his words before he spoke. Cael was left thinking on what the elven king had described and the story of how the balance needed to be maintained.

Qonos spoke. "I awoke in this world almost 400 years ago, and heard the tale I just told you. I am here to balance the evil that grows in this world. With my order of Paladins and the white sword gifted to me, I do just that. Whether you like it or not young Firestorm, you will begin your reign in a time of great challenge and strife."

They both looked at Herth as he began to snore on the low couch next to Cael. He thought on Qonos's words. King Jonothon had said things similarly to him when he was in Dalerad. His entire quest was to ensure the survival of the kingdom that he was set to rule, though he never knew why. If the king had known of some impending doom he had not shared it with him.

"My lord Qonos, pray tell me, would your guide know the location of more information on the stones of power?"

"Firestorm, he was there in the age that the council ruled Theron. If the stones yet exist, he would be the one to know. Finding him though, that could be trouble." Qonos bit into a biscuit as he finished speaking.

Matthew Cerra - Hidden Empire

"How do I find him?" Cael knew he had to be the one that would know how to finish his quest. "If I am to protect my kingdom, I need his help."

Qonos responded carefully. "I can only do so much from here Cael. Bringing you here has forced my hand when I am not ready to do so."

Cael felt himself grow defiant. He did not want to be a wandering puppet without a sense of where he was going. He balanced his frustration with respect for Qonos's authority and position before he spoke.

"I was sent to Yulan to find information from the scholars but I don't even know where to look when I get there. Anything you know would speed me along and bring me back to my family that much faster."

Qonos looked at Cael, holding him with the same glance he had in the woods hours before searching his soul. "As to where he is I couldn't tell you. He kept his name from me, but I remember him being clad in armor. It was black and was carved with creatures I cannot recall."

"How long ago did you last see him?" Cael asked.

Qonos let a quick chuckle out "The day I awoke Firestorm, centuries ago. You have to pardon me for not remembering as clearly as you might hope for."

"So my search for this creature is without a goal in mind."

"I do, however," Qonos interrupted Cael, "know where you might start your search for him. The scholars would know the location of the viable spots for him to spend his time, or where his sister the Duchess would have been found. I can offer you rations and new horses to get to Yulan to speak with them. I don't know if they will help, but, it is better than moving on without a goal in mind."

Cael nodded as he took it all in. It was difficult to think in terms of an entire kingdom, but he knew that he did not wish to disappoint his father by failing in his search. "Thank you my lord. Your help and hospitality is appreciated."

"Think nothing of it. You gave proper respects to my dead, and you need not worry about debts on your journey. If everything were to come out of balance, it would not serve my people to anger the kingdom of Dalerad. I feel we both will need allies soon." Qonos stood, motioning two of his servants towards Herth.

"Take him to his quarters to sleep off all the tea he drank, Cael." Qonos motioned to the same elf that had been giving him the look of distaste. "Valtinatha will be guiding you to your quarters. I will meet you both again in the morning before I see you off."

Cael watched Qonos leave the room, exiting through the same doorway they had entered. The servants handily picked up Herth's sleeping form, and took him through a doorway opposite of the one Qonos passed through; his snoring the only clue that he was still alive. Cael was then left alone with the displeased she-elve.

"Come human, this way." She nearly spat at him.

Cael couldn't help but like the elve though, even if she was displeased with him. He had to shift his eyes away from her as she took him towards a third exit. Though he tried not to think them, thoughts came to his mind that left his neck warm with embarrassment.

He was curious as to what he had done wrong to earn her displeasure, but he decided to wait to ask. Quickly coming out into the open air of the dark night, Cael was struck by how cold it was here. Qonos had not been making an idle statement when he spoke of the icy nights in this tree city.

Following the elf in the blue lights of the flowering orbs he took note that they were of a similar height, but she moved silently with a flowing motion as if she were part of the tree itself. He caught himself almost staring again as he was captured by the grace of her movements. Her lithe form seemed to hold back a great power that Cael was fascinated by, but he was cut short in thinking about it further, as she stopped quite suddenly, pointing at a door in the side of the tree.

"Here is where you will stay this evening, I will wake you in the morning when it is time to leave. Leave your things at the foot of your bed and the servants will care for them after you are asleep."

Cael opened the door without question, finding another warm room with a bed that looked extremely enticing, as he had been sleeping on the ground for some time during his travels. "Thank you, Valtinatha." Cael spoke before turning away, though Valtinatha seemed to ignore the kindly statement. She had begun walking even before she had finished speaking, and Cael watched her disappear up a staircase in the side of the tree. The door quietly shut as Cael stepped back into the room.

"Well I hope whatever I have done can be made right," Cael murmured to himself.

Examining the room he found the bed felt like it was grown as the bridge they had crossed earlier had been. At one side two basins sat on the table. One he immediately recognized to wash in, the other had a thin layer of water in it and showed Cael's reflection back to him. He saw the face of a weary traveler, dirt and a full days growth of facial hair were upon him.

Cael moved towards the bed, suddenly feeling more exhausted then he had realized. He wasn't sure when he laid down, or if he even took the time to wash, but soon sleep was upon him.

Cael was staring at the stone arch again. He was more careful this time, holding himself back a short distance and looking around the room he was in. Dozens of portals lined the walls of the room, a great spiraling walkway extending with them into the air to a domed ceiling far above him. Each floor appeared to have a few of the stone portals on it, some of them broken and smashed, others intact with different colors of light coming from the iridescent pools caught between their borders.

"You will pay dearly…"

Cael looked around in a panic; the voice seemed to come from everywhere at once.

"My little Firestorm babe…."

"Where are you? Who are you?"

Cael backed up, scanning the room, he realized then that he was dangerously close to the portal, just as he had been in the last dream before falling in.

"Hush, calm yourself Cael… I am waiting for you."

Cael turned slowly to face the pool, the voice echoing from beyond the flaming red and black waters it held. Leaning in closer, he could almost make out a face, and after a moment realized he was seeing his own reflection.

He turned and found himself face to face with a man taller than he was by a full foot, his hair dark and falling around his face in stringy, wet curls. His eyes glowed yellow, an inner light showing sickly and bright from within.

"You will be mine!" The dark man pushed Cael hard in the chest, forcing him to be caught in the swirling vortex of the portal. Cael screamed as the heat and pain of the portal consumed him.

Cael awoke to find Valtinatha standing over him, a glimmer of concern in her face. Cael sat up the rest of the way and noticed that she was dressed in the same greens and browns that the guards had been wearing the day before. He had thought all the elven armor was made of wood, but hers seemed to be a hard leather weave studded with bits of steel under her cloak. The cloak bore the same pattern, leaves and branches that seemed to shift as it fluttered. Cael was sure he would see no one wearing such a cloak in this forest.

"I am fine."

Her composure returned as Cael nodded and she put back on the displeased expression she had been wearing the entire time since he had met her.

"Are you well enough to travel Firestorm?" Valtinatha moved back towards the open door and Cael saw a long thin black staff she had strapped to her back over her cloak.

"I- I think so, just a nightmare again."

"You have had that dream before?"

Cael nodded "I had the dream before, but it was more... *real* this time."

Valtinatha seemed to think on what Cael said. "Herth is already waiting for us. Get yourself ready and we will go."

Valtinatha turned and shut the door behind her. Cael saw very little light other than that of the pre-dawn. He also felt a draft of the cool air that Qonos had spoken of the night before. At the foot of the bed he found his belongings laid out neatly, straightened by a servant in the night. Cael wondered at how these people moved so silently and how that much motion in the room did not even wake him.

Standing he was surprised to find the floor warm, the same vibrancy he felt yesterday in the railing of the bridge now warming his feet. He looked at the piles of his belongings, his traveling clothes cleaned and folded. Cael held them up in the morning light from the small window behind him, seeing the stains from the dirt and fight of the road had been washed away. Their tan colors still the perfect blended match for his armor.

He dressed and looked at the pile containing his studded leather chest plate and arm guards. They both looked polished and carried a dull sheen. As he put on his chest and back plates he thought about his journey and wondered how often he would find himself needing his armor. As he finished tying the armor in place he looked at the sheath for his sword.

Pulling it free he saw that it had been returned to him overnight with a new edge that was sharper then he had ever seen it carry. Putting the blade back in its sheath he grabbed his pack from the floor and headed out the door into the cold morning air.

Cael saw Valtinatha peering out over the railing at the edge of walkway. He started towards her slowly, taking time to look absorb the filtered view that the trees created in the dim morning light. Valtinatha turned towards him as he approached and motioned for him to follow, still saying nothing.

She took him around the trunk of the tree and came to a stop in front of a stairwell that led them down to the base of the mammoth tree. Valtinatha nimbly stepped down the stairs and Cael followed as best he could on the smooth wooden steps. The steep steps slowed him down as he had never been on a stairwell so steep in his life. A few more paths and stairwells later, the pair found themselves on the same landing where they had entered the tree city the evening before. Herth was waiting, his axe and swords strapped to his back over what appeared to be a maille shirt that must have been hidden in his pack.

"Ah! I see the young lord has chosen to join us!" Herth's grin was lost on most of the crowd of elves. Qonos stood off to the side and grinned at the barbarian.

Looking back to Cael he spoke, "Cael, I have provided some essentials for your trip. New horses await you at the far end of the bridge leading to the city, and in your pack I have given you enough rations to make it to Yulan."

Cael bowed "Thank you Lord Qonos, I do appreciate your help."

"That is not all. Valtinatha will be accompanying you. I think you will need more help than just Herth can offer you on this road." Qonos looked over at the barbarian who was pondering the heights of the bridge leading back to solid ground. "Though his arm is strong, you may need other help through the course of your journey, Valtinatha is a skilled warrior, and as my daughter I am sure she will be interested in what you will encounter on this quest."

Cael was perplexed, the elven woman seemed more-sick of Cael's presence than anything, surely she could not want to come along. "Lord, you do not have to send her along, Herth will be assistance enough."

"I send her because it is what must be done. We can never see the whole path that is laid before us Cael. That is something you will likely learn on this journey. Even as a king we can never be sure of the path that we walk, and we must lead our respective people down that path. She will go, and perhaps you will both learn something along the way."

Qonos looked over at Valtinatha and Cael saw her visibly stiffen under the glance. As soon as he had noticed it though, it was gone again, leaving Cael somewhat confused. Qonos continued.

"I cannot guide you out of our city again, for I have other business to attend to. Valtinatha will be able to lead you out, just make sure you can keep up, our elven steeds are different than the ones you are used to." Qonos stepped towards Cael and bowed. "It has been an honor, Firestorm. Until you return I wish you the best of luck on your journey."

Herth, Cael and Valtinatha watched the group disappear into the trees around them. One group who was obviously the city guard seemed to melt into the forest trees themselves as they walked away, and the robed figures from the night before turned and walked silently deeper into the city that was just now stirring with the dawn. Herth crossed his arms and looked back at the bridge he had walked across the night before.

"You are not losing your nerve are you barbarian?" Valtinatha asked, the edge in her voice unmistakable.

"Hardly elve." Herth walked up to the first step, slowing for the fear of it, and then continued on at a quick pace, looking everywhere he could but down. Valtinatha watched him get some distance along and continued on to the wooden bridge ignoring Cael.

Cael took a moment to look back at the high trees of the elven city and noticed the first light of sunrise hitting the highest points of the trees and ridges surrounding the valley. Below him he could see tiny tendrils of smoke, and the sounds of a city waking to a new day floated up to his ears. Turning to the bridge he followed his companions, wondering each step of the way if he would ever be able to see the beauty of Galtania again.

A menacing wind moved through the trees, twisting and broiling over branches and animals alike, and came to a stop at the ridge in the valley it had been searching for. Darkening into a single point, the figure of a man appeared, his body forming as if from a shadow in the air. He rubbed his hands over his short hair and stretched, his gray attire stark in comparison to the vibrant greens and browns of the forest. His long coat was buttoned firmly to keep it close to his chest.

"So, I see the two of them were not killed, and have added a third to their ranks." Placing his arms across his chest, he reached a hand up to run it through the short hairs of his beard. From behind him, the rustling in the brush produced an orc who stepped into the clearing on the ridge.

"Master, what is your wish?"

"Send word to the human guards at the border of Yulan, seize the three and have them taken to the dungeons in the capital."

"As you wish my master." The murky creature gave a small bow, its hissing voice lingering in the air as a dark cloud lingers before the storm.

The shape shifting man turned back to the sight of the three travelers reaching the end of the living bridge that they had been crossing. He laughed to himself.

"These are what you have sent into this world to face a member of the council; master of dragon kind? Their world will fall so very easily this time."

The figure faded into a darkened patch of air and melted away. In its place, a dark mass of swirling wind took form and flowed back through the trees with the crushing force of a gale. It headed south east. The clearing calmed and the branches stopped moving as the stillness returned. In the distant reaches of the forest, one could hear the squeal of the orcs as they began to march once more.

CHAPTER 10

Mounted on their elven steeds the miles passed quickly for the three unlikely traveling companions. It took just a few days to leave the forest and reach the vast scrub plains that bordered the desert of Yulan. Their course steered them clear of the smaller towns and villages as they rode, as Cael felt it best to help maintain the secret of the elves as long as he could. Though smaller than the war-steeds Cael and Herth were used to, the horses carried their weight just as easily. They were responsive to Cael's commands, a few times making a change before he had realized he had tried to command it.

The horses never seemed to tire during their long days of galloping and they never frothed at the mouth with exhaustion as other horses would have done with their workload. When Herth asked about their stamina,is Valtinatha's response was curt and was given as she looked down her nose at the barbarian.

"These are elven steeds. They do not tire because they run with the strength of the ground beneath them. So long as Theron still lives these horses will continue to run."

Her undertones suggested that they should not question her further. As they brushed their steeds at the end of another long day of travel, Cael turned his attention to the landscape changing around them. They had started in the deep forest, and had come to these dry scrublands. It was much different from the fertile hills of the homeland that he was used to, and seemed to bear the mark of heat and dry air. Perhaps they had once been green as the ones in his homeland had been? Earlier, they had crested one of the hills and came to a stop to observe the landscape.

"Why are we stopping?"

"We need to make sure we don't miss a border outpost. If we are to continue we need to get any help we can, unless you know the way to Yulan?" Herth answered.

"What help do we need? What are the scholars going to tell us?"

Though they were days into their journey, Valtinatha continued her aloof demeanor. Looking through his spyglass Cael noted smoke on a hill about an hour's ride ahead of them. He could make out the top of a structure though he was not sure what it was.

"If you two wish to stop, we have a direction. I see smoke on a hill about an hour from here, and a promising structure. Hopefully it is an outpost or at least someone who can direct us to one."

Cael put the spyglass away, and without looking back at his companions, he kicked his heels to make his set off towards the new goal. Cael had never been this far south, and though they had spent a few days riding in this scrubland, he still felt uncomfortable in the warm southern heat and its drab dusty browns. He knew from the maps that eventually these plains would give way to a desert, though Cael could not imagine the environment getting any more dry and barren

Valtinatha brought her horse alongside Cael as they galloped across the plains, and the soil became dustier as they pushed further southeast.

"Why do you push onward like this Cael?" she half-shouted over the sounds of the hooves on the ground below.

"What do you mean?"

"I have seen other humans, and they are distracted, concerning themselves with things that are meaningless. Yet all I have seen of you is dedicated to the single pursuit of getting to Yulan."

"You make it sound so great to be human." Cael grinned at his sarcasm. He looked over and saw that Valtinatha had not changed her expression. Cael felt a moment of discomfort and thought of a better answer.

"I was always told by my father that there is nothing more important than completing our duty and being true to ourselves. This mission was given to me by my king, and to not complete it would make me a failure to my father."

"What would your father do if you failed or had chosen to not follow your king's orders?"

Cael looked ahead at the hill, unsure of how to respond. He had no idea what his father would have done, and since he did not want to think about it he urged his horse ahead. Valtinatha did not attempt to follow. Cael was still bothered by the question; disappointing his father was something he had always sought to avoid.

The trio continued to kick up dust as they rode across the flat scrubland with the sun glaring down on them. Cael led them towards the hill where he had seen the smoke; it was,a rocky mound of shale and granite with patches of brown growth littering its surface.

As they grew closer Herth rode his horse partway up the slope and dismounted, his bow in hand and an arrow notched. Cael could see the structure he had seen earlier, and it was definitely a rickety looking wooden tower. Obviously in disrepair, he wondered if it could even bear the weight of a man inside.

"Careful Herth, don't pick a fight." Cael said quietly.

Valtinatha stayed on horseback, her ears somewhat pink in the heat of midday. "I take it we are still being careful because of the orcs you found?"

Cael nodded. He was sure that Valtinatha could fight, though he noted jealously that Herth had not tested her while they were traveling. She seemed to not know much of the world outside the elven forests of Pentath, aside from the observations of humans that she was particularly fond of dropping into conversation.

Looking up the slope he saw Herth standing at the top, a large scrub bush hiding him from view from the other side. He watched as Herth kneeled and locked himself in place to watch the activities of the other side. He stayed paused like this for some time, and then turned back down from the ridge, a few rocks and bits of dirt tumbling down ahead of him.

Cael waited till Herth was close to the bottom, the sand sliding down the hill in front of him. "What have you found?

Herth stopped and looked down at Cael. "There is definitely an outpost, but it does not feel safe."

"Safe? What do you mean not safe? It is an outpost of Yulan right?" Valtinatha questioned.

"I mean that something does not appear right. For being a nation of proud scholars this outpost seems very—" He paused searching for the word. "It seems very primal and dirty, not the refined reputation that Yulan holds in our lands."

Cael crossed his arms and tried to think of their next plan of action. "I am pretty sure we don't have any other option than going up to the door and knocking, but with one difference." Cael looked at Valtinatha as he spoke.

"What is this one difference you have in mind?"

"I think Herth and I should go in alone."

"Oh, so the human men can go in and play it tough? That is pretty smart of you," Valtinatha spat at Cael.

"Or in case we need someone to get us out of trouble. We will need someone to remain behind to make sure we can escape if need be." Cael answered as calmly as he could to counter Valtinatha's anger. She seemed to agree to the idea, though he could only assume so since she did not respond to him further.

"So what is your plan young Firestorm?" Herth asked, unperturbed by Valtinatha's previous outburst.

"You and I go inside and introduce ourselves. We get whatever supplies and directions they offer and then we come back out and get Valtinatha and continue on our way to the capital. If it goes poorly, Valtinatha finds a way of getting us out of it."

"Thank you for the vote of confidence that I can rescue you." Valtinatha kept her arms crossed to emphasize her displeasure.

Cael nodded to Herth. "Let us get prepared. Was there a gate for us to enter through?"

"There is a small gate, but not much. The outpost is not much more than some stables and a small barracks backed up against the hill. The road leading up to the gate is clear, though a little rocky."

Cael mulled the thought over in his head. The landscape they stood in was generally barren, but a small scraggly wood stood a few minutes' ride to the south. Cael felt Valtinatha could hide in it while she waited for Cael and Herth to get what they needed from the outpost. Cael pointed to the woods to the south.

"I think that would be a good place for you to wait for us. Circle around to —"

"To hide the dust from the horse? Yes, I will. How long should I give you two until I figure out how to rescue you?"

"Nightfall. If they keep us that long you will know something is wrong." Herth said.

Valtinatha remounted her horse, her light form springing off the ground into the saddle. She settled in and turned, ready to head around the hill and to the outpost. "Make this quick, we have many leagues to go before we reach the capital of these lands," she called backward.

She spoke a quiet word in elvish to her horse. The white animal galloped off into the distance, a flash of white among the browns that dominated the land around them.

Cael and Hearth watched her ride towards the west, dust floating through the air and slowly settling in her wake. Cael wondered if her help would be needed or if she would have to wait for the next few hours while they attempted to get help for the rest of their journey.

"I wonder if she will stay this pleasant, young Firestorm." Herth commented as he checked the saddle of his speckled grey steed.

Cael looked at Herth "Pleasant? What would you consider to be her in a bad mood?"

Herth smiled and looked up at Cael as he spoke "You have apparently not spent much time with women."

"What is that supposed to mean?"

Herth didn't answer, but took the reins of his horse and began to walk east around the lower base of the hill. Cael watched him go for a moment, puzzled once again by his cryptic words and behavior. He knew Herth was something more than just the primitive barbarian that lords like Kingsley would believe him to be. Cael was sure of that.

As Cael took the reins of his own horse, his mind was drawn back to Dalerad and Thera. He was curious what was happening in his absence. Though he had sent a letter to his father, being gone for so long without a trip back left him uneasy. Every step took him further from his parents' home and everything he had ever known.

Herth led him south and then east around the hill. As they rounded the southern edge, the small outpost came into view. What Herth had said of its primitive state was certainly an understatement.

On the ridge above them was a simple slat wooden fence, behind it a wooden tower that looked barely firm enough to stand. They reached the base of the hill and Cael followed Herth up the slope to get a clearer view of what he had seen inside the rickety walls. The gate was barely more than a log barring the path and the stable that was not much more than a lean-to shed to cover the horses from the afternoon sun. As they walked further, the simple structure of the barracks came into view. The strange upward-curved edges with bright red trim made the building seem strangely out of place in the colorless scrubland.

Hearth and Cael soon came to what would was once the gate. Two soldiers stood at the gap in the slat fence looking at them with bland joyless stares. Herth raised his hand and Cael followed suit as the guards each lifted crossbows and aimed them. Through a thick accent a third man spoke from the tower next to the gate.

"What is your business here?"

"We come seeking aid supplies on a trip east to Yulan. We mean no harm." Herth spoke to the guards who stood like statues in the heat of the sun.

"We do not take kindly to those trespassing or causing trouble in our lands."

"Like I said, we are not here for trouble; we are headed to Yulan on a journey, nothing more."

The man looked down at them from the tower and seemed to ponder what to say next, picking his teeth with a small stick. He turned towards the ladder and began to climb down, leather armor creaking as he reached ground level.

Cael and Herth both studied him as he landed, dust kicking up around his feet. Stepping over he examined Herth closely, and moved to Cael to do the same.

"You traveled with a third did you not?"

"Third? It is only us two you see here."

The man looked at Herth, his angular face keeping a sharp scowl. It was in broad contrast to the grin playing on Herth's features. He stood in front of Herth and looked straight at him and repeated the question.

"Where is the other member of your party?"

Herth kept his grin. "I don't know what you are talking about."

Cael surmised that by this time the commander of the outpost had been through enough. He pulled his sword and put it to the base of Herth's neck, the blade pressing in enough to draw a drop of blood which ran off the edge of the sword.

"You take me for a fool, and you are trespassing. If it was up to me I would have you both left to die in the desert."

"So you are not the one in charge?" Herth taunted the man holding the sword, which he pulled back and sheathed after pausing a moment to meet Herth's eyes.

"I have no interest in you, but my king does." He motioned to the group of guards who had gathered inside the rickety walls while Herth was taunting their commander. "Take them to the cells, leave their belongings intact. Those orders come from our master in Yulan."

Cael had to wonder what Herth thought he would gain by taunting the captain as he had, but with as unfriendly as their encounter had been from the beginning, he was glad for it. A part of him was also glad that Herth had been able to strike insults towards the commander.

He watched as the guards took their horses and arms, and soon Cael and Herth stood powerless in front of the guards.

"We will take them tonight, the orcs will bring in the girl they had with them." The commander was grinning fiercely.

Cael looked over at Herth who returned his cold glare. Cael didn't think that another human would work *with* the orcs against other nations. He wasn't given much time to think on it though as he felt a quick strike to the head, and darkness closed in before his body fell to the dusty ground..

Cael woke to find his head ringing in throbbing waves of pain. Whoever hit him had truly meant to make sure he stayed out for a long while. He gingerly rolled off his back and on to his side, raising his hand to the back of his head. As he did so, the crusty flakes of dried blood crumbled as he touched them. He brushed them off with his hand and on to his pants.

"At least they made sure to do it right." Cringing, he sat up to survey his surroundings. It was almost pitch black, except for one ray of light coming through the small window in the door opposite him. His eyes were still adjusted to the darker light, and he found they were in a stone room, and Herth lay nearby, face down in sparse hay on the floor.

Cael crawled over to the side of the room where Herth was laying, and heard him breathing steadily. His long blonde hair covered his face, but Cael could easily see the lump and a small amount of dried blood on the back of his head. Cael left him lying there, thinking it better to let him sleep for whatever they had to face later, as it did not seem they would be able to escape their cell.

Cael shifted and leaned back against the stone wall and closed his eyes, fighting back a headache from the blow he received earlier. He concentrated on the silence of the cell and thought of home; he wondered what his father would have done as they approached the outpost. Would he have fought? Moved on? Cael looked down and noted that he still had the signet ring on his hand. Though they had taken their weapons and bags they had left the obviously valuable ring on his hand.

The entire situation felt strange to him. The guards knew they were coming, but neither he nor Herth had noticed anyone watching them. Was there a lookout in the plains they hadn't noticed?

A commotion caught his ear from outside the cell door. He could hear growling and orders barked by human and orc alike. Cael used the wall to help himself stand and took a few shaky steps to the door, looking through the small slit that counted for their only window. The noise came closer and Cael saw that they were struggling with a leashed animal. It was a large cat with the colors of a lynx but with the attitude of at least a dozen of them based on how the guards were struggling to keep the animal under control.

"What are you doing?"

From the edges of the room he couldn't see, a guard slammed on the door. The loud rap rang in his head and forced him back a step.

"Get back and move to the side, we are putting her in there with you!"

Cael had started moving further back, hearing the key in the latch. "What do you mean you are putting her in here? You can't keep us in here with a wild animal!"

The door opened to reveal a chubby and raggedly dressed man, with distinctly orcish facial features mixed in. Cael gasped and pressed himself against the wall. He had never seen someone who was human with orcish features. The guard noticed his reaction, and with his whip in hand he stepped to Cael and looked him square in the eyes.

"What is it Northling? Haven't you ever seen a half orc?" his breath fell upon Cael's nose with the stench of rot and death. Clearly even being half-human did nothing to clean up the disgusting nature of the orcs.

Laughing, the guard went back to the door, yelling at the men with him to push the struggling feline into the room. The hissing and scratching was kept at bay by a long staff with a cord tightly wrapped around the creature's neck, but that didn't stop it from catching the leg of a man who got shoved too close by his comrades.

With a single swipe the man's shin was scraped clean to the bone, his scream filling the small cell. The cat landed one more paw on the side of his head and he doubled over before being pulled free. The door slammed shut, leaving Cael to face the growling beast with blood seeping from its claws. The guard's leg dropped in front of him.

Cael lowered his hands, looking at the beast with great concern. "Whoa there cat, I am not here to bother you." Cael was struck by what happened next – the cat spoke.

"Shut up Firestorm."

Cael stared at the cat, stunned, and thinking that he surely could not have heard him speak. Herth slept still on the side of the cell, and hadn't moved during the commotion.

"Did you just speak?" Cael asked incredulously.

The cat stretched and shook out its fur. Tufts flung themselves free and Cael was left speechless as a muffled pop rang out in the room. There, in the center of the room, the creature's fur was melting away and in its place Valtinatha kneeled on the floor. She stood and looked at Cael from across the cell as she began to stretch out her back.

Cael couldn't utter a word. Seeing a cat one minute and then seeing it replaced by the beautiful elven princess the next was something he was certainly not prepared for. He would have been surprised for it to occur with someone he knew for years, let alone with this near stranger he had been traveling with.

"I take it there are no animal druids in your lands?" Valtinatha said as she looked at Herth's sleeping form.

"I would have to say there is no one I know of who is capable of that. You said you are a druid?"

Valtinatha checked Herth's head, seeing the same bloody lump Cael had examined earlier. "It would have been easier for us had they kept you at the outpost."

"We are not at the outpost? How long were we out for?"

Valtinatha looked up at Cael "You have been knocked out for twelve hours at most, but rest assured I can say you are already locked away in the capital of Yulan."

"They must have drugged us after we were subdued then. Twelve hours is a long time to miss out on."

"Most likely."

Cael decided it was best for him to sit down. His head was hurting for even more reasons now that he heard he was hundreds of miles to the east of the small fortress and locked in a dark stinky cell.

"After you went inside the outpost, a great wind kicked up, blowing heavily to the west. Once it stopped a man appeared at the gates of the fort, and requested that you and Herth be brought to him so he could take you to Yulan. I watched him appear and I swear he was composed of the winds themselves; they blew and twisted as if they had carried him. He formed out of nothing."

Cael nodded. After all the strangeness he had been shown the past few weeks on this mission, having a man appear out of thin air was less frightening than it should have been for a normal person.

"Go on, tell me more of what happened." Cael asked, hoping to keep the silence at bay.

Valtinatha looked towards the door. "Once you had been dragged out to him he put your belongings over his shoulder as if they weighed nothing. I know the barbarian is heavily armed so the bag alone weighed much. But when he grabbed you both, one in each hand, and disappeared into the wind again I knew that we had been found by the danger you two had been worried about." Her last words seemed to carry some blame towards Cael for having been caught.

"What danger is that?" Cael asked looking up at her.

"I tried to follow you shortly after, but the wind that carried the man was too fast. Rest assured that once I got closer to the edges of the desert around the city I was set upon by a dust storm. I attempted to run but was knocked out somehow, and awoke with that collar and pole on my neck. I woke up in time to see that we are indeed in the city."

"To be frank I was worried about orcs, being carried by the wind was not really something we prepared for." Cael was interrupted as he tried to relieve the tension in the air.

"Then perhaps it is time to think about it. I am unsure why you were sent if you were going to be so ignorant of your situation every step of the way."

Cael felt Valtinatha's statement was unfair. "You mean you think they should have sent someone prepared to deal with men composed of the wind and had known that some new race like the elves just happened to be living inside a large swath of forest that has remained unexplored?"

Valtinatha fumed at this, "Well at least they could have sent a pair with more than a half brain to be shared between them to prevent them from running into situations to fight it out like savages."

Cael was going to respond but as he and Valtinatha were squaring off, Herth sat up and yawned loud enough to catch both their attention.

"I take it things are going well?" He asked with a smiling grimace on his face as he reached back and touched the lump on the back of his skull.

"Oh yes, wonderful. Other than getting us caught, you two have us on quite a nice journey." Valtinatha crossed her arms and stared bitterly at the now awake barbarian who kept the playful smile on his features. It looked like he was about to chuckle at the situation which Cael knew would have driven Valtinatha over the edge. After seeing that she could change into different animals he didn't think that would be the best idea to tempt her with.

"Hey, all of you shut up!" All three looked back at the guards again at the door. "You are all requested to an audience with the chancellor. We won't tie you up, but we expect your best behavior as each of you will have a marksmen following behind you." Winking at Valtinatha he added, "That goes for you too, pussy cat." Laughing, he walked out of the door, pushing it open for all three to see three humans holding crossbows trained at them each.

Cael looked grimly to his companions and stepped out of the cell, following the guard. He wasn't sure who this chancellor was but he hoped it would be a more pleasant meeting than they had received from his guards.

They were walked up a number of flights of stairs in the castle where they were being held. Cael was forced to adjust his eyes after having spent so much time in the dark underground. They came at last to what felt like the main hall and Cael looked around at the surroundings. Walls of books and scrolls lined the room, the ceiling was maybe forty feet tall and had walkways added in to help scholars reach the books on the high shelves. Murals spanned the high ceiling, though they were dark and muted and Cael could not make out the details.

The floor was tiled, and seemed to have some sort of story told in the pieces placed on the floor. No mortar held the colored pieces beneath his feet but each was locked in place as if it would take the force of a mountain to make them budge.

Their captors led them to stand in front of three seats. On each side was a robed Yulanese man, each equally ancient with wispy white hair in their long beards and strange hats on their heads. Their robes were white and the sleeves bore colored armbands. The seat in the center held a man who seemed to be the odd one out.

He was dressed in grey formal attire, but of a cut that was new to Cael. Its straight lines and the gold buttons in two columns down his chest held a long coat firmly against him. His hair was trimmed short and he had a goatee that bore a few small flecks of grey in the otherwise black hair. Cael saw the chancellor stood a full head taller than himself, and taller than even Herth. As Cael watched him closely, it seemed that a light breeze constantly moved his hair in slow wispy waves, though Cael saw nothing else in the room moving so.

"So this is the chosen 'king' of Dalerad?" The man spoke looking down at Cael with distaste. "They did so much better with previous kings."

The man straightened his long coat as he stood and Cael saw that the gold and grey lines continued on the edges of his slacks. He stepped down and examined Herth and Valtinatha, looking at them much longer than he did with Cael. There was a keen interest in his eyes as he looked upon them.

"What are you looking at, human?" Valtinatha snapped as the chancellor gazed a little too long while walking around them.

The chancellor chuckled, "Human? My dear beautiful creature, your saying of that shows how little you actually know." He kept the smile on his face, stepping again in front of Cael. Cael was unsure if he would rather face the anger he felt radiating from Valtinatha or whatever the chancellor was thinking.

"You carry the signet of the Friezen throne."

Cael nodded. "I do. I have been sent— " He was cut off by a wave of the hand.

"I have no care why you were sent, because frankly I already know more of what is going on than you do." He walked back to his high seat again, the two thickly robed scholars at his side revealing nothing as they listened to the chancellor. Cael had a hunch that they were not a danger to his group. They seemed disapproving of the chancellor's behavior.

"Why are we your captives?" Cael asked.

"You are my captives because you entered my kingdom. Yulan belongs to me."

"And you are?" Herth asked.

"Strange how you are found here, does the boy know?" The chancellor looked at Herth with a carefree glee.

Herth cocked his head in confusion, which lead the chancellor only to more laughter. "Oh this is too good to be true, so you don't know either?" He grinned at one of the scholars sitting next to him, who was obviously not as enthused about the ironic line of questioning. He cut his laughter short as the stony faced scholar ignored him and grumbled under his breath. The scholar he motioned to bring the satchel that held the map the king had sent with Cael when he had left Dalerad.

Taking the bag, the chancellor pulled out the hard casing that held the map and then pulled the curled page free. He spoke intently.

"I am someone very old, my *dear* young Firestorm, and I know what this map is a very important relic that you carry."

"You still haven't said who you are, old or not." Herth tossed at him idly. Cael began to feel that the more life threatening a situation, the more Herth tended to speak.

Looking up at the three, the chancellor spoke. "I am Persean, master of the Tower of Wind. Back from an exile that the wonderful 'humans,'" he looked at Valtinatha with emphasis on the word human, "put me in. Though I do admit they had plenty of help."

"How could you possibly be one of the masters of the Towers? The Council Wars were centuries ago!" Cael exclaimed. If this man before him was a member of the Council then Cael had to know more of what he knew of the other stones.

"How am I still here? I am one of the Zephyren, the greatest of the races that ever walked this planet. We are Masters of the Elements and of Theron itself."

"You mean enslavers. The council are evil, all of you traitors to your duty," Valtinatha snapped..

Persean tilted his head to Valtinatha, who had been suddenly driven silent. She struggled with an invisible rope at her neck and Cael watched as she was lifted from the ground, struggling to breathe.

"Whatever you are doing, unhand her. There is no reason for this." Cael yelled at Persean.

"I think she just needs a lesson in humility. It shouldn't take long." Persean smiled at Cael as Valtinatha started to weaken in her struggle. "As long as I hold her here she also can't transform. Strange little talent that. I am still trying to figure out how the Dragon King gave her that wonderful toy."

"Let her go. You are killing her!" Cael looked up at Valtinatha, whose eyes were rolling back in her head as the air continued to be blocked by Persean. Cael was unsure what sort of trick he had to do such a thing and he stepped near to her side.

Persean waved at her, and Valtinatha dropped heavily to the floor, unconscious. Cael was able to catch her shoulders before they hit the floor and prevented her head from hitting the stone tile. He pulled her up onto his lap, cradling her head as she started breathing again.

"Killing her would not have been entertaining anyways. But do I at least have your belief in my identity?"

"I think you have made your point clear." Herth answered for all of them.

"Good, then I should tell you that you are all here as my prisoners until I figure out how I want to dispose of you. You are meddling, as all humans are, and I can't have that. I can only be thankful you were not able to figure out how to properly use this map Firestorm, otherwise you would have known to stay away from here."

Rolling the map back up, Persean put it in the hard case that had protected it and looked at the trespassers. Cael met his gaze and felt hatred toward him because of how powerless he was to challenge Persean. He felt weaker than ever after seeing the power of one of the stones used for evil. Even if he did locate the last tower that had remained protective of humans, how was he to face twelve of the council when he could not challenge even one?

"Guards, take them back to their cell in the dungeon. Give them food and water though, I want them in top form before they are killed. It makes it more exciting that way, yes?" Persean laughed as the orc guards prodded at Cael and Herth to move. Cael scooped Valtinatha off the ground and carried her. He could only imagine what the orcs and human mongrels would have done to her had they been given a chance to be near her again.

Step by step they walked back to the dungeon, and Cael was left to wonder at how they would escape or survive whatever games Persean had come up with for them.

CHAPTER 11

Sao Len looked over at the small form of Mesieve lying on the cot at the side of the room. He was studying the energies moving around the boy and wondered what they could mean. The thin wispy tendrils of pain and loss leached into the air around him, the essence of sadness as the energies of the world embodied them. Their purplish haze dissipated into the realm that hid behind Mesieve, like a leak that he carried with him.

Sao Len, as a scholar of Yulan, had studied the energies of this world and how to manipulate them, but never had he seen the energy that surrounded Mesieve. Each person of this world had a distinct energy to them, each living thing and plant and animal and even the soil and stone and ocean had their own energy. Never in any of his travels had he seen what Mesieve's body was somehow doing.

Sao Len had first believed there to be a weakening of the bonds between life and death around the boy, but such was not the case; there was an actual rift that changed and appeared to be channeled through him. As Sao Len saw this he turned back to his books, wondering if there was any reference he could have seen or noted that would help him explain this. The scholars of his land could many times manipulate the energies of their own bodies, but to be attached to the world beyond as he saw this boy was nothing any of them had ever accomplished or even dreamed of. The prospect filled him with a mixture of fear and excitement. The boy was truly something special.

Flipping gently through the pages of a history of the Towers during the council wars, he caught an entry that intrigued him. The Tower of Order, led by Prios of Kalnor, had reported spirits and ghosts who had turned themselves against his forces. Though the details were not in the short note of the legend, it did say that it was feared that Prios's own victims had come back to defeat his army. If Mesieve was somehow connected to the place the spirits were flowing to, that meant he may also be a point through which they could pass.

Sao Len shook his head and rubbed his hands on his face. If he taught this boy how to see the energies of the world around him he would be faced with exposing him to the spirits he was linked to, and that left him with two options. If he taught the boy, there was a chance he could control the opening and keep it shut, or close it forever. If he did not teach him, there was a chance that they would pour forth from him uncontrolled and unfettered to wreak havoc in the world. Both options left much to be desired but they were the only options available.

The thought was interrupted by a sudden knock on the door, accompanied with yelling.

"Sao Len, open up! We don't have much time!"

Sao Len got up, and Mesieve barely stirred on the cot. He opened the door and a soldier barged in from the other side, another in the hall behind him warily holding a crossbow. His eyes turned from the room to the stairs they had come from with unease. Sao turned back to see the soldier grab a satchel off the wall and toss it to Mesieve.

"Here boy, help the scholar pack his things."

"Soldier, what is going on here?" Sao Len's stern voice demanded that an answer be given. The soldier sadly looked at Mesieve when concern before responding.

"The city has been breached. Some of the lizard creatures were pushed back off the walls but they moved in to the city center. All who can still travel are being sent from the city to Ygdrosen."

"Ygdrosen? You are retreating to the capital?" Sao Len was shocked at the news; he had half hoped that a move would be made to keep the interior from being totally under the control of the beasts that had invaded. This hope had proved to be folly though.

"How long do we have?" Sao Len asked.

"Vandahar said we were to give you five minutes, no more." The soldier said.

"That will be more than enough." Sao Len moved to the table, grabbed the history book he had been reading along with a dark wooden case by the side of the small table he kept piled with books. Motioning to Mesieve he spoke.

"Fill the bag with some of the robes in my trunk by the door, and that will be everything we need."

He watched as Mesieve complied, and the various colored robes began to fill the bag. There was enough of a mix to ensure that Mesieve would have changes of clothing as well as himself.

"Soldier, let us go then."

The soldier looked somewhat surprised that all the books and other items were being left behind. "Are you not going to bring the books?"

"They are just things, and they will only slow us down. I have the one I need." He held up the text he had been reading for emphasis before placing it in a pouch inside his robe. Sao Len motioned for Mesieve to exit the room, and he followed them out. The first soldier continued to be wary as he rapidly moved for the stairwell. Sao Len noted and watched the waves of tension filter through the room, and observed as the tendrils of painful energy around Mesieve strengthened and drew the pain away from the soldiers.

Sao Len almost stumbled as he watched. The soldier who had come into the room helped him steady himself to prevent a tumble down the stairs.

"Carefully, watch yourself Scholar."

Sao Len thought deeply as he walked, coming up to the main room of the temple rather quickly given the fast pace of the soldiers. The commanders who had been there earlier were all gone save for Vandahar, who stood at the center of the map table that they had been marking earlier. His eyes were drawn to the map, but his concentration was broken by their arrival.

Vandahar looked over at them and smiled. "Sao Len, Mesieve, I am glad to see you two are prepared. We need to get moving immediately."

"Vandahar, what is going on?" Mesieve asked. Everyone looked at him, almost forgetting that even though he looked small for his age, he was still old enough to realize what was going on around him.

Vandahar waved him forward. "We will speak as we walk young man."

Sao Len watched as Mesieve jogged forward to catch up with Vandahar and they moved out of earshot. Sao Len followed behind with the line of soldiers. Vandahar was speaking to Mesieve intently, and it appeared that Mesieve was being asked to remember something important.

Turning his attention to the bustle in the streets he lost track of their conversation. The street had numerous soldiers and civilians milling about, each seemed to be busy getting ready to leave. The city had been partially evacuated earlier in the week, but a few had tried to stick things out. Now they were forced with running before the onslaught of the strange lizard army.

Ahead of them at the base of the temple steps, there were two horses pulling a rickety cart. It looked like up until a few minutes ago it had been used to carry wounded soldiers as he saw dark bloodstains in the planks of wood in the back.

Sao Len walked down the steps and heard cries and screams from the east and northern edges of the city. Mesieve was sitting in the back of the cart and Vandahar was already on horseback, still speaking with him. As Sao Len approached, Mesieve nodded to the captain.

"Are you coming with us commander?"

"I will follow as far as the gates, but I must stay with the volunteers to hold the line here in the city. You will need time to escape and I intend to help you get it." Sao Len noted that Mesieve looked at him as he said that and looked away towards the bottom of the cart, where the bag of robes lay. The boy had known much loss it seemed, and today would only add to that.

Sao Len looked to the energy of Vandahar and saw that his mind was set, and could only nod. He pulled himself up into the cart to sit with Mesieve, while the two soldiers sat up front and took the reins. He noticed in the moonlight that a few spears had been left in the back. He lifted one and looked questioningly at Vandahar.

"I know you were trained how to defend yourself by your brethren, Master Scholar. If you are set upon you will need to defend yourself. Come let us get you to the gates."

Sao Len let the spear fall to rest on the floor of the cart, and took in the details of the night. The city had turned to chaos around them; in the distance he could see that it was burning. Black smoke towered upwards against the sky and faded into the darkness.

The moon was occasionally obscured by wisps of the smoke, and he tried to imagine he was not hearing the terrified cries of the soldiers who died to enable their Mesieve escape. He glanced over at Mesieve, and saw that he had hidden his face in the bag. The wisps of the other realm were much stronger and pulled at every nearby soldier, drawing in more energy to the infinite beyond that he was linked to.

Sao Len closed his own eyes and thought intensely about the boy. He realized that until he could return to his brethren, there was nothing more he could surmise. He turned his mind instead to meditation and prayers, and let the buildings of the bleeding city silently pass them by. He felt the cart turn, and heard more carts and marching people and understood they had reached the caravan leaving the city.

Sao Len opened his eyes and looked upon the chaos of exfiltration. Vandahar's presence helped, as soldiers pulled citizens and carts out of his path as they approached the gate. Vandahar saw that some of the carts were already leaving and turned to Sao Len and Mesieve once more.

"This is where I leave you. Mesieve, remember what I said to you. As for you Master Scholar, I entrust his care to you." Vandahar looked somewhat resigned as he spoke, the lines on his face magnified by the nearness of the unspoken end everyone knew was coming.

"Shall I carry any messages for you to the court in the capital?" Sao Len asked of him.

"Yes actually, you may. I have given directions to Mesieve that he is to follow." He reached inside his dark vest and pulled out a·folded letter bearing the seal of the Duchess of the Moon. "Sao Len, this letter ensures that you will have everything you need to take care of Mesieve. It also explains everything the court needs to hear about what happened here."

"Vandahar," Mesieve looked up, his eyes red and teary in the evening light. "Why don't you just come with us? You are free to leave."

Vandahar laughed cheerfully. "My young lad this is the end I choose for myself, and there is no shame in what I do. Remember that a life given in free will to defend others is not a death, but a path to eternity." He moved his horse close to the side of the cart and placed his hand on Mesieve's shoulder.

"I don't want to lose anyone else." Mesieve said quietly.

Vandahar looked as if he was going to say more, but cries from the walls caught his attention. Soldiers began to blow the horns of the city, drawing the soldiers on the ground towards the gates.

"What is it commander?" Sao Len asked. He knew the horns meant the enemy was approaching, and had heard them blare when the enemy first attacked the city.

"Not much time remains, you must go now and don't stop until you reach the capital!" Vandahar reared his horse off towards the gate, shouting commands that Sao Len could not keep track of as he held on to the sides of the cart. The soldier holding the crossbow released the safety on his weapon while the cart bounced towards the gate.

"Scholar, grab those spears and get ready to hand me one, the city is being hit pretty hard from the sounds of those horns."

Sao Len reached across, took a spear and handed it to the bowmen as they cleared the gate. The stone arch passed overhead like a barrier between the chaos in the city and what looked like the horrors of war on the other side. He saw archers firing arrows to the southeast, and when he followed the line of fire he saw a company of soldiers holding formation across the clearing. Small groups of the Lizardmen were engaging soldiers who protected the carts taking the south road. Sao Len took the other spear to hand in case the soldiers lost the line.

When at last he looked down, he saw the fear on Mesieve's face. His eyes were glued to the beasts slowly whittling down the strength of the soldiers. "We will be fine, the soldiers have the line."

With a great thunderous crash the jungle nearest the road opened up to reveal a large horned beast throwing a tree clear from the horns on its nose. Its feet landed, crushing several people in the other carts.

"A Rhino!" Mesieve cried.

Three Lizardmen riding the beast's back pulled on to turn the Rhinoceros toward their horse and cart. Sao Len felt a sharp prick of fear as he realized how overwhelmed the once great kingdom of Brodesia truly was. He steadied the spear and prepared to stab outward as the monstrosity passed. The crossbow sang and its bolt flew through the air. Sao Len heard the cry of a lizard as he was struck. The creature pulled the ropes as he fell and the beast veered closer to the cart. Sao Len watched in horror for a short moment and then tried to cover Mesieve as the beast struck the cart.

Sao Len felt himself thrown from the cart, with a sensation of falling slower than he should have been. He struck the ground and felt the wind leave him, and the world went dark.

Mesieve run as fast as he could through the thick jungle. Branches and vines were grabbing at him, scratching and biting as he did his best to force himself out of reach of the monsters following him. He had seen lizards the size of men strike with twisted blades and jagged teeth at the men defending the city. He saw numbers of them struck down by arrows shot from the darkness.

Mesieve's mind was filled with a sense of panic at the death he had seen and that fear kept him running. He pushed his way past another branch and felt his foot catch a root on the jungle floor. Thrown off balance and with no way to catch himself, he fell hard face first onto the jungle floor.

Winded, he tried to pull his arms underneath himself to get up. His lungs felt the burn from his exertion and the squeezing pain from his loss of breath. He heard the gleeful crashing of Lizardmen coming behind him through the trees; they were faster than he was, especially in the jungle. He crawled on his hands and knees and tried to cross the clearing, but heard them crash through the opening behind him.

He heard a hunter's squeal as they saw him, and Mesieve rolled over to see the pack of monsters as they approached. Their eyes were a beady black and yellow, and the small group facing him was colored green, yellow and red which he only saw in splashes between the dark shadows hiding them. He could see blood dripping from one of their mouths; he knew with the evil smile it was wearing that the blood did not belong to itself.

"The small one will be soft and tender," a hissing and slithery voice came from one of the creatures in the behind him.

"Please, I don't want to die. Please!" Mesieve was crying, begging and hoping that something would stop them from the fate he knew was coming. The red Lizardman in the lead stepped forward menacingly. Mesieve was struck with fear, laying on the jungle floor.

One of the others found his plaintive cries funny, and a horrid laughter filled the small clearing. Mesieve closed his eyes and covered his head, waiting for them to cross the short distance between them, knowing he did not have long to live.

Instead of feeling the bite of the monster, he heard the breaking of branches and a roar of rage pour into the clearing. Looking out from under his arms, Mesieve saw one of the Lizardmen suspended in the air. The long wispy tendrils of a grey formless cloud wrapping itself around the creature's head and face, which solidified more and more as he watched in terror. The struggle of the Lizardman was cut short as his neck snapped under the force of the mist holding it floating in the clearing.

The dark mist dropped the monster with a sickening thud. Shocked, Mesieve picked himself up with renewed panic, unsure of what exactly he had seen. He glanced back as more of the Lizardmen screamed their rage in the clearing and saw the mist reaching out for the charging monstrosities.

Mesieve was unsure what new evil had befallen him but he knew with even more firmness that he wanted to be gone from this place. His homeland of thick jungle was the place he was to die. He was not comforted by this thought, but was filled only with the fear of a child in the dark. In his case he knew what nightmares the darkness of night contained.

He tried to push his legs to run further and faster, his side aching in rhythm with the burning of his throat as he struggled for more air to fuel his escape. Finally collapsing from exhaustion, he pulled himself up onto his knees and leaned against a tree. The smooth, cool bark was the most comfortable feeling in the world following his parched marathon..

A light began to brighten the area and Mesieve felt a vaguely cool but welcoming feeling come across him. He opened his eyes to search for the source of the light, and found that the mist from the clearing was near, with its tendrils resting lightly on his shoulder.

Mesieve cried out and crawled away, leaning against another tree to face this strange vapor. He stopped his retreat when he realized the creature was trying to speak, and a vague face was forming in the creature. He was oddly fascinated by the shape forming in the cloud that floated in the clearing. Sound echoed as if miles away, but the voice came through as a whisper— and its words struck deep at Mesieve's young mind.

"Master…."

Mesieve wasn't sure how it happened, but suddenly he was so incredibly tired he felt his eyes closing. He felt tendrils slowly lowering him to lie on his side in the soft grasses, and before he knew it he was asleep.

Sao Len felt himself being dragged by one of his legs as he awoke. He nearly lost consciousness again as his head struck a branch on the ground, the stinging from the blow a sharp reminder that his life was in danger. He forced himself to squint through the pain in his body and saw that a yellow Lizardman was dragging him deep into the jungle. Blinking, Sao Len braced himself as he saw he was about to be bounced over several stout tree branches ahead.

He looked around frantically for something he could use to pry free from the monster's grip. As luck would have it a great roar filled the air, catching the creature's attention from him for a split second. The creature loosened its grip of Sao Len's ankle minutely as it looked towards the cacophony. Sao Len seized on his opportunity to escape. Kicking free, he rolled away and found a thick branch that had fallen from the trees. He held it in front of him as the yellow Lizardman turned to face Sao Len with a look of pleasure.

"You will not have a good meeting with me today beast," Sao Len said as he snapped off one of the small side branches of his make-shift staff. He faced the creature squarely and spun the staff lightly in his hand, the years of training coming back to him quickly. To Sao Len's surprise the beast began to laugh.

"Hew-mon," it hissed. "You are nothing more than lunch and a plaything for me." The creature reached to its side and pulled what a clumsily crafted sword from its belt. He began to circle Sao Len menacingly.

Sao Len nearly failed to block the quick strike from the creature, as he was so caught up in his surprise by it speaking. The invasion took on a whole new meaning in his as he parried each blow from the sword. They were not under siege by a beast of the jungle, but a sentient race no one knew existed before.

Sao Len looked for an opportunity to turn to the attack against the lizard, and found one in its clumsy sword play. Sao Len struck out, catching the creature off-balance. He swung the staff out and brought it crashing down with a crack on the reptilian arm holding the sword.

Screeching in rage, the lizard dropped his sword to the ground and clutched its obviously broken arm. Sao Len paused to gain a better footing before striking again. He brought the staff around to forcefully strike the beast at the base of its skull. It dropped heavily to the ground with this final blow. Sao Len stood over the lizard, seeing that it still breathed, but it was obviously unable to come after him again.

As the pounding blood in his ears calmed, Sao Len heard a scream that sounded like Mesieve. He turned to the jungle and saw a strange light rising above the thick canopy. He ran towards the light, using the staff to push brush out of his way. He was unsure what the light meant, but he feared that something even more evil than the lizards had found Mesieve.

He crashed through a thick stand of trees and entered a clearing filled with mist, its interior pulsing with a coolly soothing blue light. Sao Len stumbled as he tried to hold himself to the edge of the clearing, and the mist rotated face him. Though he had never seen this sort of thing before, Sao Len felt safer in its reach than he had since coming to Brodesia.

"You… protect?" The voice came like an echo through layers of time and space. Sao Len noticed that it was composed of multiple energies, possible dozens, and that they were drawing off of Mesieve and his connection to the other realm. What he was certain of was that the spirit seemed to view him positively; his senses told him more than the words the mist spoke.

"Yes, I will protect the boy." Sao looked back at Mesieve who was sleeping in the lush green undergrowth.. He stepped around the creature, which gave a sense of relaxation and rest with each pulse of light. Kneeling next to Mesieve, he saw the boy still lived, and the lines connecting him to the creature were beginning to fade.

"Must… leave…" Sao Len looked back at the creature as it broke apart and scattered into the jungle. The mist broke apart on the branches and the light faded, leaving him with just faint moonlight through the trees.

Sao Len saw the lines of energy fade away, and felt the sense of relief radiate from Mesieve as he slept. Sao Len felt the boy was resting peacefully but knew he had to disturb the restful slumber, the horns of the city bleating out the sound of a full retreat. Calril was being abandoned to the encroaching lizards.

"I am sorry, but we must keep moving." Sao Len scooped his arms underneath the boy and picked him up; he was light as ever, nowhere near the weight a boy his age should be. Sao Len headed south to finding the road. He knew that somewhere in this general direction it was winding its way towards the capital. Mesieve was still passed out in his arms.

"I think you are much more special than I first assumed," he said to Mesieve's sleeping form. "I will train you, but first you must gain some weight; you should be carrying me."

The cries from the city faded as Sao Len moved away from the city, walking one step after another. He knew he would remember this night for his entire life. The tortured screams of those unable to escape the city behind him pulled at his heart.

Sore and with wounds burning from the fighting and jostling of their escape, Sao Len pushed himself to keep going. He was truly lost as to what had happened this night, but knew that nothing would happen to the boy while he still lived.

Eventually Sao Len found the line of exhausted refugees and soldiers who were following the road south. He had been through wars and had seen refugees from his travels but being one of those refugees for once was a new experience to him.

He looked no better than most. Many were bandaged, with bloody rags hanging over their clothes. They were all coated in dirt, blood and other things he would rather not guess at, and at times he saw soldiers and other refugees helping one of their comrades off the road.

The first time he saw it he heard a child near to him comment about it.

"Look mommy, the soldiers are helping their friend to lay down and rest."

Sao Len looked over at the little girl, covered in soot and her face bearing the burn from a fire. Her mother looked over at what her daughter was pointing at.

"That is right dear, they are just helping their friend." She said turning away.

Sao Len took a moment to watch as they helped their friend from the road. They came back minutes later, one fewer than they had left the road with. He could see the sadness in their eyes as they continued their own shambling walk along the road. As the day wore on he saw it more and more; they would help an injured friend or comrade in arms off the road, and each time fewer of them came back to continue the arduous march.

They continued like this for almost a day, Mesieve sleeping in his arms, or over his shoulder, or any other way he could carry the small boy. No one offered to help him with his burden; these were people who were broken and no longer themselves. Their own survival was all that mattered to them now.

Mesieve awoke in the late afternoon of the next day at the edge of a rough refugee camp that had been constructed. It was more of a staging area than anything. Soldiers rejoined other units to guard the civilians who were finding any spot they could in the wide glade to relax and rest before continuing on.

Sitting up from where Sao Len had laid him under a tree, Mesieve let loose the tortured scream of someone who had seen things they couldn't understand. He drew eyes to him from all around with his sudden shriek.

Sao Len tried shushing the boy, but ended up slapping him across the face snap him out of his fit of terror.

"Sao Len, what happened, where are we?" Mesieve asked in confusion, rubbing his cheek where Sao Len had struck him.

Gently pushing Mesieve back down Sao Len started the story. "We have been walking for a little over a day. You were thrown from the cart when it was struck and I found you in the jungle."

Sao Len thought about how he could explain what he had seen, since he was somewhat unsure what he had seen himself. Perhaps it was best to hope that Mesieve could forget it for now.

"I had an awful dream, that some sort of cloud came and killed lizardmen that were chasing me." Sao Len let Mesieve speak, realizing that there was no longer any turning back for him. He remembered seeing the corpses of the lizardmen on the jungle floor killed and knew it must have been as Mesieve recalled. The mist somehow killed them for him.

Mesieve closed his eyes and breathed deeply. He seemed to have noticed the silence that Sao Len had maintained. "Sao you haven't said anything. Please tell me it was a dream."

"I am barred from telling you a lie about something like that Mesieve, I do not know what it was I saw."

Sitting up on his knees Mesieve started panicking and yelling once more.

"You saw it? What was that? What sort of monster was that?" Mesieve was drawing attention from the people around him. A few of the men looked at him angrily while the women were covering their children and moving away. Whispers already floated in the crowd as the story of Mesieve's outburst traveled.

"Mesieve, calm down boy, be silent!"

"No! I am a danger to these people! Sao, Sao! It called me master! Why would it do such a thing?"

Sao Len examined the men watching, and noticed the rest of the women and children being shuffled away from them. One of the gruffer-looking ones pointed at Mesieve.

"You two have some explaining to do. What is the boy speaking about?"

Sao Len looked at the man, saw that he was heavily built, and assumed he worked in the grain mills from his rough appearance and scars.

"The boy is traumatized, nothing more," Sao Len said, standing to cover Mesieve again if necessary.

A voice in back yelled forward. "He mentioned being called some creature's master, perhaps the boy sent these monsters against us!"

Murmurs in the crowd began to grow louder in a way that made Sao Len very uncomfortable. He heard ideas such as offering the boy to the Lizardmen, and worse threats he hoped he had not heard correctly. Sao Len steadied himself to face the crowd and pushed Mesieve behind him.

"This boy was under the protection of Vandahar Gates, and now I protect him. You will not touch him."

"How can we trust you, Outsider? What has Yulan done for us lately?" asked another voice, this one from a man bandaged across the chest and wielding a crutch like a long club.

"Last I heard Yulan hasn't been doing so well itself." Yelled another voice from the crowd.

Sao Len backed up a few more steps from the mob and closer to the tree. It was one thing for him to face one opponent but to face an angry crowd did not appeal to him. Mesieve was behind him, and he could feel the energy swirling around the boy.

"Sao Len we need to leave," Mesieve whispered. "We can't handle this."

Sao Len was searching for places to run when he saw the bright red hair of Siegfried, another of the royal commanders from Calril, bringing his horse up to the crowd at a quick trot. His armor had been scratched and dented, and his shoulder was wrapped in white cloth. He now bore a cut across his face from two claws of what Sao Len assumed to be a lizardman's hand.

"What is this? Everyone back away, let me through!" Siegfried's staunch voice demanded attention as the crowd fell back, giving him room to approach Sao Len and Mesieve.

Siegfried searched through the crowd, and motioned the other soldiers with him to take up points and ensure the crowd did not try anything else. Looking back at Sao Len and Mesieve he gauged them up, somewhat surprised to see them.

"Master Scholar and the Orphan of the Jungle, it is a surprise to see that you two survived this far." Siegfried examined the crowd that was being dispersed to their own places of rest in the camp.

Siegfried continued, "Though I guess it would have been cut short had my officers not noticed the commotion over here. What are you two doing here?"

"We were sent from the city by Vandahar when the final attack came. Our cart was attacked and we found our way into this refugee camp. There is not much else to be said."

Siegfried nodded, looking carefully at both Mesieve and Sao. "I take it the boy is in your care, Scholar?"

"I am," Mesieve piped up. "I am old enough to know that you are speaking to me." His voice filled with youthful rebellion.

Siegfried chuckled a bit at his expense. "I suppose you are, how old are you, Mesieve, is it?"

"Fifteen, Captain. I am small for my age."

Sao Len looked at Mesieve and saw a small measure of confident fire in him. He wasn't sure if it was the pure madness of the way the boy's life had been the past week— or that maybe he was just braver then everyone took him for— but he was truly looking more confident in that moment. He felt a strange sense of warmth and vigor emanating from him.

"Master Scholar, if he is under your care, then I will leave it as such. I don't have the time to fight for orphans when I will soon have to help the muster at the capital. I do suggest that you two take horses from the soldiers, and head for the capital ahead of the other refugees.

Sao Len bowed to the captain. "Is there a reason for this kindness, Commander?"

Siegfried had already begun to turn his horse back to the east. He stopped and looked back at the pair.

"Vandahar did many things before he made his stand. If he chose to give you his support, then you will have mine. Take the main road. Each outpost will help you with fresh horses and supplies as long as you keep that letter he gave you."

Sao Len looked confused; he had shown no one the letter, not since he had put it away in the city when he had received it.

Siegfried only smiled "Perhaps one day I can tell you the stories of mine and Vandahar's life. It was an adventure to be sure. Till next we meet Master Scholar, Mesieve."

Sao Len watched him ride off further into the swarm of the camp. He had been fascinated the few times before that he had seen the royal commanders of Brodesia. Each of them seemed an island to themselves, but always one that welcomed someone in need. Perhaps there was something more to them that he had not yet learned.

He reached into his robes, and Sao Len felt his hand brush the smooth paper of the letter Vandahar had given him. He looked over at Mesieve and smiled; perhaps they were going to have some luck yet in this journey, he thought.

"Come Mesieve, the capital is still days away, even with help and horses."

Grabbing their few things into a satchel they walked through the camp, keeping their faces hidden with the robes of the scholars. Sao Len could only imagine what was in his future now. While he wondered at the power of the letter Vandahar had written, he and Mesieve headed toward the edge of camp that Siegfried had pointed to. He was unsure what else the letter would bring once they reached the capital, but he had a feeling their story had many more chapters.

CHAPTER 12

Cael woke up in the cell in what he assumed was the middle of the night. The stones were cold, but nowhere near as cold as those he knew in his own home near the frigid north. He stretched out and pulled himself stiffly to his feet. He walked quietly around the cell and was careful to steer clear of Valtinatha's form at the far end of.

She finally woke up once they had brought her back to the cell, and had been none too pleased to have been 'man-handled by him.' She followed it up with a stream of words in her own language, which he assumed were unkind. Herth had, as usual, been entertained by the ordeal and had sat laughing at the two of them.

He looked out the cell door window and saw nothing in the hall but a torch flickering in the sconce. He heard the rough snoring of the guard just out of sight around the corner. He turned back to the room and scanned it again, trying to wrap his mind around any idea that would allow them to escape. Once again though, he came up with nothing. He was at a loss for what he could do to save them and it left him feeling empty and weak.

"Psst. Hey, you."

Cael turned back to the door in surprise. The face of a Yulanese child peeked up into the gap between the bars of the window, motioning him to come closer. He stepped forward slowly, unsure if it was another trap. The child spoke to Cael again.

"It is okay, I am on your side. We are here to help you!" he whispered excitedly.

"We? Who are you here with?"

The child grinned ear-to-ear and pointed downward. Cael pressed his face against the bars, and saw another child holding the first on his shoulders. The second child looked up at him, his chubby face smiling back at Cael from the light of the hall. Cael could see he was wearing a set of yellow robes while the first boy wore blue. The first boy speaking was much thinner and seemed to be balancing on top of the second one's shoulders.

"We are going to get you out of here! Stand back!" the child in yellow robes said.

"What are you doing, the guard is still sleeping around the corner! He is barely human."

The child in blue looked at Cael bemusedly through the bars. "Do you want out or not?"

Cael realized he did not have another option and stood off to the side, waiting to wake the other two. He wanted to save the embarrassment of knowing that two small Yulanese children had saved them.

Cael stepped away from the door, unsure what the children planned to do to get in. He could hear strange muttering from them on the other side of the door. He then heard a low screech of metal moving against itself and jumped back in surprise as the lock mechanism flew from its spot on the door.

Cael stepped out of the way as the metal mass clattered by him and further into the cell. It came to rest on the floor near to Valtinatha and she sat up abruptly at the sound. She had been asleep on hay on the cell floor. Valtinatha had the look of a hunter in her eyes while she looked at the lock laying on the stones, the mechanism spinning slowly on its backside.

Herth sat up and looked at the lock that had caught Valtinatha's attention. Then, all three of them looked to the doorway to see the two children standing there.

"Come, we don't have all night to rescue you again."

The children turned and started to head away from the doorway. Herth was the first to move, the large barbarian wasting no time in taking the offer of escape. Cael looked back at Valtinatha, her face still an expression of shock. He shrugged and turned to follow the children and Herth from the cell and out into the hall.

Cael turned the corner just in time to watch as Herth gave a running, swinging punch to the jailor. His head swung to the side and took the hit full on the jaw, dropping him back in to a pile of the half-human mass that he was. Valtinatha took a moment to spit on him as they ran past his prone form.

The children took them to the same stairwell they had used to go up into the palace the previous day. Cael was given no time to wonder where they were going as the two boys stopped on one of the many landings, this one halfway up the tall shaft.

The child in yellow looked up the spiral stairwell and listened for anyone approaching. He looked over and nodded to his partner in blue who turned and faced the wall, his eyes closed.

"What are you doing?" Valtinatha asked.

"Just watch," he said, his eyes still closed.

Murmuring under his breath, Cael watched the boy place his hands on the wall in front of himself. One hand was resting on its knuckles while the other was palm flat against the stone. Within moments the outline of a doorway appeared in the stone wall and the stones started to roll back on themselves. Folding up into the wall of the stairwell and moving silently, as if they had no surface to scratch or shake and clamor with.

The boy put his hands down and shook them out. He turned to the boy in yellow and moved ahead of him into the darkened tunnel he had revealed. A few moments later a lantern was lit and revealed that the space went on for some distance. The child looked at the three stunned adults and motioned for everyone to follow him.

Cael followed dumbfounded, wondering if he had really just watched a small boy move a wall into itself? With no other choice, he shook the confusion off and followed behind the yellow robed child who stood in the now well-lit path inside the palace walls. It was small, but free of dust and spider webs, which seemed to suggest this space was used frequently.

"Are we all here?" asked the one in yellow robes.

"Yes, now who are you?" Valtinatha demanded more than asked.

"We are students of the Scholars of Yulan. I am Sao Pan, and this is my cousin Tseng Lao," the one in blue answered from behind them. Cael could see he had somehow triggered the doorway to close behind them, and he watched as the wall rebuilt itself and left them stuck in the cramped tunnel.

"Well that answers nothing," Valtinatha

Cael jumped in and asked, "Are you the ones supposed to help me here in Yulan? The Friezen King sent me."

The boy nodded. "The Scholars will help you as they can, but they are not what we once were. As you can see, Persean has changed things a bit. But no more of that, our master will tell you everything you want to know."

"Where are you leading us?" Herth asked.

"We are going to our hideout near the docks of the city. I can tell you no more than that, as my master commanded me to say no more."

"Fair enough, since you have us sealed into the very walls," Cael looked back at the now closed entrance for emphasis. "I think we can follow you."

"Good, let us go then." Tseng Lao turned, the picture of child-like joy at their adventure thus far. Sao Pan waited for everyone to pass and followed from behind. Cael could only think as they walked along that the children rather enjoyed the challenge of the situation they were in – as if the fear of getting hurt held no meaning for them.

As they walked along, the path wound down and through what Cael felt was the underbelly of the city itself. He thought they had walked a mile very quickly, but with the gentle curving and bending of the path it was hard to be sure of how far they had traveled.

The stone pathway opened up after a time into a wide room with archways spanning the weary travelers spread out some more and Cael looked up as they walked, noting the handsome stonework fifty feet above him. The faint light from the lantern somehow pierced the darkness giving some details to the smooth stone holding the ceiling above them in place. The pillars were rounded columns, each lined with stone as they rose up above him.

The arches and pillars were scarred and broken; their stone looked like a great fist had smashed into it at intervals. It was a mess of rubble but the room felt secure. In a strange way he also had to admit that the room held itself in a sense of grandeur, a quiet defiance to what-ever had scarred the stones.

"You notice after a while that the stone is seamless, northling," Tseng Lao spoke to him.

"Excuse me?" Cael looked from him back to the ceiling noticing for the first time that the boy was right. Each piece was solid but no joints could be seen. Even the broken stones on the floor were like boulders from the side of a mountain.

"We have not yet figured out how to make it ourselves, but the stone is pure. It seems to have grown here with someone's plan in mind."

"How can stone grow?" Valtinatha questioned.

Cael looked back. He kept to the light of the lantern Sao Pan held high on a staff as they walked. The shadows cast by it were like ghosts in the murky dark that they walked.

"How can you change shape? Or how can we command the stones to move from our back in the castle? You see these things and you doubt that stone can be grown?" Tseng Lao looked at her as if she were silly. In some ways Cael was glad for the companionship of Herth and the children, as it meant Valtinatha had other targets to vent her displeasure on.

She kept quiet, and Cael wondered if it was in anger or perhaps consideration that what Sao Pan had said was quite true. He had seen enough on this quest in the short month they had been gone to not leave much room for doubting Sao Pan's words.

They walked in silence for an unknown amount of time. Cael felt lost without sight of the sky. Sao Pan stopped walking at the base of a stairwell wrapping around one of the mammoth columns that rose into the darkness above them. Cael hadn't noticed until now but a few of the other columns he could make out in the haze of the city underground also had remnants.

"This is where we stop. Above we will find our master and hopefully some of the answers you seek." Tseng Lao and Sao Pan began to hurry up the steps excitedly. Tseng Lao ran on ahead into the darkness while Sao Pan stayed and held the torch, but Cael could see he was itching to join his companion.

"Will he be alright running up the stairs in the dark like that?" Herth asked from the ground below.

Cael looked at him from a few steps above, watching as he looked into the heights above them. Tseng Lao yelled down, already a solid third of the way to the goal.

"I can see just fine!" And he quickly disappeared leaving only the sounds of his feet on the stones.

Cael let his mind wander as he took the steps, thinking on his great hope that they would get some answers. He had been traveling for weeks, and still he had more questions and confusion than he had when he got the first strange mission from Jonothon.

With a few turns around the column Cael was about halfway up the stairs. He looked down over the edge and searched the murk around them; he got a clear sense for how large a cavern they had found themselves in. He could still feel grandeur here, and in the distance he could hear the faint sound of running water. Herth tapped him on the shoulder as he and the others had passed, and the group continued up the stairs, Cael now bringing up the rear.

A little while later they arrived at the ceiling, the broad span of an arch leading to another column cut across the pathway of the stairs. Seeing that everyone had reached the top safely, Sao Pan grabbed the knob of the door and turned, pulling the door outward to let a dim light pour out onto the landing. A short stepladder was on the back of the door to help them up into the room above.

"Come, inside with you all. My master is excited to see you," Tseng Lao said while motioning them forward. Cael followed as Tseng Lao led Valtinatha to a wooden stair that went up through the floor of the building. As Sao Pan closed the door the lantern was snuffed out with one quick blow from the boy.

Cael started up the steps himself, feeling a change in the air and the smell of salt and a cool breeze.

"What is that smell?" he asked of no one in particular as he walked up.

As he reached the landing where the others stood, Cael saw Herth and Valtinatha staring out a low wide window. It revealed a tower in the distance, a fire burned at the top that brought light to the moonless night. The cool night breeze flowed freely with the panes of glass removed from the windows in the room.

"That smell, Firestorm Prince, is the ocean. Something you must have never experienced." The three companions turned to see the same scholar who had been there with Persean earlier in the day. His white robes with the rainbow sleeves were gone, and he wore a robe outfit that Cael was not sure what to call. The pants were wide and baggy and looked a bit like a long dress on the old man. He was walking hunched over a cane, and Tseng Lao appeared behind him carrying a large tray with a white teapot and small cups.

"You are the advisor to that – thing – in the castle!" Cael said, the anger from their rough journey rising in him.

The man chuckled and smiled. "'Advisor' is definitely not the word I would use. 'Puppet' or perhaps 'Figurehead' would be more fitting. Persean has never listened to my words – and for good reason."

"And why is that may I ask?" Cael inquired.

"I know more about him than anyone else. Please, come sit by the window. Let us enjoy some good tea as the night continues."

Without waiting for a response he sat at a low table surrounded by mats and cushions of green and purple cloth. They looked very soft to Cael's eye, though not luxurious. The old scholar seemed comfortable on the floor in the midst of the cushions.

Cael walked over to the table and kneeled, following the example set by Tseng Lao. The boy was already pouring tea and Cael sniffed at the small cup he was handed carefully, unsure what sort of beverage he was being offered. The scent of the tea was strange. It was a green color and smelled softer to him then the black tea of his own kingdom.

"Don't worry Cael, the tea is safe," the scholar said as he sipped his own cup carefully.

"Is it alright if I know your name? And I would really appreciate being told what is going on." Cael asked curtly.

Nodding, the scholar took another long drink of his tea, taking time to savor the flavor. He set down his cup and looked like he was trying to compose his thoughts before speaking.

"My name is Chin Lizhoa. I have worked for the high chancellors of Yulan for most of my years."

"What do you do as a scholar here?" Valtinatha asked of him.

"My task has been to study and compile all the fragments of text from the past, trying to form a coherent and complete history of Theron. We as scholars believe that through knowing the past, we shall be able to prevent history from repeating itself."

"Something that is happening anyways with Persean here," Herth stated from the window where he stood looking out into the night.

"Being a scholar of the histories, it has been my duty to give advice on the past so that the rulers can know the future. Inevitably I find that it repeats itself no matter how hard we try to prevent it. Kingdoms rise and fall, such is their state in life."

"That seems reasonable enough. So you are the court historian?" Herth asked, looking into the cup dwarfed by his large hands. Cael wondered when he had been given the tea. Tseng Lao was there next to him offering him more from the pot.

"More than just a historian, I am also a researcher. As the age of the towers grows longer, the rulers are more curious than ever about the power of that age. Every ruler pushes us further into trying to learn more about the past age, and it has been a trend that has worried me for some time."

Cael felt that Chin Lizhao was holding something back from them still. He prodded, "You said you had been pushed further into researching the towers, yet you don't say what you had been asked to find."

Chin Lizhao smiled at Cael's observation. "In our reading of the books of the libraries this time we found the location of a relic that had been created during the council wars, and used on the council member that had ruled Yulan in ages past."

"Persean ruled Yulan once before?" Valtinatha asked with an edge to her voice.

"Oh yes, every corner of Theron was ruled by a Council member. Yulan happened to have been the home of Persean, the master of the tower of wind. He once controlled all the land from Storm Sea to the west, to the end of the dunes in the east."

"And somehow you let him back into power? What made you think that was a good idea?" Cael asked, his mind still fresh with Persean's treatment of Valtinatha. If Persean had left any impression on Cael it was that he would not suffer being unable to have at least what he controlled before, if not more.

Lizhoa looked at Cael through his aged eyes, a small smirk on his face. "You can be assured his release was not what we had intended."

"Then what was?" Cael asked, keeping the edge from his voice.

"After we began to search for the relic we found it in a cave in a small series of dunes. The entrance looked like it had been recently uncovered from beneath the sands. Inside we found that the cave had been a temple, built to be hidden away from all prying eyes, and as I soon learned, meant to stay buried."

Chin Lizhao sipped his tea, looking out into space and reliving the memory, or so it appeared to Cael. Whatever happened there seemed to be a great burden for the aged scholar. After a few moments of silence he continued.

"On a platform at the heart of the temple sat the point of a spear, a foot in length. Clearly as sharp as anything ever made and pointing to the ceiling in a pool of light coming from a glowing, pulsing orb hanging in the air. On the stone, red glowing runes slowly pulsed, obviously important had we paid them any heed."

Lizhoa took another sip of his tea. Cael watched him, curious about the importance of the spear.

"Without taking time to study the runes marking the walls, I committed a great folly. I grabbed the spear tip and held it in my hands while looking at the craftsmanship in awe. I stood there enthralled, the light faded, and a wind kicked up. It gained in strength and spun those of us in the temple towards the center of the room, a great whirling maelstrom locked in a room no larger than a home. The sand was biting and we all covered our eyes and waited in fear for the fate that had befallen us."

"The wind faded a few moments later, and a man appeared out of it. He stood before us naked, and looking at us with a mixture of relief and pain. I do not know who was more shocked, him or myself and my companions. At first, he spoke to us in a language we did not understand, but he seemed able to learn ours quickly. It was a short time till he began to speak to us in a way we could understand. He asked us about countries we had only heard of in legends, and when we told him what we knew of the history we have in the library, he grew angry."

"What was he angry with?" Herth asked gently, seeing the strain on the scholar's face from telling the story so far. Cael found himself more irritate than forgiving as Herth seemed to be.

"He was in a rage that so much time had passed it seemed. He had not expected it to have been so long, and his lands had fractured into multiple kingdoms. How would any ruler gone for so long react to such a homecoming?"

"You released him on accident then, and he took over your country? How did you let that happen, surely you knew the importance the relic had for him?" Cael prodded the scholar. He was somewhat surprised at himself, he could not help but feel protective of those he knew, but he felt especially so of Valtinatha today.

"It was not at first. Do not assume that we stood by and let the filth of the council walk right in. In what we assumed was a fit from his rage, he grabbed the spear tip from me, and ran from the temple and cave. We followed him outside into the desert sun and watched him throw the spear out into the dunes to the east. His strength was so that we could not even follow the blade as it flew; even his arm was a blur. He had the audacity to thank me for removing the blade, and said he would be back for us, and for the capital. Though he did not directly threaten us I knew that his return did not bode well for the scholars and our chancellor."

"When did he return? And what became of the blade?" Herth asked.

"He returned almost 30 years later, and some of us had begun to forget him. A sandstorm heralded his coming; like a dark wave the storm slammed the city and forced all to find shelter. In the midst of the dark maelstrom he formed out of the wind on the steps of the palace, his disgusting half-orcs with him. They marched into the palace nearly unopposed, and killed any who came within sight of him bearing arms. He did not even give our chancellor the opportunity to surrender or stand down, preferring only to attack him as he did your elven friend Valtinatha" He looked at her for emphasis, his eyes apologetic.

Chin Lizhao continued, "It has been two years since he returned. And things have become as you see them, his time spent mixing the forces of orcs he has breeding and the half-humans he found in his travels. He is building an army of what we see as monsters. I cannot say which way he is going to march first, but he is ever worried about keeping to his schedule. Everything is about his schedule, as if he is trying to get some task completed in a great race."

"What of the blade?" Valtinatha asked. "Did you try to recover it?"

"The idea of searching the desert for a blade such as we had found did not appeal to the chancellor at the time. That and without the support of the college of Master Scholars my hands were tied. Being so young at the time, they ignored my inquiries as youthful adventurism.

"Did your college not recognize the danger of what you had done? You released a member of the old council." Cael asked again, incredulous that they had not acted.

"The desert is known as a great eraser of people and places, Cael. Even the scholars would not have been able to find the blade after it was thrown so far," Herth stated in assurance. Cael looked back to the scholar, feeling a little better that Herth had vouched for them in his own way.

"Take heart though, my prince. A few months ago some of the traders that wander the desert came to the school for the scholars, saying they had found something that they felt should be brought to us. My two charges here brought me the package." As if by unspoken cue, Sao Pan walked from the room; Cael noticed but did not turn to watch him.

"It was wrapped in layers of cloth, more to protect those handling it than to protect the object. Surely enough, as they brought the blade before me I knew its source and its importance. I sent them from the scholar houses immediately." As Chin continued the story, Sao Pan had entered the room and set a bundle of cloth on the table. "To bring the blade here, where it remains hidden from Persean."

Herth leaned forward to unwrap the blade as the others watched. As soon as it came uncovered, Cael knew it to hold special significance. The blade had the dull shine of polished steel, and the etchings of clouds and winds floated on the blade when light hit the steel, shifting and moving across the blade as it lay in the cloth wrappings.

"It is beautiful," Herth said, clearly awed by the sight of the blade.

"The beauty of that blade is nothing compared to its importance," Chin Lizhao stated.

"What would that be?" Valtinatha asked curious from her edge of the table across from Herth.

"To a being as powerful as Persean, this relic is a source of fear for him. The fact he fears it so much is a testament of its strength and for that reason it must be his bane. It seems to have been the binding force that held him imprisoned in that temple. If it has control over him I cannot say, as I did not attempt to experiment with it. I thought it best that it remain hidden since we had no idea of its power, or what to do once we did."

Cael watched as Herth touched the blade, his hands playing over the smooth surface and staying clear from the sharp edges. "You have shown us a relic of some importance, but what can you tell us about the locations of the other towers?" Cael looked up at the old scholar who looked pleased at being asked such a question.

"The historic locations of the towers are known to us, but all were hidden and fell slowly in their own time so I cannot say for sure where their stones came to rest. There were a total of twelve original towers, and a thirteenth was built shortly before the fall." Chin Lizhao covered his mouth as he coughed. Throat clear, he went on. "Here, let us consult the map you brought with you and perhaps we can find something about where the stones now lie."

Herth and Valtinatha looked confused as the scholar was handed the hard traveling case from Tseng Lao. Cael wondered how much these apparent children were allowed access from the underground city they had walked through earlier in the night.

Unstoppering the case, Tseng Lao pulled out the leather map still held in a tight roll and placed it on the table. Sao Pan pulled the tray holding the tea off the table and removed it from the room.

"Should I ask how you got your hands on this?" Cael asked.

"It is my duty to Persean to study all relics; this one however was not as important to him since he needs the key for it."

"A key for the map? How would a map need a key??" Valtinatha asked, looking on as the map was smoothed out. Everyone studied the faint borders appearing on its surface.

"This is no normal map. This is a map created ages past to help a traveler discern his path. With the key, the holder can reveal the world around himself in ways he cannot see for himself. Though its range is limited, it can see areas that the holder has not yet been to."

"Well then we are in luck, Cael has the key for this map already." Herth spoke up cheerfully.

"You do?" The scholar asked, getting excited at the prospect of the map and key being together.

Valtinatha gave him a curious look, causing Cael to pause slightly before answering. "I do, it is the ring the Friezen king gave me before we departed."

Cael held his hand out for the group to see, and the symbol of the Friezen rose glinted in the light of the lanterns hanging above them. The scholar reached out to look more closely at the ring, making no attempt to remove it. He met Cael's eyes and seemed full of questions.

"This is truly remarkable. And you are sure this is the key to this map?"

Cael nodded. "Yes, just before we were captured by the elves, Herth had me use it to reveal them surrounding us in the great woods northwest of here. I ran my hand over the spot we were in and it revealed the terrain and the beings standing around us on the leather here."

Cael continued to look at the map and realized that something was not right with it. The center had shifted. This map was different from when he had last looked upon it in Pentath.

"Something is wrong, this map is not the same as the one before. Mine was centered on—" Cael drew his hand back as the map shifted, showing the spot he was thinking of, the borders of the great wood and Dalerad. Yulan had now shifted out of view once more.

"What happened?" Cael asked.

"You are the holder of the key for the map. If you want to see it, it will show you. This is a very exciting thing for us, as no one else can use this map unless you wish it."

"How does it work?" Cael was curious, though wary, about having a map that would change at will. He was much more used to the stable and unchanging paper and leather maps of home.

Chin Lizhao was encouraging. "If I am correct it is limited though to your own personal strength and what you already know of the world. You wanted to see what was there before, so it changed. To see things further out may not be possible until you are stronger or have seen more of the world."

"That doesn't help me much," Cael added.

Smiling, Chin Lizhao spoke up. "Why don't you try just asking it a question we need to know for now? This is your journey."

Cael looked down at the map again, his mind unsure of what to do now that he knew that his thoughts controlled what he would see. He thought of his father, the king back in Dalerad, but then he thought about a question he really needed answered.

"Where would we find the locations of the Towers?" He said it more to himself than to anyone else. He reached over to the edge of the map and watched it shift again. A name appeared and the view showed the ocean south of Yulan, a great blank spot on the map, but the coast and Yulan were still very clear at the top of the map.

"Brodesia," Herth read aloud.

The scholar nodded to himself with glee. "That in a way makes sense."

"What makes sense? The map went blank," Cael said in wonderment.

"Firestorm, have you ever been to Brodesia?" Chin Lizhao asked.

"No."

"Then how could you see its location on the map, or know what was there? You asked the question."

Cael had to admit to himself that Lizhao was right in a way. The map was blank because he had no knowledge of where he was going.

"Since I cannot take you to the libraries and show you the maps of the ancient locations of the towers, this map has shown you something better. It actually would be helpful to me if you went to Brodesia."

"Helpful to you?" Valtinatha asked? Cael could hear an edge in her voice about being asked to do Chin Lizhao's bidding.

"My father, Sao Len, went there and has not been heard from in some time," Sao Pan said excitedly as he joined the conversation.

"Yes, his father was sent after the exact information you seek. In Brodesia they revere the being known as the Duchess of the Moon."

"Being? Duchess sounds rather feminine to be just a 'being.'" Valtinatha asked.

"Yes, it does. However 'being' is more correct. The Duchess was not human, nor was it Zephyren like Persean. It merely chose to take a feminine form. Her and her brother created life on Theron and her temple is in Brodesia."

"That sounds awfully similar to the man in armor that created the elves," Herth said, still studying the blade of the spear.

"Man in armor? Do you know the color?" Chin Lizhao asked, a serious tone in his voice.

"Black. My father said when he awoke that the color of the armor was black and was carved in a way he could not recognize. He was barely able to remember because it had been so long ago."

The scholar let out a string of what he assumed were curses before speaking. "Your father saw the brother of the duchess. The thought of meeting him would be the greatest honor."

"What is so great about him?" Valtinatha asked.

"He created your race, and many others of this world. And, he fought the council personally during the fall. He would know the locations of the stones."

Cael thought for a moment and a few pieces of the puzzle connected for him. "And his sister's temple is in Brodesia."

"Correct." Chin Lizhao let the conversation settle into a pause while they all considered the situation.

Cael knew that he needed to get to that place now more than ever, as too many of the pieces were leading there. He had the passing thought that the king may have known his journey would be winding and long, as it was turning out to be.

"So, Sao Pan's father went there to find out about the towers?" Cael asked.

"In a way, he knew the location of the towers could be there, but he was more concerned in getting a clear picture of the history of the world, which involved some study of the towers and their history. Last I heard he was studying texts at a temple for the Duchess of the Moon."

"So if the map showed us Brodesia," Cael went on for clarification, "then either Sao Pan's father or someone else there knows the locations of the Towers?"

"Correct. It is our luck that a ship bound for the area leaves this morning. Booking passage for all of you may be complicated, but I think it can be managed." Lizhao looked at Valtinatha as he said the word 'complicated.'

"What will be complicated about me booking passage, Scholar?" Valtinatha asked, though more curious then irritated.

"Save for those of us in the room, none have seen an elve. With the city on edge due to Persean's raids and the constant presence of armed soldiers and orcs, pointed ears such as yours will raise questions that could be dangerous," Chin Lizhao responded calmly.

"He is right Valtinatha," Cael added. He knew in his heart that Chin Lizhao was correct that people would panic at seeing her if they were already on edge.

"Is there a way we can just cover her ears with a cloak or something until we are clear of the shore?" Cael was surprised that Valtinatha had not responded when their conversation was particularly personal for her.

"I think we can manage student robes for you, but for Herth, I don't think anyone here is as big as he is. Barbarians are not welcome this far south."

Cael looked at Herth and wondered what they were going to do with him. His size would make it difficult to hide him. An idea struck him and smiling, he turned back to Lizhou. "Do you have a cart we can use? This is a trade vessel we are traveling with, is it not?"

Lizhou nodded to Cael. "I believe we can arrange to have a cart take us to the harbor. Are you thinking we will be taking some cargo with us?"

The group looked over at Herth, who was still examining the blade. He looked up at the group quizzically, having lost track of the conversation. "Excuse me?"

Cael looked out at the city underneath his yellow hood. The buildings rose like red tiled towers into the sky. Though not as tall as the white and brown palace in the distance, the structures rose as much as forty or fifty of the kings feet into the air. Each floor had a ring of tile under the edge of the windows that pushed the walls inward, making each a tall thin steeple by the fourth floor.

The buildings consisted of painted wood beams, and what looked like plaster coated the walls between them. Many of the buildings bore scorch marks and cracks from the orcs and half-orcs he had seen patrolling the streets. The people themselves were downcast, and Cael felt a defiant pall over the city folk they passed. They were dirty, and many looked angry at their occupiers. The city was a dangerous place after all.

The city guards seemed to let Chin Lizhao pass without interference; he was known to serve their master Persean, so why wouldn't they? The smell of the ocean was growing stronger as they pushed forward, and the crowd thickened. The smell of sweat from the day's heat was mixing with the sea breeze and made Cael's nose sting.

Valtinatha sat facing out from the rear of the cart, while Herth laid inside wrapped in cloth. He was not particularly joyed by the process of being wrapped in the cloth, but he did accept his fate as he stood much taller than all the people of the city. Even Cael and Valtinatha pushed the height limit they could get away with. Cael knew they had to get there quickly to keep him from suffocating from the heat. Cael could already feel the heat radiating off the boards of the cart as they rode along.

"How do these people put up with this sort of environment?" Valtinatha asked. Cael followed her eyes and saw an orc patrol hassling a merchant and tossing things about in his cart at the side of the road. "It is angering to watch this. Is there nothing they can do to defend themselves?" she continued.

Cael was surprised by her concern and responded, "They are just trying to get by, Valtinatha. What is a single man going to do to protect his cart while the foulest monster of his children's nightmares is now right outside his door?"

She bristled, her anger obvious at having to stand by and do nothing. "I can understand he is outnumbered, but my people are all taught to fight in some form. I would never allow myself to be stuck in this sort of place."

Cael looked over at her, seeing in the way she held herself that she meant it deep in her heart. He wondered if such a thing could be kept true in this world where they found themselves. Would even her elven pride be tempered by a stronger foe?

Feeling the cart slow, Cael turned toward Chin Lizhou and the boys at the front, seeing soldiers yelling for them to stop. Cael put his head back down and tried to listen in on what was being said.

"What are they doing?" Valtinatha asked through her teeth.

"Quiet. He is saving our skins. Our escape would be noticed by now."

Lizhou spoke to the soldiers. "Sergeant, what can I help you with today?"

"You are not in the palace with the Master Scholar. What business do you have in the harbor district today?"

The man speaking, if he could be called a man, had the sickly green skin of an orc, with the shape of a Yulanese man, and twisted black teeth in his mouth. His armor was of dirty, black-studded leather, grime coating it in a disgusting pall to Cael's eye.

"Another of my brethren from across the sea requested some things be sent to him." Chin Lizhao continued his story, attempting to keep the guards from searching the cart and making them miss the ship.

"To what port are they going?"

Cael continued to eavesdrop. He glanced off to the side and saw the boots of other soldiers coming around behind the cart. He kept his head down and hoped they did not raise his or Valtinatha's hoods.

"Adavad is their port of call. Many old things there hold a great interest for him."

Cael looked at the orc who was closely studying Valtinatha. He was reaching to grab her hood and he could see her starting lean away from him. Cael needed to do something quickly, for if she was sighted they would be lost for sure.

Dropping his hood, Cael spoke. "Can I help you soldier?"

The orc snapped his head up. His green-tinged face was covered with scars, *undoubtedly signs of affection and status in orc culture*, Cael thought.

"What is it to you, human whelp?" he growled through his gnarled teeth.

"Mild curiosity is all." Cael could barely keep his face free from displaying the disgust he felt at being so close to the orc.

Chin Lizhou yelled from the front, "All is well, sergeant, can we be on our way?"

The orc stared at Cael, his human counterpart, and the sergeant before putting the point of his spear near Cael's neck.

"I say we check the other student here first, then they can go."

The orc grinned at Cael and reached for the hood covering Valtinatha's head. Cael nodded to Chin Lizhou who grabbed the reins for the horses in preparation for the flight they would now have to make. Cael looked back just in time to see a look of surprise as the orc squealed at the sight of Valtinatha's ears.

"It is the elve! It's them!" Cael brushed aside the spear at his neck and Chin Lizhou started the cart rambling down the path.

They could hear people screaming as the horses barreled suddenly down the road.

"Down!" Cael pushed Valtinatha into the cart's footwell as arrows from the orcs began to rain down around them. He heard the dull thuds as the arrows stuck into the wood panels of the cart.

"Get off of me!" Valtinatha yelled, trying to push away from Cael. He pushed her back down as an arrow notched the wood where her head would have been.

"The arrows are poisoned! It might not kill you depending on the mix, but you will wish you were dead!" He yelled over the screaming and the crashing of the cart as it barreled down the lane. It lunged to the side, catching the edge of a stall spilling wilted fruit into the roadway. Cael saw a few of the arrows strike people on the road, and felt a wave of pity and anger at the sight. He knew they would not survive.

Amid the tumbling, Herth unwrapped himself from the mass of cloth. Still partially covered, Cael saw his sword, strike through the wrappings to create an opening that allowed the barbarian to push his way free.

"I am not going along with a plan like this again," Herth claimed calmly.

"Then make sure we go somewhere where you are not the tallest creature alive," Cael spat back as he was handed his sword.

Cael turned back to see that Valtinatha was keeping her head down, balling up some of the cloth Herth had been in to use as a rudimentary block for the arrows that were coming. She had taken Cael's warning seriously. The arrows were slowing now though, as the range had increased and they were falling short at this point. Cael tied his sword belt on and looked back at the orcs still running down the docks toward them.

"We are nearing the docks! Get ready to run for the boat!" Chin Lizhou yelled.

Cael turned, and sure enough saw the sails and the ramp to the boats coming up ahead. But their cart only held a few minutes' lead on the soldiers on very crowded docks. He jumped off the cart as it began to slow, his ears catching a scream behind him. He reached back, found Herth already next to him, so he grabbed Valtinatha as she stumbled off of the cart. Cael's blood ran cold as he saw the black feathers and dark wood of an orc bow buried in her shoulder.

"Ah! It hurts, the burning..." Val couldn't go on, she was gasping in pain.

Cael laid her down and watched the wound begin to burn and smoke, the blood coming away from the edges of the wound a sickly yellow. Already her veins were blackening around the wound. It was not a poison he had seen in some time, but it was one he was familiar with. He pushed down the fear of seeing it again and focused on the moment.

"Valtinatha, take my hand, I am going to have Herth remove the arrow."

"We don't have time for this!" Chin Lizhou said, starting to come around the edge of the stopped cart with the two students in tow.

"If we don't get the arrow out now, she won't make it to the ship. The arrow is soaked in a poison that's killing her. The longer it is moistened by her blood the more of the poison will find its way into her," Cael growled.

Herth looked at Cael. Valtinatha's writhing body and outbursts of pain drowned out the noise from around them, and the bustling of the harbor obscured the cart. "Hold her as still as you can, Cael." Herth looked down at Valtinatha, and placed a hand on her shoulder to force her back against the ground. Gripping the arrow with his other hand, he nodded to Cael.

"Valtinatha hold on tight." Cael took Val's hand tightly and felt her squeezing back firmly with the last of her strength. Cael could already feel the fever starting from the poison that had worked into her system. With a quick flick of his large hands Herth pulled the arrow free. Cael held Valtinatha down as she cried out in terrible agony, and placed his hand and a remnant piece of cloth on the wound to stop the flow of blood.

"Come, we can fix the rest of this on the ship," Chin Lizhou said, the two small boys already pulling the rest of Herth's numerous weapons from the bottom of the cart and carrying them towards the boat.

Cael lifted Valtinatha off the ground while Herth took his bow and readied an arrow for the first soldier to come within range. With everything in hand the group ran down the docking towards the small ship waiting at the end. Cael continued in the path created by Lizhou and the two boys. They were already speaking to the captain who was barking orders at his men.

The captain, a burly man with a full beard and a stocky round chest, looked welcoming to the group running down the ramp. "Welcome lad, let's get 'er down in the hold."

"The captain is a sympathizer with the scholars from before Persean, Cael. You will be safe with him," Chin Lizhou added from the dock, his two students already out of sight.

"I can't thank you enough Chin Lizhou. I will make sure to return here if I can," Cael said.

Chin Lizhou smiled, waiting for Herth to pass and board the ship. "My friend, I can take care of things here. When you get to Brodesia, seek out Sao Len, or those who know of him. Your answers lie with him on your quest." Lizhou backed down the ramp, waving Cael and the captain off. The sound of Herth's bow twanged as the soldiers reached the pier.

Cael followed the captain below decks to finish his work on Valtinatha's wound. Though the arrow had been removed, she was not entirely safe from harm yet. He would take the time to look at his first sailing vessel when her life was no longer in danger.

ABOUT THE AUTHOR

Matthew Cerra has the day job of teaching science and mathematics, and also bringing understanding to the physical realm into the minds of his students. When not teaching, he can be found spending time with his wife and daughter, travelling and going on any roller coaster his daughter is tall enough to ride. He also spends time gardening while attempting to keep his four dogs from digging up the fruit, vegetables, flowers, and trees he has just raised from seeds.

When not creating his own worlds Matthew is an avid reader of fantasy, science fiction, and science facts. His particular favorites involve cosmology and history. He also dreams of one day completing a Doctorate, though he has not decided on a course of study for it yet.

HALF LIGHT PUBLISHING

 Half Light is founded by T.M. Williams, who has 15 of her own titles in print and whose books have sold in 170+ countries. All of her titles will now be housed under the Half Light umbrella, and run the gamut from zombie thrillers and twisted fairy tales to Marketing How Tos. We are searching for unique projects and authors, and we support each project with two professional editors, a proofreader, submission director, marketing expert, and graphic designer for covers and book trailers.

Come Join Our Family Of Authors

www.HalfLightPublishing.com

To learn more about how you also can be published

And to view more about this work, scan this QR Code and
learn about Half Light Publishing

ABOUT THE AUTHOR

Matthew Cerra has the day job of teaching science and mathematics, and also bringing understanding to the physical realm into the minds of his students. When not teaching, he can be found spending time with his wife and daughter, travelling and going on any roller coaster his daughter is tall enough to ride. He also spends time gardening while attempting to keep his four dogs from digging up the fruit, vegetables, flowers, and trees he has just raised from seeds.

When not creating his own worlds Matthew is an avid reader of fantasy, science fiction, and science facts. His particular favorites involve cosmology and history. He also dreams of one day completing a Doctorate, though he has not decided on a course of study for it yet.

HALF LIGHT PUBLISHING

Half Light is founded by T.M. Williams, who has 15 of her own titles in print and whose books have sold in 170+ countries. All of her titles will now be housed under the Half Light umbrella, and run the gamut from zombie thrillers and twisted fairy tales to Marketing How Tos. We are searching for unique projects and authors, and we support each project with two professional editors, a proofreader, submission director, marketing expert, and graphic designer for covers and book trailers.

Come Join Our Family Of Authors

www.HalfLightPublishing.com